INVITATION TO A BALL

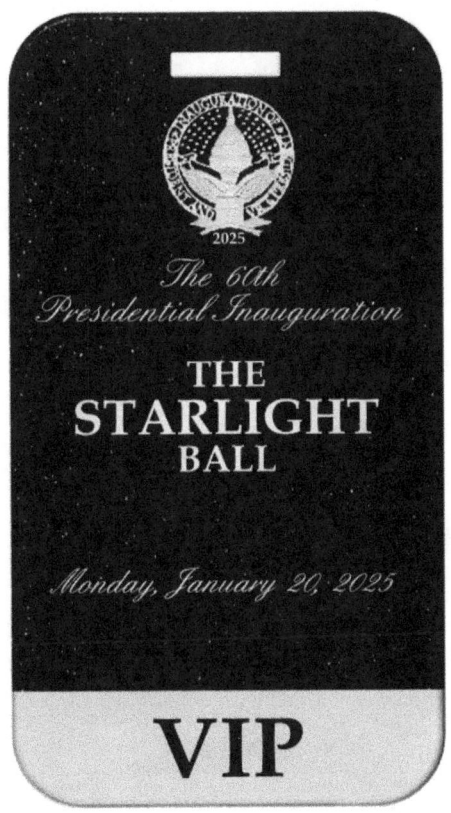

Invitation to a Ball

By
W. B. Speir

Progressive
RISING PHOENIX PRESS ®

Published 2025 by Progressive Rising Phoenix Press, LLC
www.progressiverisingphoenix.com

ISBN: 978-1-958640-77-7

Printed in the U.S.A.
1st Printing

Front Cover Artwork by W. B. Speir. All Rights Reserved:

Interior Illustrations by W. B. Speir. All Rights Reserved.

Chapter Heading Illustration "Vector Silhouette of Horse Family on Meadow," by majivecka. ShutterStock Vector ID: 1613778274, used under license from ShutterStock.com.

Horse Head Image: "Creative Horse Elegant Logo Symbol Design Illustration Vector," By Sugivarto. ShutterStock Vector ID: 1443709205, used under license from ShutterStock.com.

Cowboy/Cowgirl Image: "Horseback Cowboy and Cowgirl," By Cattallina. ShutterStock Asset ID: 1349824859, used under license from ShutterStock.com.

Cowboy Hat Image: "2 Cowboy Hats, 1 Feminine and 1 Masculine," By AI. ShutterStock Asset ID: 2572031725, used under license from ShutterStock.com.

Cover and Interior Design by W. B. Speir
Visit: http://www.williamspeir.com

To my beloved LAS through all the seasons of our lives. You are the love of my life and my best friend. Thank you for the freedom to write and for almost twenty-seven glorious years!

To the people who taught me to ride horses, and to the people who made me fall in love with Texas.

And to the fans, because you are the greatest, and I love sharing my stories with you.

TABLE OF CONTENTS:

CONTENT WARNING:

Invitation to a Ball is an adult Romance novel. The story includes elements that may not be suitable for all readers. In addition to depictions of violence, this story contains scenes of a strong sexual nature. Readers who may be sensitive to these depictions please take note.

THE
INVITATION

The Committee for
The Presidential Inaugural
Washington, D.C. 20599

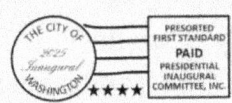

PRESORTED
FIRST STANDARD
PAID
PRESIDENTIAL
INAUGURAL
COMMITTEE, INC.

THE CITY OF
2025
Inaugural
WASHINGTON
★★★★

###
******************************ACRLOT**C005
Mr. Alexander M. Barclay
22 Barclay Ranch Road
Justin, TX 76247

DO NOT BEND

CHAPTER 1

*A*lexander (Alex) McIntyre Barclay, a 46-year-old Texas business owner and rancher, sat in his home office, staring at the pile of mail that had just been brought up from the gatehouse. On top was a large envelope with the return address of The Committee for the Presidential Inaugural, postmarked Washington, DC.

He grabbed the letter opener on his desk and slit open the top of the envelope. Inside were several items: his official invitation to the inauguration on January 20th, a souvenir invitation with the President and Vice-President's names on it, a souvenir program for the ceremony, his two tickets to the seating area where he and the other mega-donors would be watching the ceremony, his tickets for the parade viewing area after the ceremony, and his VIP passes for The Starlight Ball. There was also a sheet of paper showing all parking areas, where to be and when to be there, and other information he'd need to make certain that he didn't miss any of the ceremonies and other festivities allowed by the enclosed tickets and passes.

"I can't believe that Charley is being sworn in as Vice President of the United States," he thought to himself as he read the souvenir invitation. Charles Angwin Glass had been Alex's roommate at Purdue University when they were undergraduates. Alex was studying industrial engineering, and Charley was studying aeronautical engineering. Alex graduated and went on to found his own phenomenally successful consulting company. Charley entered the United States Air Force before resigning his commission and embarking on a career in politics.

Alex looked at the other name on the invitation: Thomas James Watkins. Alex had met the new President several times over the years, and he had been a major donor to Tom's campaign. As a token of the new President's gratitude for Alex's donations, Alex was being invited to the inauguration ceremony, the parade, and the most prestigious of the three inaugural balls taking place that night. The passes for the ball even included a VIP parking pass for the deck directly behind Union Station, where the ball was taking place.

Alex glanced up at the photo in the frame on his desk for a moment. Then he took the contents of the envelope, placed them in a neat stack—smallest to largest—put the stack on top of the envelope, and moved the stack to the left corner of his desk. Then he picked up the frame and stared at the photo of Penny Ramsay and himself, taken on a trip to Colorado several months earlier.

After a few minutes, he opened the back of the frame and removed the photo. He closed the frame, stared at the photo for a while longer, and then placed it in the trashcan underneath the credenza behind him. He put the frame in one of the credenza drawers, reached for his desk lamp, and turned it off. He stood and left the office, turning off the overhead lights as he exited.

As he walked back to the main house, looking at the Christmas decorations around the Residence, he thought, *"Now that Penny's gone, who do I take to DC with me? I guess I'll call my cousin, Sarah. She's usually up for accompanying me to events like this, and I'm sure her husband won't mind her being gone for a few days."*

Alex continued walking around the pool area to the house, wishing he had someone other than a relative to take to DC with him.

Delaney (Laney) Erica Connor, a 32-year-old attorney with a small firm in Fort Worth, Texas, knocked on the door of her managing partner, who had summoned her to his office a minute earlier. "You wanted to see me, Dwight?" she asked when he looked up.

Dwight motioned for her to come into his office and sit down in one of the chairs across the desk from him. "Thanks for coming so quickly, Laney," he said. "What's your workload right now?"

"Mildly swamped," Laney replied, smiling. "Nothing I can't handle. All of the contracts should go out on time."

Dwight nodded. Then he reached into his top desk drawer and pulled out a large envelope. "How'd you like to take a trip to Washington, DC on the firm in January?"

"I think I'd freeze my ass off," Laney replied.

Dwight turned the envelope so she could see the return address. "Even if you got to go to the inauguration?"

Laney stared at her boss. "You're kidding!"

Dwight shook his head. "The firm donated a lot to the campaign, and I received an invitation to the ceremony, the parade, and the ball. But Linda, my wife, broke her leg in two places over the weekend—"

"Is she all right?" Laney interrupted.

Dwight shook his head. "Not really. She's getting plates and screws put in her leg to hold the bone together, and the doctors tell me that she'll still be recovering well into February. I have no desire to go to DC without her, and since you're going to be the next partner added to the firm this summer, and since you worked on Watkins' campaign, I thought you might like to go in my place. It'll be fun for you, and it'll be great exposure for the firm having you there representing us. Win-win!"

Laney held out her hand, and Dwight gave her the envelope. "Don't lose anything in that envelope," he cautioned. "I hear getting replacements is nearly impossible at this late date."

"I promise, Dwight. And thanks for thinking of me."

Dwight handed her an itinerary he had printed out. "Here is your flight information and hotel confirmation. I'll have the reservations changed to your name. You'll be staying at the Waldorf Astoria on Pennsylvania Avenue, right next to The White House. They have shuttles running to the Capitol, where the inauguration will be held, and it's a short cab ride to Union Station, where the ball will be."

Laney took the itinerary and glanced at it. Then she looked inside the envelope. "There are two passes to the ceremony, the parade, and the ball, and the flight reservation is for two people."

Dwight nodded. "Do you have a plus-one?"

Laney shrugged. "I'll let you know so you can cancel one of the reservations if you have to."

Dwight nodded and gestured that the meeting was over. Laney stood and thanked him again.

She started to exit the office, then turned and asked. "January in DC is a crap shoot, weather-wise. What if I get stuck up there for a few days?"

Dwight smiled. "Then extend your reservation at the hotel, reschedule your return flight, and enjoy yourself. The trip is a reward for all your hard work. If you stay up there longer, either because you need the time off or because the weather isn't cooperating, that's fine with me. Just let me know when you'll be back so I can let your clients know."

"Should I take my laptop with me just in case?"

Dwight snorted. "You need to unplug for a while, Laney. You're a great associate, and you'll make a great partner, but you're no good to me, the firm, or the clients if you burn yourself out at your age. I want that laptop locked in your desk when you leave here to go to DC, understood?"

"Understood," Laney confirmed. She walked back to her office on the other side of the lobby Christmas tree.

"Liam and I have only been dating for a couple of months," she thought to herself as she sat down behind her desk. *"We're getting together tomorrow night, so I can ask him then if he wants to go with me. But what if he thinks it's too soon to take a trip together? I don't want to blow this relationship, but I also don't want to go to DC alone... especially if there's a chance I'll get stranded up there for*

a few days."

She jotted a few notes on her calendar, put the envelope in her briefcase, and returned to the client contract she was drafting when Dwight called her into his office.

The honor of your presence
is requested at the ceremonies attending the
Inauguration of the

President and Vice President
of the United States

January twentieth
Two thousand twenty five

The Capitol of the United States of America
City of Washington

by the
Joint Congressional
Committee on Inaugural Ceremonies

Amy Klobuchar, Chairwoman,
Charles E. Schumer, Deb Fischer,
Mike Johnson, Steve Scalise,
Hakeem Jeffries

11:30 a.m.

Inaugural Invitation

The committee for
The Presidential Inaugural
requests the honor of your presence
to attend and participate in the Inauguration of

Thomas James Watkins

as President of the United States of America

and

Charles Angwin Glass

as Vice-President of the United States of America

on Friday the twentieth of January

two thousand and twenty five

in the City of Washington

Souvenir Invitation

Inaugural Ceremonies Program

The Capitol of the United States of America

January twentieth
Two thousand twenty five

Souvenir Program

Invitations to the Ceremony and The Starlight Ball

WASHINGTON, DC

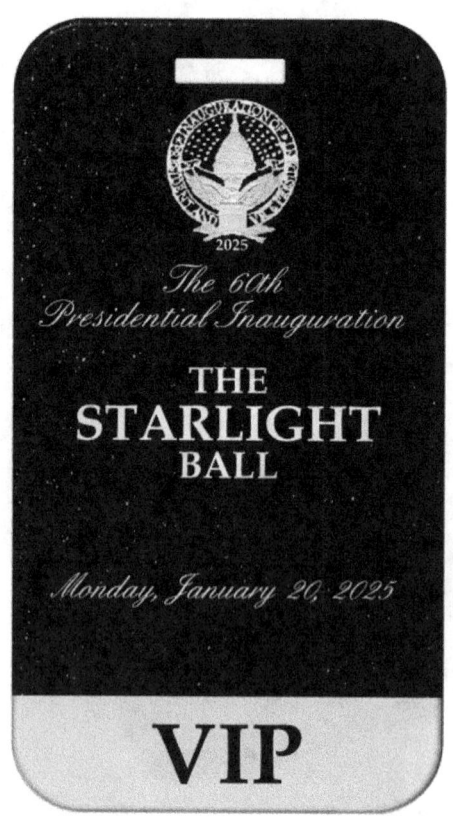

2025

*The 60th
Presidential Inauguration*

THE
STARLIGHT
BALL

Monday, January 20, 2025

VIP

CHAPTER 2

At 8:00 AM on Sunday, January 19th, Alex and his security team arrived at Perot Field Fort Worth Alliance Airport. Alex kept his private jet at Alliance because it was close to the ranch and because the company that maintained the aircraft had operations there, allowing Alex to keep the jet properly maintained without having to employ the ground crew himself.

Mike Billingsley was the head of Alex's security detail, as usual, and Travis Dennison and Ray Jennings were assisting Mike to keep Alex safe on his trip to DC. Gordon Hopkins was driving the SUV and would return it to the ranch once Alex was safely in the air.

Alex never went anywhere without a security detail. As the fourth richest man in Texas, the threat of kidnapping for ransom was too great of a risk. He had two GPS trackers implanted under his skin in case his detail ever got separated from him, and when in Texas, Alex was typically armed, as were the members of his detail.

As they pulled into the hangar where Alex's Gulfstream G700 was waiting to fly him to DC, he saw the flight crew standing at the base of the stairs. The pilot, Henry Powell, was a former naval aviator, and his co-pilot, Anne Stone, was a former Air Force pilot. They had been with Alex ever since he had purchased his first Gulfstream jet several years earlier. When he upgraded jets the previous autumn, they stayed with him. Jenny Blankenship was Alex's current chief steward and had been part of the flight crew for just over two years. Her assistant steward was Keith Jordan, who had been part of the crew for six months.

Mike, Travis, and Ray exited the SUV first and performed a security sweep of the hangar and the aircraft. When Mike was satisfied that it was safe, he signaled Gordon to let Alex board his jet. Gordon slid out of the driver's seat and opened Alex's door.

"Thanks, Gordon," Alex said as he stepped out of the SUV. "I'll call you if there are any changes to our itinerary."

"Thanks, Boss. Have a great trip, and I'll be here to pick you up when you get back."

Alex nodded and patted Gordon's arm. Then he walked toward his aircraft. "How's the weather look?" Alex asked Henry as he approached the flight crew.

"Smooth flying, Mr. Barclay," Henry responded, shaking his boss' hand. "It's a two hour and 45 minute flight to Reagan-Washington National, so assuming no detours or reroutes, you should be at your hotel in time for lunch."

Gordon got back into the SUV. Travis and Ray retrieved the luggage, and Keith helped them load everything into the aircraft. Once the luggage was in place and the cargo hatch closed, Jenny escorted Alex to the center seating area, which was Alex's preferred place to sit when he flew in this jet.

Mike took his seat across the aisle from Alex, Travis sat in the seating area ahead of Alex's, and Ray sat in the seating area behind Alex's. Keith closed the main hatch, and then he and Jenny took their seats in the forward crew compartment. Alex felt the aircraft pressurize, and then it rolled out of the hangar and onto the taxiway.

In less than five minutes, the aircraft was airborne and heading east toward Northern Virginia.

Jenny served coffee and orange juice while Keith prepared breakfast in the forward galley. As Alex sipped his juice, he pulled out the envelope with the instructions and invitations to the inaugural events.

"The SUV you rented will be waiting for us when we land?" he asked Mike.

"Yes, Boss," Mike confirmed. "It'll be waiting in the hangar, and it has all of the usual refinements we requested. I've worked with this company before, and they're reliable."

"And the three of you have worked out who's going to do what while we're there?"

"Yes, sir. Travis and Ray will alternate driving and patrolling perimeters. I'll remain with you when you're outside your hotel room, and then the three of us will alternate guarding the hallway outside your room. You have us booked across the hall from you, there are no rooms on either side of yours, and you're on the top floor, so protection should be straightforward. Of course, we cannot be armed at the inauguration or the ball, but we'll make it work."

Mike hesitated for a moment, then continued. "It's too bad your cousin, Sarah, couldn't make the trip. I'm sure you'd rather be with her at the ceremony and the ball than with me."

Alex chuckled. "She's a much better dancer than you are, but with both kids sick, there's no way she could leave home right now. Still, it's not the first time I've gone stag to an event like this, and I'm going for Charley and Tom. It's their big day. I'm just there to cheer them on."

"It's too bad about Penny, too, Boss, if you'll forgive me for saying that. The break-up was bad enough, but right before Christmas? I can't even imagine what that felt like."

Alex looked at Mike, and then he nodded. "I thought it was going well, but in the end, her career was taking off, and I was in the process of retiring. She would have given up too much to make it work."

"Are you going to keep working with that matchmaker?"

Alex sighed, noting the disdain in Mike's tone. "No clue. I'm still getting over Penny. I'll see how I feel in a few months."

"Yes, Boss."

Keith and Jenny served breakfast, and Alex put the envelope back in his briefcase, satisfied that all arrangements had been taken care of. Mike had been the head of his security detail for years and always knew what to do to keep Alex safe.

Laney hated air travel, and this morning bitterly proved her point.

Because DC was going to be frigid, she had to pack her heavy winter coats and clothing, and she had to pack for a few extra days in case the weather front moving into the mid-Atlantic area forced her to remain in DC longer than planned. She also had her new ball gown, which took up a lot of space in her garment bag. She had too much luggage to carry it all onboard, so she'd have to check her bags at the airport and pray they all arrived safely at her destination when she did.

The car service was supposed to arrive at 6:30 AM on Sunday morning, but it was twenty minutes late. It took nearly ten minutes to load her luggage in the trunk, and it was 7:00 AM before the car finally left her Mockingbird Estates townhouse in East Fort Worth.

Laney knew it would take at least thirty minutes to reach Dallas-Fort Worth International Airport, and it could take another hour to check-in, get through security, and reach her gate. Her three-hour flight was scheduled to leave at 10:00 AM, leaving her just enough time to grab a coffee and board the plane with the rest of the first-class passengers.

The ride to the airport was smooth, but once the car entered the airport, traffic was a nightmare. She knew her flight's departure gate, and as the car turned onto the terminal's passenger drop-off lane, it seemed like every other passenger was departing from the same terminal.

After waiting in a line of traffic for nearly fifteen minutes, the car was finally able to pull up to the curb. She paid the driver and grabbed her bags from the trunk. After making sure she had everything, she went inside and headed for the airline counter to check-in.

Laney stood in the first-class check-in line for about ten minutes before a check-in agent motioned for her to approach the counter. She presented her ID to the counter agent, who printed her boarding pass and checked her bags for the flight.

As the check-in agent handed Laney her boarding pass and ID, along with the luggage claim checks, she said, "Everything's a little backed-up this morning. Don't be surprised if your flight is a bit late taking off."

Laney nodded and headed for the security entrance to the departure gates.

She reached her gate thirty minutes later and found an empty seat in the crowded departure lounge. She looked at her watch; it was 8:45 AM—forty-five minutes before her flight was to begin boarding. She looked at the departure information displayed above the gate... and watched it change from a 10:00 AM departure time to a 10:45 AM departure time.

There were groans from the other passengers when the gate agent announced the flight delay. Laney did the math in her head. *"With the time change, we won't land at Reagan-Washington until 2:45 PM. Figure thirty to forty-five minutes to get my bags and get a cab to my hotel, that puts me checking into my room between 3:30 PM and 4:00 PM. It'll be dinner time before I get settled."*

"I hate air travel."

At 10:20 AM, the gate agent announced that first-class passengers could board the aircraft. Laney grabbed her briefcase and her coat, stood, and headed for the gate. A few minutes later, she was in her first row window seat, and the flight attendants were serving coffee, juice, and other beverages. Laney requested a mimosa. *"At least first-class has its perks."*

She looked at the empty aisle seat next to her. *"If only Liam knew what he was missing. We get together, and I'm about to tell him that I've got tickets to the inauguration, and then he tells me that he's breaking up with me. 'I just don't see this going anywhere, and I'm not a fan of your politics.' It never occurred to me that he voted for the other guy. Why should it have even mattered to him? Clearly, I dodged a bullet, but it'd be nice to have some companionship on this trip. Hopefully, there will be someone to dance with at the ball. No way I'm missing that just because Liam is a jerk."*

Laney stared at the empty seat, remembering Dwight's reaction when she told him he could cancel the other flight reservation, because she was going to DC alone. *"Dwight has a terrible poker face. I know he was ecstatic that I didn't have anyone to go with. He's terrified that I'll meet someone, run off, and get married. He wants me to be a partner, and he knows he'll get the most use out of me if I'm single and have nothing distracting me from my career. And there was a time when I was happy to put my career above all else. College, law school, being a new associate... I was driven to excel at being a lawyer. Nothing else mattered. He saw that in me, and he mentored me to continue being that way for the rest of my life, or at least until I totally burned out and ended my career. But lately... I don't know. It's not enough. I want a life partner. I want a family. But I can't have that AND my career because there's not enough time in the day for both. Something's got to give, and I'd better figure it out before I'm forced to either accept or reject the partnership."*

Laney sipped her drink and watched the rest of the passengers board the Airbus A321. *"But will rejecting the partnership give me time for a family, or will I have to alter more of my career to fit another person into my life?"*

After what seemed like an eternity, all of the passengers were finally onboard and seated. The main hatch was closed, and Laney heard the engines starting.

The plane pushed back from the gate a few minutes before 11:00 AM, and after taxiing and waiting in the take-off queue for over thirty minutes, the plane finally took off and headed for Washington DC. Laney took out a book from her briefcase and started reading to pass the time and to take her mind off the decision she knew she had to make soon but had no idea what to choose.

Alex's plane was 30 minutes from Reagan-Washington National. The trip has been quick, smooth, and pleasant. Jenny and Keith were busy picking up the glasses, plates, and utensils as part of their landing preparations.

Mike leaned over, so he wouldn't be overheard, and asked, "Now that you don't fly every week, Boss, what are you going to do with the jet? It made sense when you were constantly traveling to visit your staff in the field and to attend sales meetings, but now that you're retiring and selling your shares of the firm to the other partners, do you still need your own plane and flight crew?"

Alex smiled. "I've been wrestling with that for a couple

of months. I like the convenience of having my own plane, and I can certainly afford to keep it, but it seems like a waste of talent for the flight crew to go from flying to a different city every other day to flying once every month or so. I want to do right by them, but I also want to have my own plane available for when I travel. Henry and Anne approached me a few weeks ago about letting them accept charters with the jet, and I'm leaning toward that. There are details to work out, but it might be the best solution for them and for me."

"That sounds like a good plan, Boss," Mike admitted. "As long as they don't have a charter scheduled when you need the jet."

"That's one of those details to work out," Alex said.

Mike was about to say something when Henry's voice came over the intercom. "We'll be landing in twenty minutes. We have a priority approach into Reagan-Washington National, so we'll be at the hangar approximately ten minutes early."

Alex leaned back in his seat and said, "I can't imagine flying commercial. This plane has everything I could ever want for air travel. If I didn't love the ranch so much, I'd keep traveling every week. But I love spending time with my horses and the land, so I need to find a way to keep the jet *and* let the flight crew stay busy so they won't go work somewhere else."

"You'll figure it out, Boss," Mike stated. "You always do."

The landing was smooth as silk, and Alex muttered "Go Air Force," under his breath. It was a standing joke when he flew. He blamed hard landings on his ex-navy pilot, who was trained to use a tail hook for carrier landings, and he credited smooth landings to his ex-Air Force co-pilot. Alex guessed that Anne was at the controls for this landing.

As they taxied into the hangar, where the jet would be kept while Alex was in DC, Alex saw the rental SUV waiting for them. A rental car for the flight crew was parked next to it. His SUV was equipped for VIPs. In addition to bullet-proof glass and door panels, it had Kevlar tires, GPS monitoring, and two-way communications and panic alarms linked to a security company that could dispatch assistance anywhere in the DC metropolitan area.

Once the jet came to a stop, Henry left the cockpit and came back to talk with Alex.

"Tell Anne that was a perfect landing," Alex joked as Henry sat across from him.

"I will, Mr. Barclay." Henry smiled. "Fortunately Reagan-Washington National has long enough runways for Air Force alumni. On another note, I need to confirm when you plan to return to Fort Worth."

"Not before Wednesday the 22nd," Alex stated. "But I understand there's a weather front expected in the next day or so. Is that going to force us to change plans?"

"It might push our departure to the weekend, if it's as bad as they're predicting. I've been monitoring the weather service reports, and it's supposed to hit sometime in the morning after the inauguration, so unless you want to leave immediately after the ball, I think we can assume we'll be staying here longer than planned."

"Will that cause a problem for you and the crew?" Alex asked. "I don't want all of you to be in a bind if I decide to stay longer than expected. I do love being in DC."

"I think we can accommodate any delays you have in

mind, Mr. Barclay. I've checked with the rest of the crew already, and no one has any scheduling issues for the next three weeks."

"Well, if I end up staying here longer than that, I'll let you take the plane back to Fort Worth for a few days so everyone can take care of their commitments, and then you can bring the jet back to pick me up."

Alex looked at Mike. "Does the security detail have any scheduling issues if I decide to stay here for a while?"

Mike shook his head. "None at all, Boss. And if something comes up, Henry can bring a second team back with him, and we'll take a commercial flight home once the second team arrives. We'll accommodate your schedule."

Alex nodded. Turning back to Henry, he said, "I'm sorry I couldn't get y'all into the Waldorf Astoria, but it was booked solid. The apartment I rented in Arlington for the flight crew came highly recommended. If it's not to your liking, or if there are issues that can't be corrected easily, let me know, and I'll find you something better."

"It should be okay, Mr. Barclay," Henry assured him. "We've stayed there before, and it's a great place."

Alex heard Jenny and Keith open the hatch and extend the stairs. Henry stood and announced. "Time to deplane, gentlemen."

Travis and Ray exited the plane first, followed by Mike. They did a quick security screen of the hangar, the SUV, and the other vehicle for the flight crew. Once that was completed, Mike let Alex know that he could exit the aircraft.

Alex thanked each member of the flight crew, and then he exited the plane as Travis and Ray were removing the luggage and placing it in the back of the SUV. Alex got into the back seat. Mike sat next to him, and Ray sat in the front passenger seat. Travis got behind the wheel, started the SUV, and drove out of the hangar. The flight crew remained behind to coordinate with the ground crew and finish cleaning the aircraft.

Alex looked at his watch. It was 12:50 PM Eastern Time. After a short drive to Pennsylvania Avenue, the SUV pulled up in front of the Waldorf Astoria. Bellhops rushed out to help unload the luggage. Travis and Ray stayed with them while Alex and Mike entered the hotel lobby to check-in. Once the bellhops were finished unloading, Ray went with them to the lobby while Travis parked the SUV. Ray was to remain with the luggage until it had been delivered to Alex's suite and the room where the detail was staying.

Alex entered the Elite Guest queue and was quickly escorted to the check-in desk.

"Good afternoon, sir," the hotel staff member at the check-in desk said pleasantly. "I'm Juliana, the desk manager. How may I help you?"

"Reservation for Barclay," Alex replied. "The Franklin Suite and the suite across the hall from it."

Juliana smiled. "Ah, Mr. Barclay, welcome back. I see you've enjoyed the Franklin Suite before." Her eyes glanced at Mike. "And three occupants in the suite across the hall for your staff. Everything is arranged."

Alex handed her his credit card while she encoded the room keys. Alex asked, "Should the weather turn nasty, and I end up having to stay in DC for several extra days, will the Franklin Suite and the other suite still be available for my use?"

Juliana handed Alex his credit card back. "Let me check on that for you." She typed several commands into her computer and looked at the information for a moment. "Both rooms are available for an additional 17 days, but no longer than that. Do you want me to reserve them for you? You won't be charged unless you do extend your stay."

Alex nodded. "Yes, please. Better safe than sorry, and the Franklin Suite is my favorite suite in the hotel."

Juliana smiled and entered the information into her computer. "Done. Is there anything else I can help you with?"

"Just the keys," Alex replied.

Juliana handed over the keys. "You remember where the Franklin Suite is located?"

"I do," Alex confirmed, taking the keys.

"Then have a pleasant stay at the Waldorf Astoria Washington DC, Mr. Barclay." Juliana handed him one of her business cards. "And if there's anything I can do to make your stay more enjoyable, please call me."

Alex looked at the card and slipped it into his shirt pocket. "I will. Thanks!"

Mike followed Alex to the special elevator bank that went to the top floor of the hotel, and they rode up to their suites together.

It was nearly 3:30 PM local time before Laney's plane landed and taxied to the terminal. This was one time she was grateful to be in the front row; she'd be the first one off the plane.

After waiting nearly thirty minutes for her baggage, which all arrived safely, she put on her overcoat, headed for the ground transportation area, and stood in line for a taxi to take her to her hotel.

It was a quick trip to the Waldorf Astoria, and the line at the check-in desk moved quickly. Soon, she was heading up the elevator to her deluxe king-bed room.

The room was beautiful. Laney put her things away, making sure that the ball gown was hanging by itself so any wrinkles would shake out, and then she sat down in the overstuffed chair by the window.

The clock on the nightstand said 4:30PM. Realizing she was hungry, she picked up the room service menu, selected what she wanted for dinner, and ordered the meal to be brought to her room. Looking around, she thought, *"I'm finally here... in DC... by myself. Just as Dwight wanted. Well, I'm going to enjoy myself on this trip, and I'm not going to let Liam's issues—or Dwight's influence—ruin the experience for me."*

CHAPTER 3

lex woke up early the next morning. He thought about trying to get more sleep, but the excitement of the day's events made that impossible. He got up, showered, dressed, and then ordered breakfast from room service.

The Franklin suite, while not the largest suite at the hotel, was still two-thousand square feet and included a large living area, a dining area that seated six, two marble bathrooms, a private study with desk, and an oversized king-bed in a separate bedroom that had a walk-in closet. The blue and white decor had a calming effect on Alex whenever he stayed there, and the layout reminded him of his first apartment after graduating college.

Alex went to the door of his suite and looked outside. Ray was on duty, standing just to the left of the door, which gave him a clear view of anyone trying to approach Alex's room.

Ray heard the door open and turned to face Alex. "Good morning, Boss. Sleep well?"

"Reasonably," Alex replied. "Have you been here all night?"

"Just since four this morning," Ray replied. "I'll take a nap after the ceremony, and then I'll be all good for tonight. Is there something you needed?"

"I just ordered breakfast from room service," Alex said. "Wanted you to know that someone will be coming up in the next fifteen to twenty minutes."

"Thanks for the heads-up, Boss. I'll be on the lookout." Ray bent down and picked up the newspaper that the hotel had delivered an hour earlier. "Here's todays paper."

Alex accepted the paper, thanked Ray, and went back inside his suite. He sat down on one of the couches in the living area and started reading about the inauguration preparations while he waited for his food to arrive.

Laney rode the elevator down to the lobby level and headed for the restaurants. She took one look at the lines of people waiting to get in and decided to grab something from the coffee stand, which sold a variety of pastries. She took her coffee and croissant sandwich back to her room, preferring to be away from all the noise of the crowds trying to get a table for breakfast.

The coffee and sandwich were quite good, and she finished both quickly. Then she turned on the TV to see if there had been any last-minute changes to the plans for the inauguration. Apart from the cold temperatures, it was supposed to be a sunny day with calm winds. The heavy winds and bitterly cold temperatures weren't supposed to hit until around three the next morning.

Laney opened the envelope that Dwight had given her and pulled out her ticket for the ceremony. The embossed ticket had a green border, and it specified that the ceremony started at 11:30 AM, she was in Section 6— Green, and her ticket numbers were 0146 and 0147. She looked at the map of the ceremony viewing areas and confirmed that Green 6 was a sitting area, rather than a standing area. Looking at the map, she saw that green ticket holders were to enter at the gate located near the corner of South Capitol Street SE and D Street SE.

"That's definitely too far to walk in this crowd." Laney called the front desk and asked about the hotel shuttles that were taking ticket holders to the ceremony.

"Yes, ma'am, the shuttles will be running as planned," the front desk clerk acknowledged. "What color is your ticket?"

"Green," Laney replied.

"Green... Okay. Your shuttle leaves the front of the hotel at 9:40 this morning. You should be down here in line no later than 9:15. Otherwise, you'll have to take a cab or walk."

"Thank you." Laney ended the call. She glanced at her watch. *"8:30. I'd better get ready."*

Alex sat with Mike, Travis, and Ray at the dining table in his suite. He wanted to review the plans for the ceremony before getting ready to leave.

Mike looked at the tickets and the map of the viewing areas. "You're in Green Section 6, seats 0068 and 0069. Good place to watch. Not so close that you'll get a crick in your neck looking up, and not so far that you won't see what's happening."

Mike noted where the green ticket holders were to enter the ceremony security gates. "I think the best drop-off and pick-up spot is the Capitol South Metro Station on First Street SE, between C and D Streets SE. It's a short walk from there to the green entry gate, and there's plenty of parking—a lot and a deck."

Alex nodded. "Who's staying with the car?"

"I am," Travis said.

Alex looked at Ray. "And where will you be?"

"Washington Avenue, Boss," Ray replied. "It's close to the security screening checkpoints for green and orange ticket holders. I'll get as close as I can to the First Street SW intersection, since that's probably the way you'll leave the ceremony. Mike will let me know where you are so I can intercept. Then we'll head back to the car from wherever we meet up. I doubt the roads will be opened to traffic by then, so it'll be a short walk and then a meandering drive back to the hotel."

"Is it still your plan to skip the parade, Boss?" Mike asked.

Alex nodded. "I hate marching bands, and Tom and Charley will be in their limos, so there's really nothing to see. I'd rather get back here, eat, and get some rest before tonight."

Alex looked at the map again. "It's going to be a lot of walking today, isn't it?"

Mike nodded. "Yes, Boss. It's a good thing you live on a huge ranch. It'll also be cold."

"Another reason to skip the parade," Travis noted.

"When do we leave?" Alex asked.

"Nine-thirty," Mike said. "We need time to get there, park, walk to the gate, and then walk to our section. It could easily take us an hour to get to our seats once we arrive, depending on the crowds."

Alex nodded. He wasn't a fan of crowds, but this was a once-in-a-lifetime event he didn't want to miss.

Mike glanced over to the coat rack and saw a familiar black cowboy hat on top. "Wearing the Stetson today, Boss?"

Alex grinned. "Gotta keep my head warm, and alpine hats like the one you wear just don't work for me."

The shuttle left the hotel on time, and it dropped Laney and the other green ticket holders off at the Capitol South Metro Station. All of the streets closer to the Capitol were closed off for security reasons.

Laney followed the signs to the green gate, and then she followed the signs to the security screen checkpoint. The air was quite cold, and Laney was wearing tall boots, wool slacks, a Norwegian ski-sweater, ski-gloves, and her heavy wool overcoat. Her muffler-style scarf was wrapped tightly around her neck and head. She opted to leave her purse in the safe of her hotel room, keeping her wallet and her identification in her pants pocket.

After getting through the security screening, she

followed the signs to Green Section 6. She found her seat and started people-watching to pass the time.

She saw two men sit down a few rows in front of her. One was wearing a beautiful black cowboy hat, and the other was wearing a dark gray herringbone hat. The man in the herringbone hat had a curly wire going from an earpiece down into his overcoat.

"Must be a VIP," Laney mused. *"He brought security with him. And that cowboy hat makes him look like he's part of the Texas delegation."*

Laney had already spotted several familiar faces from her work with the Tarrant County Party and the State Party. As she continued staring at the cowboy hat, she heard someone call her name. Turning, she saw Elizabeth Talbot, the Texas State Party Chairman, and her husband Elliot moving down the aisle toward her.

Laney stood and gave Elizabeth and Elliot a hug. They had met on several occasions and had become friends.

Once seated, Elizabeth asked, "What are you doing in Dwight's seats?"

"Linda broke her leg in two places back in December, so Dwight asked me to represent the firm today."

Elizabeth nodded. "Well, good for you! You know... I was hoping to have a conversation with you in the next week or so, once the dust settles from all of this." She gestured to the crowds. "Perhaps we can chat today."

"How about now?" Laney suggested.

Elizabeth laughed. "You lawyers are always so focused on getting things done sooner than later. All right, let's chat. We've been watching you for some time, and you've done great work for the party in Tarrant County. So much so that we think you're ready for bigger and better things."

"What *kind* of bigger and better things?" Laney asked cautiously.

"We want you to join the State Party Leadership Committee. Take what you've been doing in Tarrant County and help us do that state-wide."

Laney was stunned at the offer. She wanted to work at the state level—possibly even the national level at some point—but she didn't think her career would allow her to devote that kind of time to any outside activities.

"I'm honored, Elizabeth," she said after a moment. "I need to think about it, if that's okay."

Elizabeth smiled knowingly. "Yes, being the newest partner at your law firm will place a lot of demands on your free time. But we're willing to work around all that. That's how badly we want you on the committee."

The musical prelude to the ceremony began. Elizabeth leaned close so she could be heard. "I don't need an answer now. Just think about it. Are you going to the ball tonight? I know Dwight had passes to The Starlight Ball."

Laney nodded.

"Good. We'll be there, too. We have a table for the Texas mega-donors. Join us there, and we can talk more. There are some important people I want you to meet who'll be sitting with us. It'll be good exposure for you."

"Dwight used those exact same words when he gave me his tickets."

"He knows I want you on the committee," Elizabeth said. "I've made no secret of that fact. Perhaps he knew we'd run into each other today."

The ceremony was beautiful, if long. The Vice President was sworn in first, and then the President. The President's inaugural address was stirring, but Alex found himself wondering how much of the President's agenda would actually get accomplished. He had heard too many inaugural addresses in his life to believe that everything would be done. Still, he knew Tom, and he knew Charley, and if anyone could do all that had been promised in the address and during the campaign, it was Tom and Charley.

After the ceremony was over, Alex and Mike left the Capitol and headed toward First Street SW and Washington Avenue SW, where Ray was waiting. Mike communicated with Ray and Travis as he and Alex made their way through the crowds. They spotted Ray close to the green security screening checkpoint, and the three of them headed toward the Capitol South Metro Station.

They arrived several minutes later. Travis had the SUV running, and the heat was on full as they climbed inside.

"How was it, Boss?" Travis asked as he pulled onto First Street and started working his way around the city back to their hotel.

"Cold, but great," Alex confirmed. "The seats were perfect, and it was good to see Charley sworn in as Vice President."

Laney made her way to the shuttle bus pick-up location. She was so busy thinking about what Elizabeth had offered her that she almost walked right past the bus. If it weren't for the Waldorf Astoria logo painted on the side, she wouldn't have noticed, and then she'd have to either walk or try to catch a cab back to the hotel.

She climbed onto the bus and found an empty seat. The shuttle bus left a minute later. It was a short ride to the hotel, and when the shuttle arrived, Laney wasted no time getting out of the cold and inside the warm lobby.

As she headed toward the elevators, she saw the man in the black cowboy hat heading for the top floor elevator bank. There were two men with him—both with earpieces. One was the man in the herringbone hat, and one was wearing a charcoal fedora.

"He has more than one person guarding him. Must be a MAJOR VIP. I wonder if he's going to one of the balls tonight."

Just before the man in the cowboy hat disappeared around the corner, she caught a glimpse of his face. *"He looks familiar. I know I've met him before, but I can't remember who he is."*

Her elevator arrived, and she rode it up to her floor, still wondering who the man in the cowboy hat was.

CHAPTER 4

lex exited the bedroom of his suite at 6:30 PM on the evening after the inauguration. He was wearing a classic tuxedo—white shirt, black bow tie, black dinner jacket and pants, black waistcoat, black shoes, and black cufflinks and shirt studs. His American Flag lapel pin was the only splash of color on his outfit that night.

After returning from the inauguration, he ordered crab cakes from room service for lunch, and then he took a nap so he'd be rested for the ball. He felt refreshed, and he was looking forward to the evening's festivities.

Mike and Travis were standing in front of the TV in the living area, watching the news. They were also wearing classic tuxedos, even though only Mike would be entering the part of Union Station where the ball was being held. Ray, who had gone downstairs to bring the SUV around to the hotel entrance, would be staying with the car, and Travis would be patrolling the outer perimeter of the venue inside Union Station.

"Look at this, Boss," Mike said, pointing to the television. The screen showed huge lines of people, wearing their finest tuxedos and evening gowns, lined up in the street and fighting the cold.

"What am I looking at?" Alex asked.

"That's the crowd of people trying to get into the Commander in Chief Ball and the Liberty Ball. They're both being held at the Washington Convention Center, and that's the line waiting to get through security."

"Are we going to face something like that for The Starlight Ball?" Alex inquired.

Mike shook his head. "No, there's a drop-off at the main entrance to Union Station, and there's another entrance for those coming from the parking garage. The lines to get into the ball's venue area itself are all inside the building. No standing outside in the cold, waiting to get in. They don't want to piss off the mega donors."

"But they don't mind pissing off the people going to the other two balls?" Travis asked. "That doesn't make sense."

"Hopefully it's a snafu with the venue and not something the organizers planned," Mike offered.

"Or someone is trying to piss off the people who voted for Tom and Charley," Alex said. "Whatever the cause, we should get going."

Everyone grabbed their overcoats and put them on. Alex reached for his cowboy hat, then he hesitated. *"No, not tonight,"* he thought. He pulled on his gloves, checked to make certain that he had the passes to the ball and his identification, and then followed his security staff into the hallway.

As they rode down the elevator, Alex asked, "Are we being dropped off at the main entrance, or are we coming in through the parking garage?" Alex had been assigned a reserved VIP parking space on Level 2.

"Main entrance," Mike confirmed. "It's a much shorter walk to the venue space."

When they reached the front of the hotel, Ray was already waiting for them outside the lobby doors. Alex got into the back seat first, followed by Mike. Once his seatbelt was fastened, Alex handed Ray the VIP Parking Pass for the Union Station parking garage, and he handed Mike his Guest Pass to the ball.

"Thanks, Boss," Ray and Mike both said.

Travis entered the SUV, and then Ray pulled away from the hotel.

Ray traveled down Pennsylvania Avenue NW away from the hotel and The White House, turned onto 12th Street NW, then onto E Street NW to Columbus Circle, where Union Station was located. In spite of the number of cars waiting to drop off passengers, the line moved quickly, and soon Alex, Mike, and Travis were walking through the main entrance. Ray looped around to Massachusetts Avenue NW and then followed the signs to the Union Station Parking Garage.

They checked their coats so they wouldn't have to carry them around, and then Travis moved off to the right to begin his patrol while Alex and Mike headed left to the security checkpoint. It was shortly after 7:00 PM, and the signs at the checkpoint said that entry would be allowed at 7:30 PM. They stood in the middle of the growing crowd of guests who were also waiting for the ball to begin.

When the clock showed that it was 7:30 PM, security

began allowing the guests to enter. Alex and Mike waited their turn and were finally able to reach the security checkpoint.

After presenting their passes and IDs, the guards used metal detecting wands to check both of them for weapons. The guards looked at Mike's communications devices and noted that he had clearance from Secret Service to keep the equipment with him.

Once allowed into the venue, they stopped to get their photo taken, and then they were given wide white satin lanyards for their guest passes, which were to remain visible at all times. Alex hooked his pass onto the lanyard and put the lanyard around his neck. Mike did the same. Then they entered the ball area.

This was not Alex's first time inside Union Station, but it was the first time he had attended an event there. A number of round and square tables were set up around the venue, and there was a large stage at one end where the President and Vice President would enter and dance their first dance. The main dance floor was directly in front of the stage. There were several bars and buffet tables around the outer perimeter of the tables, and waiters were busy bringing drinks and finger foods to the tables.

"Do you see Elizabeth Talbot?" Alex asked.

"Not yet," Mike replied, surveying the tables. "I see Senator Barlow and his wife, though. Won't Elizabeth be sitting at his table?"

"Let's go find out."

"You go ahead, Boss," Mike said. "I'll find a spot where I can keep an eye on you. Signal me if you need anything."

"Thanks, Mike." As Mike headed off, Alex walked toward Senator Barlow, who recognized Alex immediately.

"Alex Barclay! Good to see you, old friend. How have you been?"

Alex shook the Senator's hand and kissed his wife on the cheek. "Doing well, Senator. You?"

"Glad today is almost over and we can get to work starting tomorrow."

"Weather permitting."

"True," Senator Barlow acknowledged.

Elizabeth Talbot and her husband walked up. "I see the Texas delegation is beginning to arrive," Elizabeth said, giving Alex and Senator Barlow a peck on their cheeks and hugging the Senator's wife. "You remember my husband, Elliot?"

Alex and the Senator shook Elliot's hand, and then they all sat down at the large round table where Alex had found Senator Barlow and his wife. Elizabeth pulled out a Texas flag on a small wooden stick and placed it in the vase that was part of the table's centerpiece.

"Now it'll be easier to find our table," she explained.

Several more Texas mega-donors arrived and joined Alex and the others at the table. Alex knew all of them from fundraisers he had attended and hosted over the years, as well as from the Cattlemen's Association meetings and events he had attended. Soon there was only one empty seat left, and it was the one next to Alex.

"I invited someone to join us," Elizabeth said. "She works with the Tarrant Country Party, but I'm trying to get her to join the State Party Leadership Committee. She's here representing Dwight, who's her boss. Evidently, Linda broke her leg last weekend, so Laney got Dwight's tickets."

"Laney?" Senator Barlow asked.

"Laney Connor. She's one of Dwight's associates who's

going to be his newest partner in a few months. She's the sharpest contracts attorney I've ever met. You'll like her."

Elizabeth looked toward the venue entrance and smiled. "Speaking of Laney, here she comes now."

Alex turned to look. What he saw was a strikingly beautiful brunette walking toward him, wearing a deep blue asymmetrical dress that seemed to shimmer as she moved. She was tall, her eyes sparkled, and her smile was intoxicating. *"What a beautiful woman! Why couldn't that matchmaker have introduced me to HER?"* As the woman approached the table, Alex thought, *"There's something familiar about her, but her up-do and that dress is making it hard to place where we've met."* He checked her left hand and didn't see a wedding ring. Then he thought back to Elizabeth saying that Laney was a contracts attorney who worked for Dwight. *"That's Delaney Connor!"* he thought. *"She drafted the trust contracts for the ranch two years ago. I certainly don't remember her looking like THAT, and I didn't know she went by Laney. My God... her beauty is mesmerizing!"*

Laney arrived at the table. "Am I the last to arrive? Sorry about that. The line outside is *huge*, and they ran out of hangars at the coat check."

Without thinking about anything other than how much he wanted to spend time with and get to know this woman, Alex stood and pulled out the empty chair for Laney. She smiled as she sat, and he pushed her chair in and then sat next to her.

"Hello, Delaney. I don't know if you remember me—"

"You're Alexander Barclay," she said immediately. "I did some contract work for you a while back... something for your ranch."

"Setting up a trust for my ranch's operations," Alex reminded her. "And I prefer 'Alex'."

"That's it. And please call me Laney." Laney stared at him. Then she asked. "By any chance were you wearing a black cowboy hat at the ceremony this morning?"

Alex nodded. "I opted to leave it at the hotel tonight. It just didn't seem right to wear it in here."

Laney laughed. "I was sitting a couple of rows behind you with Elizabeth and Elliot, and then I saw you in the Waldorf Astoria lobby afterwards."

"That was probably me," Alex confirmed.

"Laney," Elizabeth interrupted. "Let me introduce you to the rest of the table." Elizabeth introduced everyone, and then she proceeded to take control of the conversation.

"What time are the President and Vice President supposed to arrive?" Elliot asked Senator Barlow a few minutes later.

"Sometime between 8:30 and 9:00, depending on how much time he spends at the other two balls," the Senator replied. "The Commander in Chief ball is for the military, so there will be a lot of pomp and ceremony when the President arrives. The Liberty ball is for the President's campaign staff and transition team, so he'll need to stay long enough to speak with them. Fortunately, both of those balls are in the same place, just one floor apart. Then he comes here, and he'll stay here until he returns to The White House."

Elizabeth was about to interject when Senator Barlow looked at Alex and said, "So, Alex, I'm dying to know if the rumors are true."

"What rumors are those, Senator?" Alex inquired, ignoring the annoyed look on Elizabeth's face.

"That you're retiring."

The other mega-donors, who knew Alex and what he did for a living, stared at Alex with their mouths agape. Even Elizabeth was shocked into silence.

Alex nodded. "It's true. I'm selling my consulting company."

"How can you just walk away from something you built and is so successful?" Barlow asked.

"I'm not just walking away, Senator. I'm selling it to the partners of the firm over a three-year period. As of this past December, they own a third of the firm. I've stopped getting involved in the day-to-day operations, and I only meet with the partners monthly. After this coming December, they'll own two-thirds of the firm, and I'll only meet with the partners quarterly. Then, as of December of next year, they'll own the entire firm, and I'll be out. I've spent years putting the right people in the right positions, and it's time to see what they can do on their own. The reason I'm letting them buy me out over three years is so there's time to make adjustments to the partnership if we find that someone isn't as ready as I thought they were."

"But after this December, you won't be in charge if you only own a third of the company," Elliot pointed out.

Alex smiled. "Actually, the partnership agreement is a unique one. As long as I own a single partner share, I control all votes. It's still my company until they buy the last share from me at the end of next year."

"Clever," Senator Barlow said. "But why retire? You're only... what? Mid-40s? What are you going to do with yourself?"

"Enjoy my ranch, Senator," Alex replied. "I built a state of the art facility, and I never get to spend any time there. I'm going to raise my horses, ride every day, and enjoy my land."

"I forgot about your ranch," the Senator commented. "Your spread is north of Fort Worth, isn't it?"

Alex nodded.

"What is it... fifty thousand acres?"

"Sixty-four thousand," Alex corrected him. "A hundred square miles."

Barlow stared at Alex for a moment. Then he said, "You didn't answer my original question, Alex. *Why* are you retiring?"

Alex took a deep breath and let it out slowly. "I started consulting right out of college, and by twenty-five, I had started my firm with twenty associates. I had five hundred associates within three years, and in the past twenty-three years, it has grown to tens of thousands of associates and hundreds of partners across the English-speaking world. I built an amazing company, and it has helped many clients while making my staff and me very rich. Now I'm in my 40s. I'm wealthier than I ever imagined I'd be, and I have a beautiful home out at the ranch. Plus I have Barclay Aerospace and my real estate investments. But I have no one to share all of that with. I traded work for relationships... and I live alone. I have no one to inherit what I've built. I sacrificed having a family to be successful, only to realize that family is required to be a successful person. I'm missing half of my life, and if I want that half, something has to give. Since I'm not getting rid of the ranch, and since Barclay Aerospace is a family business, that really runs itself without me, then I had to walk away from my career to have room in my life for the one thing I want the most but don't have—a wife and children. So that's why I'm retiring. I want a family while I'm still young enough to enjoy and appreciate them. I want someone to pass on my name to, my fortune, and my ranch. I'm tired of my worth being judged by wealth; I want it judged by my happiness and the joy that comes with having a family. My career got me where I am, sure, but it can't give me what I'm missing. To pursue one, I have to leave the other, so that's what I'm doing. End of story."

The senator looked unconvinced. "I see that you're here alone. Have you identified your future wife yet?"

"Not yet, Senator," Alex replied. "I thought I had, but I was mistaken. One thing I know: if I don't step back from working full-time, I'll never find a wife."

The Senator just stared at Alex. "You're serious. You want a family so badly that you'd walk away from billions to get it?"

"Were you married before or after you entered politics?" Alex asked.

"Before," the Senator replied, squeezing his wife's hand. "We got married in college."

"So you had your family in place before you pursued your careers, and you were able to grow them at the same time."

Senator Barlow nodded.

"I was too busy in college to date, then I was too busy building my company to date, then I was too busy running my company to date, and now I have a great company and no life. We are not the same, Senator. You knew you needed to seize the opportunities as they presented themselves to you. I chose to avoid all distractions to my career, only to realize that my career would never make me happy. Rich? Successful? Yes. Happy? No."

"So you're just walking away from it all?" Laney asked.

"Yes. The family business stays in the family, but like I said, I don't get involved in the day-to-day operations of that. My cousin runs my real estate investments. The consulting company, which took all of my time, is in good hands now. I'd rather go out on top than die and be remembered only for my business accomplishments."

"You're also an author," Elliot pointed out.

"Mostly business books," Alex acknowledged. "I've only recently started writing novels. But that's just a creative outlet. It doesn't give me what I really want."

Senator Barlow shook his head. "If I didn't know you, I'd never believe it. But hearing you explain it all, I think I understand. I'm still shocked to the core that you'd be willing to do something so drastic, but I understand why. I wish you the best of luck, old friend. May you find what you're looking for."

The waiters brought over drinks, and Elizabeth seized the opportunity to dominate the conversation again. She was about to pull Laney into a new topic when the United States Army Band began playing. A few of the guests headed for the dance floor.

Alex suddenly felt like dancing, and he couldn't help himself from wanting to feel Laney in his arms. He didn't know why that desire hit him so hard, but he decided not to fight it. Turning to Laney, he asked, softly, "Would you like to dance?"

Laney stared at him for a moment. Then she smiled and nodded.

Alex stood and held out his hand. Elizabeth glared at him as Laney took his hand and followed him to the dance floor. Elliot and Senator Barlow just grinned.

CHAPTER 5

Alex and Laney danced until the song ended, and when the band began playing another song, Alex suggested they keep dancing, and Laney quickly agreed. She felt something she had never felt before when she was in his powerful arms... an attraction, but more than that. It was as if her whole life had brought her to this place at this moment, and it was to find herself in his arms. *"It may sound silly, but that's how this feels,"* she thought as he led her around the dance floor. *"What would Dwight think if he saw me now?"*

Laney glanced back at the table and saw Elizabeth talking animatedly about something, and Laney had no desire to listen to Elizabeth's attempts to secure her role as State Committee Chairman for another year. She wanted to be dancing with Alex for the rest of the night.

"What brings you to the ball by yourself?" Alex asked, bringing Laney's thoughts back to the ball.

"The guy I had been dating for a couple of months broke up with me the day I was going to ask him to come with me," Laney admitted. "He said he didn't care for my politics. Honestly, is that any reason to break up with someone?"

"It's not a very good reason, but if his views are very different from yours, then there are probably other incompatibilities that would surface eventually. Sounds to me like you dodged a bullet."

"I did," Laney agreed. "And what about you? Why are you here by yourself?"

"A couple of reasons," Alex replied. "In early December, I broke up with the girl I had been dating for a few months, and my cousin, who usually comes with me to events like this, has two sick children at home and had to cancel on me last minute."

"But you came anyway?"

Alex nodded. "Charley Glass is a good friend, and he and I were roommates at Purdue. I wasn't going to miss seeing him sworn in as Vice President, and Tom Watkins is also a friend. I'm here for them."

Laney couldn't help but think about Alex retiring from his business to start a family. She felt she was approaching the point where she was going to face the same choice. *"Would I have the courage to do what he did? Could I AFFORD to do what he did?"*

Looking at Alex's face, which she enjoyed looking at very much, she said, "You mentioned at the table that you were retiring to have time for a family. I'm curious about how you met the girl you broke up with, if it's not too personal to ask about it."

Alex chuckled. "It's personal, but I'll answer on one

condition."

"What condition?" Laney asked, seeing the mischievous twinkle in his eye.

"I'm still a client of your law firm, right? So anything I say to you is protected under attorney-client privilege?"

Laney smiled. Relationship topics were a gray area for a contracts attorney, but this was clearly important to him. She decided to play along. "Yes, it's protected."

"Good. To be completely honest, I used a matchmaker. I sat down with this woman and told her what I was looking for—not in terms of physical traits, but in terms of the kind of *person* I wanted to be with, her... qualities for lack of a better word. She immediately decided that I needed to be paired with someone *much* younger, and she introduced me to a 24-year-old internet content creator from North Carolina."

"Someone young enough to be your daughter?" Laney thought that was a strange choice.

"I asked the matchmaker about that, and she said I needed someone to make me feel young, someone who didn't have a lot of experience and baggage, and someone... as she put it... fertile enough to have and raise children as I got older."

"I guess that makes sense," Laney admitted. "What was she like?"

"Penny was a petite little fireball who loved snowboarding, hiking, and partying with her girlfriends. Frankly, I thought she was adorable. We hit it off immediately. Bethany Haskins, the matchmaker, had an... shall we say... unorthodox process when pairing one of her clients with a potential match. She's one of those matchmakers who demands that her clients have a certain net worth. She won't compromise on that. Her process is like nothing Penny or I had ever experienced before, but it seemed to work because we became very close very quickly. She was living in Charlotte at the time, and after spending a couple of weeks with her out there, I brought her back to the ranch to see how she'd like living in Texas."

Alex paused. "You know, I've never talked about this before. If it's too much information, let me know."

"No, please go on," Laney responded, more curious than ever.

The band started playing another tune, and Alex and Laney stayed on the dance floor.

"Well, things were progressing nicely. She loved the ranch, we found a horse that was the perfect size for her, and she enjoyed riding. We travelled, and she taught me to be more adventurous." Alex dipped Laney. "The first problem showed up when we were in Europe. One of her social media sponsors is a camera company. They insisted that she record and post all of her travels, and the camera automatically geo-tagged the videos. My security detail went nuts when they found out that she had taken video footage of me, and then posted it immediately with geo-tags that showed where I was. They insisted that she take down the videos and remove the tags, but that violated her agreement with the camera company. She also didn't like having a security detail with her when she got together with her girlfriends. She felt they were spying on her, rather than protecting her. I was willing to work with her on these issues, but her career was on the rise, and she felt that my security concerns, not to mention the fact that the ranch is in the middle of nowhere, were too limiting for her. As she put it, they were clipping her wings. In the end, we decided to part ways, and she moved back to Charlotte the week after Thanksgiving."

"That sucks," Laney said.

"It does, but she had to do what she felt was right for her, just as I have to do what I feel is right for me. Security is a real concern. So is privacy. What I need is someone who understands that and can work within those parameters. Not an unreasonable request, but clearly something Penny was... too young to handle."

"Are you going to try again?" Laney asked.

"Eventually," Alex stated. "Probably. I don't think I'll use Bethany's services again, but I might try a different matchmaker or try to find someone on my own. I want to try again. I didn't decide to retire just so I'd have even more time by myself."

Laney almost asked if he might like to date her, but she quickly realized that question was inappropriate... and probably a little creepy... and *very* pushy. She also found what Alex went through to be fascinating... especially about using a matchmaking service. "You have me curious. What was so unorthodox about your matchmaker's process?"

At that moment, the band began playing "Hail to the Chief," and Alex saw the First Family and the Second Family step out onto the stage. There was thunderous applause from the guests that lasted several minutes.

"I'm afraid that's a conversation for another time," Alex said. He led Laney back to their table as the newly sworn-in President and Vice President began dancing with their wives.

Laney watched the President dancing with the First Lady, but she also glanced at Alex several times. *"I know he cited attorney-client privilege before he told me those things, but he still opened up to me, saying things he'd never told anyone before. It's sad what he went through, right after he made the decision to retire, and it seems to be affecting him more than how Liam ending our relationship affected me."*

She watched Alex and decided that he was about the most handsome man she had ever met. She knew his reputation as a force to be reckoned with in the business world, she had seen videos of him delivering speeches to crowds of listeners, and she remembered the intricate details he wanted in the contracts she prepared for him. But looking at his face—his eyes, the slightly weathered look of his face, the set of his jaw, the streaks of gray lightening his dark hair—she tried to imagine him in a denim shirt tossing hay bales to his horses. She knew him as a brilliant and successful man, but getting to know him on a personal level while they were dancing showed her another side of him. *"He's someone I could fall for in a heartbeat,"* she thought.

As she continued watching Alex, and what was happening on the stage in front of her, she had another thought. *"I really want to know what was so unorthodox about that matchmaker's process. I may want to try it myself someday."*

After the President and Vice President finished the first dance, both men spoke to the crowd of enthusiastic mega-donors and family members. Then they started making their way around the room to greet the guests.

When the Vice President saw Alex sitting with Senator Barlow, he and his wife came over to the table. Alex stood, and he and the Vice President hugged. Alex then kissed the Second Lady on the cheek and introduced everyone at the table.

"Good to see you, buddy," Charley said to Alex.

"Good to see you, too, *Mr. Vice President*," Alex responded. Turning to Charley's wife, he said, "Gina, I assume you're still happy that I introduced the two of you."

Second Lady Gina Glass beamed. "Best thing you ever did for us... apart from all those donations you made to the campaign."

"Ah, spoken like a true politician's wife," Alex joked.

The President approached the table with his wife, Carol. "Good evening, Mr. President," Alex said. He gave Carol a wink as he introduced everyone to the President.

Tom shook hands with everyone around the table. "It's good to see Texas so well represented," he said to Senator Barlow. "I can't thank you enough for all the support you gave to Charley and me. We're both very grateful."

With that, the First and Second Families, and their security, moved on to the next table of donors that they needed to greet.

"Is anyone else hungry?" Elliot asked. "I'm starving. I think I'll check out the buffet tables. The appetizers they keep bringing around just aren't doing it for me."

"I'll go with you," Alex said. Looking at Laney, he asked, "Can I bring you anything?"

Laney stood. "May I join you?"

Alex smiled and nodded. Then the three of them headed for the buffet.

Once they were away from the table, Elliot said, "I'm

sorry about how Elizabeth is acting tonight. She came to DC with an agenda and forgot that everyone else here has their own agendas, too. Laney, she really does want to bring you onto the State Committee, and it's for all the right reasons. Don't let how pushy she's acting dissuade you. The entire committee voted to bring you onboard."

"Thanks, Elliot," Laney said as she grabbed a plate and started loading it with food. "And I'm still considering the offer. I just need to see if being a law partner will allow me to give the time to the committee that it needs."

"I understand," Elliot said. Looking at Alex, he added, "And don't let Elizabeth be an irritant to you, Alex. It's not personal, and sometimes I think she forgets that other people are also used to getting their way. She knows what you did for the Party, and the state and national campaigns, and she certainly doesn't want to jeopardize your future generosity."

Alex laughed. "No worries, Elliot. I'm used to her way of operating. I'm just not going to give in to it."

"Perfect," Elliot said. "It'll do her good to know there are people she can't push around who are vital to the Party's success."

When Alex, Laney, and Elliot had their food, three waiters took their plates and carried them to the table. After depositing the plates, napkins, and utensils, the waiters moved on to help other guests.

After Alex and Laney had finished eating, Alex asked her if she wanted to dance, and she agreed.

Once they had left the table, Elliot gently put his hand on Elizabeth's wrist. "Relax, dear. You may have come to the ball to conduct business, but those two came to enjoy their evening and to celebrate the inauguration of two great men. Right now, they're enjoying each other's company, and I think they deserve to be left alone. Plenty of time to conduct business after we get back to Texas."

Elizabeth glared at her husband, and then her expression softened. "You're right. Plenty of time... later."

Alex and Laney spent most of the next several hours dancing. As the clock on the wall showed that it was just after midnight, Alex asked, "How did you get here? Did you drive or take a cab?"

"I took a cab."

"I imagine it'll be hard to find one back to the hotel. I have a car in the parking deck. I'd be happy to give you a ride back when we leave."

"Your security detail won't mind?" Laney asked, grateful for his offer.

"I'll make it work. The fact that you're one of my attorneys will help considerably."

Laney laughed, but she hoped he wouldn't continue to think of her as just one of his attorneys. "How long are you staying in DC?"

"I was going to fly home Wednesday, but if the weather gets as bad as they're predicting, then we might not be able to leave until the weekend. What about you?"

"My flight is scheduled to leave Wednesday late-morning," she replied.

"Do you have plans for tomorrow?"

Laney's heart skipped a beat as she shook her head. "None that I know of. It'll probably be too crowded for sightseeing, and if the weather's bad, it'll be foolish to leave the hotel."

"Would you like to have breakfast with me?"

Laney looked into his eyes and smiled. She wanted

nothing more than to spend more time with him. "How about brunch? After all this dancing, I'll probably sleep in."

"Brunch it is. Say... ten-thirty?"

"That works for me. I assume casual will be fine. I don't like getting dressed up like this every day."

"Casual is perfect, although I must say that I absolutely love that dress on you. It's... well, it's stunning."

Laney blushed. "And you look dashing in that tux, but it's an after-six tux and not really proper for brunch."

"A woman who knows her formal wear," Alex grinned. "That's refreshing. The only time I get to wear a morning suit is at early or mid-day weddings. But at least being semi-retired lets me wear boots and jeans almost every day. It's a nice change from business suits."

"That I'll have to see." Laney chuckled. "You wear that tux like it's part of who you are. I can't imagine you dressed like a rancher. I've only seen you in suits and formal wear."

"I'll have you out to the ranch when the weather gets warmer, and you'll be surrounded by people who look like ranchers. Do you ride?"

"Horses? I used to. Not much time since I started law school."

"We'll have to do something about that," Alex stated. "Riding is how I clear my head. It's amazing how answers seem come to you when it's just you, the horse, and beautiful land to ride on."

The band stopped playing and announced that they'd return in ten minutes.

"It's getting late," Laney said. "When are you planning to leave?"

"Whenever you're ready," Alex answered. He looked around the venue and saw Mike watching him. Alex gestured for Mike to join him.

"The head of my security detail is coming over here. If you're ready to head back to the hotel, I'll let him know."

"I'm ready as soon as I get my coat. We should probably say goodnight to the others at the table first."

Alex agreed.

Mike walked up. "About ready to go, Boss?"

"Yes, Mike. Laney, this is Mike Billingsley, the head of my security detail. Mike, this is Laney Connor from Fort Worth. She's actually one of my contract attorneys. She's staying at the Waldorf, too, and I offered her a ride. She and I will also be having brunch together in the morning."

Mike smiled. "I'll take care of it." Speaking into his communication device, he said, "Travis, we're getting ready to leave with the Boss and a guest. Ray, we need the car brought around to the main entrance."

Turning to Alex, Mike said, "If you'll give me your claim checks, Boss, I'll retrieve your and Miss Connor's coats."

Alex and Laney handed Mike their claim checks, and he headed for the entrance. Alex and Laney returned to their table to say goodnight to everyone.

"You're leaving together?" Senator Barlow asked.

"We're at the same hotel, and I have a car here. It's the neighborly thing to do, don't you think?"

Barlow nodded, hiding his smirk.

Elizabeth whispered something to Laney, and then Laney and Alex left the venue. Once they had retrieved their coats and scarfs from Mike, they headed toward Union Station's main entrance. Alex introduced Laney to Travis when he joined them.

There was a small crowd at the main entrance, waiting

for cars to pick them up, and a sign pointing to the taxi queue had an even longer line.

"I'm glad you offered me a ride," Laney said. "I'd be here all night waiting for a cab."

Mike listened to his earpiece, and then he said, "Ray is double-parked outside. Shall we go?"

They exited Union Station and immediately felt a blast of icy wind blowing around them. The SUV was one lane over from the line of cars waiting for pick-ups. They crossed to the SUV, and Alex helped Laney into the back seat and then joined her. Mike entered the back seat last, and Travis got into the front seat. Then Ray pulled away from Union Station and headed back to the hotel.

They made good time to the Waldorf Astoria, and Ray dropped everyone off at the main entrance before parking the SUV.

"May I escort you to your room?" Alex asked.

Laney beamed, and she felt her heart skip a beat again. "What a gentleman! Yes, I'd love that."

Mike turned to Travis. "Go up and do a sweep of the Boss' room. I'll meet you in the hallway outside his room in a few minutes."

Travis nodded and headed to the elevators that went to the top floor. Mike stayed with Alex and Laney, although he took a couple of steps to the side out of respect for their privacy.

They rode up to Laney's floor. "Where is your room?" Alex asked once they exited the elevator.

"About halfway down the hall," she replied.

Alex looked at Mike, who stopped and returned to the elevator to wait for Alex to return. Alex then walked with Laney to her door.

"I'll come get you at ten-thirty in the morning. If anything changes, call my room."

"I will, Alex, thanks." Laney stared at him for a moment, and before they knew it, they were wrapped in a tight embrace. Their lips met, and it was like they were transported to another plane of existence. Neither knew who kissed first, and it didn't matter. In their minds, the whole day had been leading to this moment.

After what seemed like several minutes, their lips separated and they looked at each other. Alex smiled and said, "So I'll see you at ten-thirty?"

Laney, her cheeks flushed, nodded. "Yes, thin-turty, I mean ten-thirty, will be nice. Goodnight, Alex."

"Goodnight, Laney. Sleep well."

"You, too."

Laney entered her room and closed the door behind her. Alex walked back to Mike, who pushed the button for the elevator. Alex ignored the wide grin on Mike's face.

Alex knew he'd be thinking about that kiss all night.

Laney knew the exact same thing.

CHAPTER 6

$\mathcal{A}$lex and Mike took the elevator down to the lobby at ten-twenty the next morning. Alex was wearing jeans, casual shoes, and a sweater.

He appeared to be well rested, but he was anything but. It had taken him forever to fall asleep the night before, and he woke up several times, thinking about Laney, the kiss, and how attractive he found her.

"Am I actually thinking about dating someone I met at a ball? The reason I hired a matchmaker is because I don't know how to date someone. If I try to date Laney, assuming she even wants that, I'm swinging on a trapeze without a net—no process, no managed expectations, just two people figuring it out as they go. Am I really willing to take that risk? Am I confident enough in myself to do this the old-fashioned way? I can convince a board of directors to spend a billion dollars to merge with their largest competitor, but how do I make a woman want to

be with me? Or maybe I don't try to make her want anything. Maybe I just let things unfold naturally. But how does that work? I guess I'll worry about this later."

When he reached the lobby, the scene was not what he expected to see at such a posh hotel.

The predicted weather front hit about three-thirty that morning, bringing 30-mile-per-hour winds and dumping several inches of snow. The snow was still coming down heavily. The three major Washington DC airports—Dulles, Reagan, and Baltimore—were all closed due to wind and field conditions. All of the people who attended the inauguration and were planning to fly home on Tuesday were now stranded. People were crowded at the front desk, trying to extend their stay at the hotel while talking to the airlines on their phones to reschedule their flights. Those not standing at the front desk were in line waiting for tables at one of the restaurants.

It was chaos.

Alex and Mike surveyed the disarray for a minute before heading to the elevator bank that would take them to Laney's floor.

Once inside the elevator, Mike asked, "What's the plan, Boss? You'll never get a table down there, and I doubt the sidewalks are passable, even if any of the local restaurants are open."

"I think room service is the only way to go," Alex replied. "It may take a while, but at least we'll be in comfortable surroundings."

"You're going to bring her back to the suite?" Mike asked.

Alex nodded. "Do you have a better idea?"

Mike shook his head. Then he spoke into his

communications device. "Travis? Ray? Boss is bringing his guest back to the suite. Do a quick scan of the place and straighten up what you can."

Alex smiled at Mike's attention to detail. "Thanks, Mike."

"No problem, Boss."

They arrived at Laney's floor. Mike remained at the elevator, and Alex walked to her room. He knocked on the door, and Laney opened it almost immediately.

"Good morning, Alex," she purred. She was wearing white leggings, low-top sneakers, a light blue sweater, and her hair was pulled back in a ponytail. She looked completely different than she had the night before, but Alex thought she was still striking. The leggings showed the shape of her legs beautifully, and being a leg man, Alex found them irresistible. *"My God, she's beautiful. It wasn't just the dress, the hair, and the setting last night. It's everything about her."*

"Good morning, Laney," Alex said, focusing his attention on her face and her hypnotic eyes. "Change of plans."

"How do you mean?" she asked as she closed her room door.

"It's a madhouse downstairs," he explained as they walked toward the elevator. "We'd be lucky to get a table before the dinner service. But... my room has a dining table that seats six, so I was thinking we order room service. It may take a while for them to bring up the food, but at least we'd be comfortable while we wait."

Laney nodded. "Sounds like a good plan. I looked out the window, and going outside today is definitely not an option. Is the lobby really that crazy right now?"

"You're about to see for yourself," Alex said as they got into the elevator and rode downstairs.

If anything, it was even crazier when they reached the lobby than it had been when Alex and Mike came though.

"Oh, yes, room service is definitely a better idea," Laney said as they walked to the elevators that went to the top floor.

A few minutes later, they arrived at Alex's suite. Travis was standing guard outside. Alex turned to Mike and said, "I don't think I'll be needing anything for a while. Room service will be here at some point, but apart from that, I think we're good."

Mike nodded, and Alex opened the door of his suite so Laney could enter.

"Good God, this is your room?" Laney sounded stunned. "This is my first time staying at a Waldorf Astoria, but I never imagined that a hotel suite could be this grand. This is nicer than my townhouse."

"And it's not even the biggest suite in the hotel," Alex informed her. "But it's my favorite. I always try to book it when I'm in town."

Laney looked around. "I'm not even going to ask what it costs a night. I don't think I want to know."

"You don't," Alex confirmed, "but it has all the comforts of home, apart from not having its own kitchen."

After giving her the tour, they sat on the couch. Alex grabbed the room service menu, a notepad, and a pen. "Let's figure out what we want to eat and get it ordered. The longer we wait to do that, the longer it'll take to get here."

They went through the menu and selected what they wanted for brunch. Alex wrote everything down, and then he called the room service number to place the order. When he hung up the phone, he said, "They say it'll be here in thirty minutes. We'll see, but I hope they're right. I'm starving."

"Me, too," Laney said. "But at least we have time to talk before the food arrives."

"Talk? That doesn't sound good," Alex thought. He turned to face her. "What do you want to talk about?"

"First of all, I want to thank you for last night—not just for dancing with me and making the night so special that way, but for opening up to me. You shared a lot, and I appreciate you trusting me enough to do that. Your secrets are safe."

"You're welcome," Alex said. "And thank you for listening. Like I said, I've never told anyone what I told you. It actually felt good to share it with someone. And thank you for making last night special for *me*. I went to the ball to see Charlie and Tom, but meeting you and having you as a dance partner made the evening different from anything I could have expected. I'll never forget it."

Laney nodded. She looked like she wanted to say something else, and Alex guessed what it was. "About that kiss?" he asked.

Laney blushed. "Yes... that kiss. I was thinking about it all night."

"You were? Me, too. It was wonderful."

"More than wonderful. It was the perfect end to a perfect day." Laney looked into Alex's eyes. "I don't want to overthink things—"

"Then don't," Alex interrupted. "We shared something that clearly we both wanted. There's nothing else to be said about it... unless it was too much... or not enough."

Laney blushed furiously, and Alex knew he had guessed correctly. "Okay, it wasn't enough. For either of us. That's not a bad thing, is it?"

"No... not a bad thing... just... oh hell." Laney sat back and stared at the ceiling. "Can I be honest with you? I mean completely honest, like you were with me last night?"

"Of course," Alex replied.

It took Laney a minute to start. "I'm going through the same thing that you went through before you decided to retire from your company," she finally said. "I sacrificed a lot to get where I am. I graduated college at twenty, I finished law school at twenty-three, and I've been an associate for nine years. This summer will be my tenth year, and I'm going to be made a partner on my anniversary. I never had time to date in college, no one has time to date in law school, and new associates at law firms barely have time to sleep, let alone be in a relationship. If you want to be a lawyer and have a family, you practically have to have the family first. I became a lawyer first, and now I'm feeling the emptiness that comes from having a great career but no one to share it with. And to top it off, I think Dwight wants it that way, so I'll be a slave to the firm with no social life to distract me."

Laney leaned forward. "Listening to you tell everyone about why you were retiring opened my mind to ideas I never had before. Like you, I'm at a crossroads between getting everything I ever wanted from my career and getting what I really want to give my life meaning. They're not the same thing, even though I had almost convinced myself that they were... until I listened to you last night at the table. I want a life partner. I want a family. I want it all, but I can't have it all, so what am I willing to give up? My career that I worked so hard for? My desire for a family that's getting stronger every day? After Liam dumped me, I decided to focus on career and forget about family, but... that kiss... shattered every decision I thought I'd made. Now I'm struggling. What do I really want?"

Laney threw up her hands and leaned back in silence.

Alex understood what she was going through. He had been there himself. "Do you mind if I ask you questions like I would with a client? I've found that helps to clarify one's thinking... most of the time."

Laney nodded and gestured for him to proceed.

"Okay," Alex began. "What is your work schedule right now? What kind of hours do you work in a week?"

"It's a small firm, and I do contract law, which isn't as time consuming as some specialties. I work between sixty and eighty hours a week, which includes many weekends."

"And let's say you make partner this summer. How much more of your time will that job take?"

"Partners are supposed to bring in clients, in addition to servicing clients, and they're supposed to mentor the new attorneys. Some of my client work will get assigned to one of those new attorneys, but between sales and mentoring, my hours would probably increase to ninety hours a week."

"So that's between twelve and fifteen hours a day?"

Laney nodded.

"And you still have to sleep?"

Laney nodded.

"And eat?"

Laney nodded.

"And work for the Tarrant County Party and possibly the State Party Committee?"

"That's the million-dollar question," Laney responded.

"And you'd have to fit in errands, hair appointments, car repairs, shopping, and getting gas whenever you can?"

Laney nodded.

"That leaves you barely enough time to survive, let alone have any sort of life outside of work. Now... let's say you want a family, or just extra hours away from work so you could actually have a life. What would you have to trade to get and keep that?"

"The partnership would be out of the question. Staying with a law firm would be, too," Laney answered after a minute. "There's no way I could even keep my current hours and try to have a life."

"And if you keep your current hours, or if you make partner and increase your hours, how long before you burn out completely?"

"I'm nearly there right now," Laney admitted. "Maybe a year at my current hours. Six months if I make partner."

"So remaining an attorney where you are now is unsustainable, regardless of whether or not you decide to pursue a life outside of work, right?"

Laney cocked her head to one side. "Why did you ask the last question like that? 'Where you are now'? What did you mean by that?"

"Look, you spent a lot of time and effort getting where you are. If you're about to make partner, then you're clearly good at what you do. It would be a shame to walk away from your career altogether, even though that's an option if you want a family badly enough. So, if you can't stay where you are, because you're on the verge of burning out, then where could you go that would allow you to practice law, reduce your hours, and have the life you feel is missing?"

Laney scowled for a few minutes. "You mean like going into private practice?"

"You tell me," Alex replied. "Private practice is different from being a corporate attorney, and both are different from working at a law firm. A private practice would make you a partner immediately, and you'd only have to acquire and service enough clients to pay for just you. Would that leave you enough time for a life, if you only had yourself to pay, and would you make enough to live on if you only worked... half of your current or projected hours?"

"Do I have to be the sole bread-winner to start a family?" Laney asked.

Alex shook his head. "It depends on who you choose as a life partner. If he makes a good living, or if you both make about the same, it depends on the life you want as to how much money will be required to make it work."

There was a knock at the door. "That was quick. I think our food is here," Alex said. He stood and opened the door.

Travis nodded to Alex, meaning that he had searched the room service cart, and let the room service waiter enter the suite.

Alex pointed to the dining table. "Set it up there, please."

The waiter complied. Once the food was on the table, along with the beverages and utensils, Alex signed the check.

"When you're finished, please call room service, and we'll send someone up to collect the dishes," the waiter said. "Please don't place any dishes in the hallway."

Alex nodded, and the waiter left. Alex gestured toward

the table, and Laney stood and joined him.

Alex held out the chair at the head of the table for Laney, and once she was seated, he sat in the corner chair next to her.

There was little conversation while they ate, and soon all the food was gone.

"That was wonderful, thanks!" Laney said.

Alex smiled. "I think that room service is better than the restaurants here, but don't tell anyone I said that. You can't get crab cakes like these in any of the restaurants downstairs."

Alex called room service, and five minutes later, another waiter arrived to clear the dishes. When he had left, Alex and Laney returned to the couch, stuffed and happy.

After several minutes of letting their food settle, Laney asked, "There's a lot of risk in what I'm contemplating, isn't there? I mean... if I go out on my own and don't make enough to support myself, I could be in real trouble financially. If I make enough to support myself but don't find a life partner, I could miss out on a lot of career opportunities that could only happen by staying with a law firm. Things could go terribly wrong for me."

"Or they could go wonderfully right," Alex pointed out. "You're on an express train to burnout if you stay where you are—regardless of whether or not you accept the partnership. If that happens, your career is over. So the options you need to focus on are the ones that keep you from burning out. Risk is a part of life. If you spend your life avoiding risks, you aren't actually living. You're just existing, and there's a big difference between the two. You don't want an unfulfilled life, believe me. If you accept the premise that you can have everything you want, if you're willing to modify *how* you do things, then it's a matter of rebuilding your life to leave room for the things you want and don't currently have. You *can* leave the law firm and become a corporate attorney or go into private practice. This will allow you to remain an attorney, but it'll leave you more time for yourself. If you're worried about finding someone, you can always use a matchmaker like I did."

"But that didn't work out for you."

Alex nodded. "True. The first match didn't take. It's rare to find the perfect match on the first try. It's a matter of refinement based on experience, just like dating, or so I'm told. I'm not willing to abandon the search just because there was an unfortunate result with the first attempt, but I also need a bit more time before I try again."

"So you don't regret using a matchmaker?"

Alex shook his head. "Not really. I don't see myself using Bethany again, but I can't deny that the first match almost worked out. The problem was one of careers. Hers was taking off as mine was winding down. There was an inherent incompatibility there, unless she was willing to walk away from her career, and I'd never ask her to do that. And just because the first one failed doesn't mean that the next one will."

"Do you think I should use your matchmaker?"

Alex laughed. "I don't think you make enough to meet her client requirements. But there are others out there who might work for you, if you wanted to pursue that."

"How much would I have to make to use your matchmaker?" Laney asked. "If you don't mind me asking."

Alex hesitated before answering, and then he said, "A net worth of ten figures or higher."

"You have to be a billionaire?"

Alex nodded.

Laney remembered reading the list of the ten richest men in Texas. Alex was number four, meaning that he was more than just a billionaire. *"Alex is not like anyone else I've ever met. He's incredibly rich, but he's also so down-to-earth—so personable and approachable. He's one of the few men on that list that didn't inherit his money or make it from oil. He worked hard for it and earned every penny. He could be the perfect man. But why would he ever be interested in someone like me?"*

She started to ask a question, but she stopped. Then she asked, "Do you mind if I ask you something personal?"

"Attorney-client privilege is still in effect, right?"

Laney nodded.

"Go ahead and ask."

Laney blushed slightly. "What's so unorthodox about your matchmaker's process?"

Alex looked surprised. "Wow, when you ask a personal question, you really ask a personal question."

"What do you mean? How personal can it be to talk about a process?"

Alex laughed. "Ask me that again when I tell you what she put me through."

Laney looked confused.

Alex took a deep breath and then let it out. "Okay, but remember, you asked. Her process has several checkpoints. The first phase is called 'Getting to Know You,' and that lasts for about two to three weeks. At the end, there's a checkpoint to see if the couple wants to continue. If so, the second phase is called 'Getting to Know the Match,' and it requires the client to spend three to four weeks with the match to see how the match lives. At the end there's another checkpoint. If the couple chooses to continue, the next phase is called 'Getting to Know the Client,' and this requires the match to come live with the client for a month. If the couple continues after that, the next Phase is called 'The Final Checkpoint.' By the time this checkpoint is reached, the client and the match have lived together for four months, and they should know almost everything there is to know about each other. If they decide to move forward, then this is the point where finances, assets, net worth, etc., are finally discussed—not before. If the couple still wants to continue, this is usually when the couple will get engaged, and the match will move in with the client completely. The match will not have a home other than the client's home. Then it's up to the couple to set a date, draft any prenup agreements, and so on."

Laney was puzzled. "I expected something different, or weirder. That doesn't sound all that unorthodox to me... other than the living together part."

"Ah, that's because I didn't tell you what the first phase is *really* all about."

"What's the first phase really all about?"

"Sex," Alex replied. "Non-stop, daily, endless, exhausting sex."

"You're kidding."

Alex shook his head. "No, I'm not. She believes that sexual tension can kill a budding relationship. She also believes that sexual compatibility needs to be determined first, because without it, the rest of the process will prove meaningless."

Laney was shocked... and slightly aroused. "Do you agree with that?"

Alex shrugged. "Let me put it this way. She told me a story about a friend of hers. This friend had dated her boyfriend since they were ten and eleven. Their parents were friends, and both families had been wanting to merge the families and the family businesses ever since the couple were toddlers. They lived next door to each other, they spent every waking minute of their lives together, and they were going to be married at Christmas during her Freshman and his Sophomore year in college. They were from very religious families, so they never fooled around at all before the wedding. They got married, according to their parents' plan, but on their wedding night, she discovered that she couldn't stand making love to him. She wanted time to get used to being physical with him, but he wouldn't give her the time. His sexual tension had reached an overload; he wanted her to submit to him right then. She refused. When they got home, she begged for an annulment, and he refused. Enraged, she divorced him. A year later, she met an older man, and he knew how to please her. She found that she loved sex with him, and they married soon after. When you look at the relationship from that single perspective, it makes sense for sex to precede marriage, if for no other reason than to ensure compatibility before the relationship goes too far."

Laney nodded slowly. She felt her nipples hardening, and there was a warmth coming from the area between her legs. "And having sex for two to three weeks straight...?"

"She believes that, initially, the sex is supposed to be

romantic, but it's usually riddled with tension and performance anxiety. The more you do it, though, the more comfortable you get with each other. Then, as time progresses, you can focus on learning about each other's bodies, pleasure points, thresholds and limits, likes and dislikes, the lines that won't be crossed for any reason... By the time you reach that first checkpoint, all of the sexual tension is removed, and the relationship can either end or proceed without distraction. The sex from that point on is based on choice and desire—nothing else."

Laney was having a hard time wrapping her head around this focus on sex so soon into a new relationship. *"I've never really enjoyed sex before,"* she thought. *"None of the boys or men I've been with were very good, and they only focused on themselves, rather than doing anything to ensure I was having a good time. That's why it has never been that important to me. And I've always thought that having sex first cheapened the relationship and made it harder to focus on romantic love. Friends first, then lovers. This matchmaker's process flies in the face of that and makes having sex first a mandatory step. But how would that work out for me if I don't enjoy sex? It could end up being a miserable couple of weeks."*

"And the... the moral implications?" she asked.

Alex's shoulders slumped. "I still struggle with that. She was absolutely right about the sexual tension being removed, but to jump into bed with someone you barely know, that you've never dated... Let's just say that there was more performance anxiety that first time than I've ever experienced before, which doesn't really answer your question about the morality of it all. I will say that once we got past that initial awkwardness, we both discovered that we had things to learn and things to teach, but it was... still *very* awkward at first. And according to her rules, you have to be completely naked the whole time. You can wear a bathrobe when you're not having sex, but apart from that, you cannot have any clothing on until after the checkpoint. The purpose of the phase is total vulnerability and the total exploration of the other person's body, so none of it can be covered or hidden."

Alex paused before continuing. "I guess it was the moral issue that made it so awkward to begin with. I was anxious about being with someone I barely knew, and I was anxious about being any good at what we were doing. It had been a long time for me since I'd been with a woman, and the age difference didn't help at all. If anything, it made me even more anxious. But as we got past the initial nervousness, and gave into Bethany's approach, we got much more comfortable with each other, and I... kind of... forgot... about the morality of it all. However, having gone through the entire process, I have my doubts about how firm a foundation Bethany's approach actually builds, and I'm singling out the first checkpoint. I'm not sure a strong relationship can be built upon it. Yes, she has her reasons for insisting on that part of the process, but I think the over-emphasis on sex so early in the process is... misplaced."

"So you made it all the way to the... the Final Checkpoint?"

Alex nodded. "I wanted to continue, and I was prepared to propose to her. But when we sat down to discuss how things were going, I let her go first. As soon as she started talking, I knew that she was saying goodbye. It was for the best, but it hurt. One thing I did learn from the experience is that women in their twenties are too young. Yes, I want someone younger than I am—especially since I want children—but it has to be someone with actual life experience... someone more mature, established, and understanding of what has to be sacrificed to have it all."

Laney laughed. "It sounds funny to say it like that—having to sacrifice to have everything."

"But it's true," Alex insisted. "I want my ranch, I want an income, and I want a life partner and a family. To make room for the life partner and family, my income had to decrease substantially. I still have income, I still have my ranch, and now I have room in my life for everything else I want. I had to sacrifice, but that doesn't mean I have to give up *all* of something."

"*So I wouldn't have to stop being a lawyer to have a family, I'd just have to change the way I practice law to have room for a family, and that could impact my income.*" Laney nodded. "That makes sense. So do you have issues following your matchmaker's process again?"

"I wouldn't follow all of it, but most of it, sure. Oh, I have no doubts that there will be performance anxiety with the next person, like there was with the last one, but that's to be expected. It's a different body to learn, with different pleasure threshold and limits, and that person will have different desires and ways she wants to be touched and... stimulated. But once all that is learned, sex from that point on will be incredible. Once the guesswork is handled, what remains is just pure pleasure, pure release, and frankly pure fun. But I don't necessarily agree that the sex comes first. I think there has to be an attraction first before sex is appropriate."

Laney thought about this. "*So he's advocating for a*

process that's not about just experiencing pleasure with a virtual stranger, it's about giving pleasure to someone you're already attracted to. Maybe that approach would finally help me find someone I can enjoy having sex with.." She looked at him. *"Now I wonder just how much I'd enjoy sex with Alex."*

Laney and Alex stayed in his suite all day, talking, sharing stories about their past, and laughing at all the funny things that had happened to them over the years. They ordered room service for dinner, since the restaurants downstairs were still crowded with stranded guests, and the snow was still coming down quite hard.

After dinner, they sat on the couch while their food settled, and before they knew it, they were locked in a passionate embrace, kissing each other as if their very lives depended on it. There was a bit of exploring with their hands, but they didn't let anything go too far.

It was close to midnight when Alex walked Laney back to her room.

"Would you like to spend the day with me tomorrow?" Alex asked.

"I'm supposed to fly home tomorrow," Laney reminded him.

"Or you could cancel your flight and fly home with me," Alex suggested. "Besides, your flight tomorrow will probably be cancelled, so you're here for at least another day or two."

"I'd give anything to spend the day with him... or

spend the week with him." Laney thought. "Let's have breakfast and see what's happening with the flights out of Reagan. If my flight is cancelled, then I'd love to spend the day with you, and I may even agree to fly back to Fort Worth with you. I could use the time off, and I enjoy your company. A lot."

"I enjoy your company, too," Alex said. "I'd definitely like to spend more time with you."

They kissed one more time, and then Laney entered her room and closed the door.

Alex walked back to the elevator, where Mike was waiting.

"Are you having company again tomorrow, Boss?" Mike asked as they rode the elevator down to the lobby.

"For breakfast, yes," Alex replied. "As for the rest of the day, it depends on the airlines."

Laney curled up in the chair by her window, watching what she could see of the DC skyline, but not really paying attention to what she was seeing. Her mind was far away and filled with thoughts she could barely keep organized.

"I'm not ready to fly back to Fort Worth. I'm not ready to go back to work. And I'm definitely not ready to leave Alex. But I may have to."

She pulled the blanket tighter around her. *"Alex. What an... exceptional man. He gave me a lot to think about. He opened my eyes to ways I can practice law AND have a family, but there's a lot of risk there. And when he talked about his matchmaker's process, it was all I could do not to jump him and make love right then and there. That's not me. Not only have I never had good sex before, I've never had sex with someone so soon after meeting him. I've never even thought about doing that before. Now I'm thinking about it nonstop. I don't know if this is good or bad, but I want to be with him more than I've wanted to be with any man in my life. And it's not because he's rich, it's because he's such a unique person. The money doesn't mean anything to me. He does. I don't know what to do. I'm standing at a crossroads that will determine the rest of my life, and it's the airline that's going to be the deciding vote on which path I take next."*

CHAPTER 7

Laney was still on hold with the airline when Alex knocked on her door the next morning. She opened the door and motioned for him to come inside while she waited for the customer service representative to come back on the line.

Alex sat down on the edge of the bed as Laney sat in the chair by the window, scribbling notes in her notebook. Her hair was down, rather than up in a ponytail, and she was wearing black leggings, low-top sneakers, a white ribbed long-sleeve t-shirt—with the sleeves pulled back— that hugged her stomach and breasts as snugly as her leggings hugged her legs and butt.

"So no flights today?" she asked when the airline representative told her that her flight was canceled.

Alex couldn't hear what the airline representative was saying, but he saw Laney's face, and she was not happy. "What if I make my return flight open ended so we don't have to keep going through this every day?"

Laney listened for a moment. "And what would the price difference be?"

Laney shook her head and looked at Alex.

Alex whispered, "Fly home with me!"

Laney nodded. Then she said to the representative, "All right. Cancel my return flight altogether. I'll make other arrangements to get back to Texas."

Laney scribbled more notes in her notebook, and then she ended the call. Looking at Alex, she put down her cell phone and said, "Well, that didn't go well. I hope you're serious about giving me a ride home, because I'm going to need it."

Alex was elated to be able to spend more time with her. "Of course I'm serious," he said. "I'd like to stay until the weekend, if that's not a problem. Will your firm let you be gone that long?"

Laney nodded. "Dwight even suggested that I take some extra time while I'm here. I just need to let him know that I won't be in the office until next week, and I need to extend my stay here at the hotel."

Laney suddenly looked shocked. "What if I can't extend my stay here?"

Alex leaned forward and patted her knee. "Don't worry about that. Just call downstairs and see what's available. If they're booked, they're booked, and we go with plan B."

"What's plan B?"

Alex smiled. "Call the front desk first, and we'll worry about plan B later."

Laney picked up the room phone and pushed the button for the front desk. A moment later, Laney said, "Thanks to the weather and the airlines, I need to extend my stay. Is there any way I can keep my room until Saturday or Sunday?" There was a pause, and then she said, "There is? Is there a way I can have the extra days billed to a different credit card? The initial stay was billed to my boss." There was another pause. "Yes, the card I used for incidentals." After another pause, she said, "Perfect. Thank you so much!"

She hung up the phone and smiled at Alex. "The room is mine until Sunday morning."

Alex smiled. "See? All that worrying for nothing. Always ask first. Then, and only then, if you don't get the answer you want, come up with a plan B. It's a waste of energy to make a plan B if you don't need one."

"That's all good if you're quick on your feet," Laney said, closing her notebook. "But for lawyers, we have to plan out all the angles in advance to make sure that nothing is overlooked."

"And when working for a client, that makes perfect sense," Alex agreed. "But life isn't a courtroom. Keep your life simple. Not every situation requires a battle plan with multiple contingencies built in."

Laney laughed. "Consulting taught you that?"

"Lord, no! Horses taught me that."

Laney started to stand, but Alex held up his hand. "You need to call your boss and let him know you won't be back until next week. Then you need to agree to spend every day with me until we fly home."

Laney grinned, picked up her cell phone, and called her boss. The call went to voice mail. Laney left a message, and then she ended the call. "Satisfied?"

"All except for agreeing to spend every day with me."

"I'm happy to agree to that."

Alex stood. "Good. Let's go to my room and order room service."

Laney stood and followed him to the door. "Will I need a sweater or jacket?" she asked.

Alex, who didn't want her covered up any more than she was, replied, "I doubt it, but if you do, we'll come back and get it. I'll make sure my room is warm enough for you."

Alex was wearing jeans and a western-style outer shirt with the sleeves rolled up to just below his elbows. A black crew neck t-shirt was visible underneath the outer shirt.

Mike was waiting at the elevator as always. "Good morning, Mike," Laney said pleasantly.

"Good Morning, Miss Laney," Mike replied, holding the elevator door open for her.

Alex and Laney spent the entire day talking, ordering room service, and laughing. They also found themselves kissing several times and letting their hands do a bit more exploring, but they still managed to stop themselves from crossing any lines.

Alex walked her back to her room just before one o'clock the next morning. As they stood outside her door, Laney asked, "What time do we get together in the morning?"

"The weather's going to be better, and many of the tourist spots'll be open, according to the weather report. Why don't we get together at seven, and then we can plan what we want to do? It might be good to venture out of the hotel for a bit."

"I'd like that," Laney said, smiling.

"Then I'll see you at seven. Good night, Laney."

Laney kissed him, and the kiss lasted for several minutes. "Good night, Alex," she whispered. Then she disappeared into her room.

Alex sat on the couch when he returned to his suite. His mind was racing too fast to attempt sleep. He turned on some music, but he kept the volume low. He just needed the noise to block out the other sounds of his hotel room.

"Is this real, or is it just one of those flings two people have when they're away from home and feeling lonely? We both recently suffered break-ups, we're both in DC by ourselves to attend a huge event, and we're both staying at the same hotel. Is proximity driving this? Are we caught up in the events happening around us, or are those events just the catalyst that brought us together? Is it fate, or is it simply a matter of circumstance? I need to know, because I have feelings for her, and I don't want to act on them and then find out that, once we leave DC, the feelings were left behind. She's an amazing woman, and I can easily see myself with her, but is it real? What will she have to sacrifice to be with me, and is she willing to do it? What else will I have to sacrifice to be with her, and am I willing to do it?"

The next day, Friday, Alex and Laney spent much of the day touring the Smithsonian. Neither had been there since they were in school, and they barely scratched the surface of all the exhibits the museums had.

Alex knew that he was falling for Laney, and it scared him as much as it excited him. He wanted to explore a relationship with her, but he didn't know how to broach the subject. He finally decided to watch for the right opportunity to say something to her. He hoped that she'd feel the same way.

That night, after returning to the hotel and changing clothes, they went to dinner at The Prime Rib on K Street NW for their first dinner outside of the hotel. Alex wore a dark gray business suit with a black shirt and crimson tie, and Laney wore a slim blue dress that stopped just above her knees, with white trim and half-sleeves, and riding boots. The food was wonderful, and they were stuffed by the time they returned to the hotel for the night. It had been a perfect day.

When they reached the hotel, Alex invited Laney up for a nightcap, and she agreed. Once they were in Alex's suite, Alex poured them both a drink and then joined her on the couch.

"You've had something on your mind since dinner," Alex said. "What is it?"

Laney nodded. "Two things. One, tomorrow is January 25th, and we fly home on Sunday the 26th, meaning that tomorrow is our last day here. Frankly, I'm not ready to return home, and I don't really want to return to my old life. I'm enjoying being with you too much."

Laney paused, and Alex waited for her to continue.

"And second, I've spent more time with you this week

than I've spent with any boyfriend I've ever had. I could date someone for six months and not spend as much time with him as I've spent with you. I feel like I know you—the *real* you—and I like you... a lot. I'm just not ready for all this to end."

"She feels the same. This might be the right time to tell her how I feel." Alex put his drink down on the coffee table. "What are you saying, Laney?"

Laney looked directly into his eyes. "I'm saying, 'who needs a matchmaker?' I'm saying I want more than just a week in DC with you... a happy memory that I can cling to as I slowly burnout from my job. I'm saying that I want you, I'm falling for you, and I hope you want me and are falling for me, too."

Alex took her hand in his, trying to hide how happy he felt. "I've wanted you since our first dance, Laney, and I've been falling for you every moment since. But I knew you had some career and life decisions to make, and I wanted you to make them before I said or did anything that might cause you to make an... an impulsive decision that you'd regret later."

"You're the right decision, Alex," Laney said. "We're the right decision. I'm certain of it."

"And what about your career?" Alex asked. "For us to work, you can't spend 70 to 90 hours a week at the office. That won't leave you any time for us, and the commute from the ranch will be hell."

Laney nodded. "But what if I quit the firm and things don't work out between us?"

Alex thought about this for a minute, and then an idea came to him. "What if you could find out if we're going to work out without quitting your job?"

Laney looked confused. "How could that happen?"

"Take a leave of absence from the firm. Let your boss know that you're having to make some serious life choices, and you need time to make the right one. If he's okay with that, then take a... a four to five month leave of absence. We should know by then if we're right for each other. If we are, you can go part-time, or quit the firm and go into private practice, or do whatever you want to do with your career. And if we're not, you can go back to the firm, accept the partnership, and we part ways knowing we took the chance."

"And how would that leave of absence work?" Laney asked. "Would we follow your matchmaker's process?"

Alex shifted nervously. "If that's what you want to do. I think we could adapt her process to our situation, since we already know each other, we've technically already dated, and we clearly have feelings for each other. We could probably skip the endless sex checkpoint, since that's better handled as *part* of a relationship. We can also skip the checkpoint dealing with me spending time in your world, since we both live in North Texas, and your world consists of working all day in a law firm. Besides, I've already seen you as a practicing attorney, thanks to the contracts you drew up for me. That would leave the third checkpoint—you living with me at the ranch for a month— and then the fourth checkpoint—you living with me at the ranch for another three months after that before we talk finances, prenups, and make the final decision about staying together or parting ways."

Laney nodded. Then she blushed furiously and asked, "If we eliminate the first checkpoint, what do we replace it with? The way your matchmaker set it up may not build a strong foundation for the future, but should we abandon it entirely?"

Alex laughed. "Did you have something specific in mind?"

Laney shook her head, trying not to show her embarrassment.

Alex stared at her. *"There's no question that I'm attracted to her, and for her to bring up the first checkpoint indicates that she's attracted to me. I've wanted to sleep with her several times this week, but I have no desire for sex without commitment. Now that she's suggesting a level of commitment, it puts sex into a different context."* He felt himself getting aroused.

He took a drink and said, "Bethany's rule was that the first checkpoint take place in a neutral location. I rented a house in Charlotte for Penny and me across town from her place." Alex looked around the hotel suite. "We could extend our stay here at the hotel and call it a long vacation where we get to know each other on a deeper level and see if we can build a firmer foundation than Bethany's process does. I don't have to check out until two weeks from tomorrow. My security detail and my flight crew have no scheduling conflicts for the next two weeks. If you're really sure about this—and I mean *really* sure—we can make it work. And if we don't want to continue at the end of the two weeks, I'll still give you a ride home, and we'll part ways amicably."

"And if we do want to continue?" Laney asked.

"Then you'll stay with me at the ranch for at least a month... possibly four months... until we reach the final checkpoint and see where we are and where we want to go."

Laney thought about this for a minute. "So I can tell Dwight that I'm taking an additional two weeks of vacation, which I have coming to me but didn't think I'd actually get to take. At the end of that, I can either go back to work or tell him that I'm extending my time away from the office by taking a leave of absence for... between a month and four months."

Alex nodded. "So we're doing this?"

"Do you want to?" Laney asked.

"Very much. Do you?"

"Very much. But can I admit something to you?"

"Of course," Alex said.

"I'm terrified." Laney's voice trembled. "I've never really enjoyed... intimacy before. I've never had a decent partner, I guess. And spending the next two weeks with you is as frightening as it is exciting."

"I'm terrified, too," Alex confessed. "It's something I want, but that doesn't make it any less scary. The unknown is always scary. But at least we'll be facing our fears together. You're not in this alone. I'd like to think that I'd be the right person for you, and you'd be the right person for me, but there's really only one way to find out."

Laney reached for his hand and squeezed it. "Thanks, Alex. Somehow, just knowing that I'm not the only one feeling anxious, and that we're going to work through that anxiety together, makes me feel better."

Alex looked into her eyes. He was still holding her hand. He pulled her toward him until their lips met. He hadn't planned on what happened next, but the heat of passion became overwhelming, and he surrendered to his desires. She did the same.

He let go of her hand and wrapped his arms around

her as they kissed. Before he knew it, he had unzipped her dress, and his hands were exploring the smooth skin of her back. He unsnapped her bra and pulled her dress down to her waist. His hands began exploring her breasts as she leaned back against the cushions on the couch. Her hands loosened his belt, unsnapped and unzipped his slacks, and then she reached for his growing erection.

Alex removed his shirt and tie, and then he removed Laney's bra. His hands slipped down beneath her skirt, moving aside her panties so he could stimulate her clit. He was rock hard from her grip, and all he wanted was to be inside of her.

Laney moaned as his fingers stimulated her clit more forcefully. Then he pulled off her boots, dress, and panties, and pulled off his shoes, pants, and undershorts. He stood, picked her up off the couch, and carried her into the bedroom.

He jerked the covers off the bed, set her down, and joined her. "Is this what you want?" he whispered.

"Yes," was her reply.

He moved down and licked her nipples for a minute. Then he moved lower until his tongue reached her clit. He stimulated her, flicking his tongue against her swollen bean while using his fingers to stimulate the inside of her pussy. He was gentle with her, not knowing her thresholds yet.

After she had experienced several orgasms, he moved up and penetrated her, entering her slowly until she could get accustomed to the size of his erection. She had another orgasm quickly, causing her legs to tremble.

After several minutes of deep penetration, she whispered, "I want to ride you."

Alex flipped over until Laney was on top of him,

without losing the connection. She straightened and began moving up and down on him. She had several orgasms in this position. Then Alex rolled her off of him and onto her hands and knees. He penetrated her from behind, and with his hands just above her hips, he moved her forward and backward on his erection, causing her to orgasm several times.

They were both bathed in sweat as Alex felt himself getting closer to his own release. He flipped her over so he could face her. He penetrated her again and thrust deeply until he could no longer hold it back. He released inside of her, and she squealed as she felt his hot liquid shoot deep inside of her.

Alex remained inside of her until he felt his erection soften, Then he pulled out and lay next to her, breathing deeply.

"That was incredible!" Laney whispered. "I had no idea it could be that good."

"And we've barely scratched the surface," Alex said softly. "There's so much more to learn about each other. So many ways of pleasing each other still to determine."

Laney snuggled up close to Alex. "Can I stay with you tonight? I want to feel what it's like to actually sleep with you... to hold you all night."

"Of course," he replied. "I hope you'll stay with me for the next two weeks, so we can get used to being together before we get back to the ranch."

"I want that, too."

CHAPTER 8

Alex woke up to a strange sensation. Not only was he completely erect, but there was a hand on him, gently moving up and down.

He looked over at Laney, who hadn't realized that he was awake yet. Glancing at the clock, he saw that it was just before 5:00 in the morning.

"You decided to start without me?" he asked softly, enjoying the sensations.

"I couldn't wait anymore," she said, looking up and giving him a kiss. Then she moved on top of him, and Alex could see her face in the low light from the nightlights around the suite. "Are you ready to begin the day?" she asked, sounding nervous and excited at the same time.

"I am if you are. Do we need to set some ground rules?"

"Like what?"

Alex put his arms around her. "Are you on birth

control?"

"Yes."

"Good. Because I don't use condoms, and as you discovered last night, I don't pull out."

Alex felt her shiver, and then he continued. "Also, you're probably aware that most men reach orgasm, and then they're done... or at least they're done for a while before they can go again."

"Right," Laney confirmed.

"Well, there are some people who can keep going after they've had an orgasm. Some can even keep going after several orgasms."

"Are you one of those people?" Laney was shivering even harder, and Alex knew that she was very nervous and excited by this time.

"Yes. My record is seven."

"Good God! Isn't that... you mean inside? Isn't that... messy?" Laney started trembling slightly.

"Very," Alex confirmed. "That's why we need lots of washcloths and hand towels in easy reach, bottles of water, and we might need bath towels, depending on whether or not you..." Alex didn't finish the sentence.

"Whether or not I what?"

"Squirt."

"Ha," Laney laughed. "That's not a real thing."

"Oh, yes it is," Alex countered. "Trust me, it's very real."

"I don't believe you," Laney said.

"You want me to prove it?"

Laney stared at him. "You're serious, aren't you?"

Alex nodded. "I'm told it's the most incredible sensation you'll ever feel. All I know is that you'll spasm uncontrollably and make a huge mess, depending on how far it... goes. For some women, it happens very naturally. For others, it has to be coaxed by someone who knows how."

Laney had goosebumps all along her arms. "And you know how?"

"I learned from... someone... who was very fond of that particular sensation. But I have to warn you. It's more intense than anything you've probably ever experienced before, and it's not for someone who likes their lovemaking...vanilla... gentle... all the time."

Laney was quiet for a while. Alex asked, "Do you have any ground rules?"

Laney looked down at him. "Just one... There's one thing I don't do. Well, two actually. No anal, and no multiple partners. I don't care if it's men or women, I want none of it. I'm a one person girl and that's final."

"Good," Alex said. "I don't care for any of that either."

Laney continued lying on top of him, not speaking and not moving. Finally, Alex asked, "Is there anything else we need to discuss before we..."

"No." Laney rolled off of him and got out of bed. "I'll go get the towels and the water."

Laney walked into the living area and got four bottles of water from the mini-fridge. She placed them on Alex's night table, and then she went into the bathroom.

Alex admired the view of her incredible body as she returned with the towels—her gentle curves, slim hips, toned legs, flat stomach, perfectly shaped butt, perfect breasts, shaved pubic region, and erect nipples. She put the towels down on the bed, and then she lay down next to him.

Alex put the washcloths and hand towels on both sides of the bed so they'd be in easy reach. He noticed that she had brought a couple of the bath towels out as well.

"These are bath towels, Laney," he said.

"I know," she purred.

"These are only if you squirt."

"I know that, too."

"You know it's pretty intense, right?"

Laney leaned over and kissed him. "I want to know what it feels like."

"Are you sure? We can take it slow and easy to start with. There's no rush here."

"I'm sure." She reached down and grabbed the object of her desire. "But first, lay back. This is for you."

Alex obeyed, and Laney moved down until her mouth was next to his erection. She kissed the tip, and then she used her tongue to stimulate the head and shaft. She shifted positions and put it in her mouth, letting her lips move up and down on it. Her lips tightened as her head moved, sending sensations from his toes to his chest.

He knew this was for him, but he wanted to please her, too. "Turn around and face the other way," he whispered. "Please."

Laney spun around so Alex could lick her clit while she continued working on his erection. As his tongue began exploring her clit, she gasped, but then her lips tightened again, and she moaned as her head moved up and down on his shaft. A couple of minutes later, she cried out as the first orgasm hit her. Alex began to stimulate her more quickly, and she had to alternate between her mouth and her hand to keep from biting down on him.

Soon, Alex felt his release building, and he leaned back

onto the pillow as she brought him closer to the climax. His hands caressed her butt, and when he felt that the release was imminent, he clutched her hips and held on as he filled her mouth with the hot, salty, sticky liquid.

Laney giggled as she felt him release, and she continued moving up and down on him until she had every bit of it. She grabbed a washcloth, wiped off her mouth, and then wiped Alex off. She spun back around and smiled when she saw the look of satisfaction on Alex's face. Before she knew it, she was on her back, and Alex was moving down between her legs. He grabbed one of the bath towels and spread it out, tucking it under her butt and legs.

"Are you...?"

"Yes, I am. You deserve to experience it after what you just gave me. But remember, no matter what you feel, or think you feel, don't try to stop me. You'll understand when it's over, okay?"

Laney nodded and leaned back on her pillow.

Alex grinned. "Hang on."

His tongue began stimulating her again, and he continued stimulating her this way until her clit and the surrounding area were quite wet. Then he inserted one finger into her pussy and began stimulating her inside.

After a while, he inserted two fingers and increased the stimulation. Laney had several orgasms, and she was quite wet, but Alex continued what he was doing, knowing that she wasn't quite there yet.

After a few minutes of this, Alex moved his head out of the way and began to move his fingers in and out rapidly. She squealed as the orgasms became more intense. He began alternating between stimulating her inside and moving his fingers across her clit from side to side. Her legs were shaking by this time, and her stomach muscles clenched and unclenched rapidly.

"I'm going to pee," she whispered.

"No, you're not. Just let it happen."

Alex began stimulating her more vigorously, alternating between internal and external stimulation. He felt her have several minor squirts that splashed her inner thighs, but he knew the grand squirt was building. He continued stimulating her as her legs began flailing and her stomach muscles were getting the workout of a lifetime.

Suddenly, Laney raised her hips and cried out as a stream of liquid shot out of her onto the bath towel.

"Bingo," he said as he moved up and penetrated her without warning. His erection provided plenty of stimulation, but he also stimulated her clit with his thumb. He pulled out as she squirted a second time, and then he penetrated her again. This went on nearly five times before he turned her over, pulled her up so she was on her hands and knees, and penetrated her from behind.

She didn't squirt in this position, but she did have several orgasms. Then Alex broke the connection and told her to get on top of him. She did, and he penetrated her immediately. She didn't squirt when she was leaning forward, but as soon as she leaned back, she squirted again, sending the liquid all over Alex. He didn't mind. He had already climaxed four times inside of her, and the white sticky liquid was running down her inner thighs and pooling on him.

Alex flipped her onto her back while still penetrating her. He climaxed two more times, and she squirted three more times in that position.

Finally, she said, "Enough. I can't take anymore."

Alex pulled out, and she sat up and began stimulating him with her mouth. After a couple of minutes, he climaxed, and she fell backward into her pillow, panting like someone who had just run a marathon. Alex grabbed the hand towels and started cleaning up the mess all over the two of them.

As he looked down at her when he was finished, he said, "Normally, I wouldn't have done that to you so soon, but you seemed curious. I don't advise we do that every time, just because of the mess, but sometimes it can be... entertaining."

"You're a beast, you know that?" Laney asked. "What you did to me... I've never felt anything like that before. How is that even possible?"

"I don't know, but I'm more curious about how it was discovered in the first place." Alex gathered up the soiled towels. "I suggest we take a shower and get all these fluids off of us. Then we can order breakfast and let housekeeping bring us new towels and make the bed with fresh sheets."

"Together?" Laney asked, pointing toward the bathroom.

"The shower's large enough for two," Alex said. "I'll wash you if you wash me."

Laney nodded, and she struggled to sit up. "Wow is my stomach tight!" She stood and followed Alex into the bathroom, admiring the view.

They got into the shower, and Laney noticed that Alex was still slightly erect. Unable to resist, she sank to her knees and began stimulating him again. It didn't take long for him to climax. Still erect, he turned her around, bent her over, and penetrated her from behind. He climaxed again, and Laney giggled as she felt the hot liquid run down her legs.

She turned and gave Alex a kiss. "No more until we've eaten, or I'll pass out."

Alex nodded. He began washing her. He started by removing the sprayer wand and turning up the pressure all the way. Then he had Laney spread her legs so he could spray inside her pussy. The sensation made her climax, but she felt cleaned out when he was done. Then he washed her body while she washed her hair.

Once Laney had rinsed off, she washed Alex's body while he washed his hair. When he was rinsed off, he grabbed a towel and began drying her as he used the towel to run his hands all over her body. She did the same for him. When she stepped out of the shower, she ran a brush through her hair, and then they put on the two hotel robes and slippers hanging behind the bathroom door. Alex put a couple of washcloths in each of the robe pockets before they exited the bathroom.

"Are you still nervous about being with me?" Alex asked.

"Not anymore," she replied. "Not after everything you did to me and for me."

"And did you enjoy yourself?"

"More than I ever thought possible," she replied.

Alex stripped the bed and put the soiled sheets with the used towels in the bathroom. Laney grabbed two bottles of water, and they went into the living area to recover.

Alex couldn't help but notice that Laney's hair was actually more curly than wavy when it was wet, and he liked it. *"Must be the Irish in her."*

"How many times did you cum in me?" Laney asked as she cuddled next to him on the couch.

"Total? Including the shower?"

Laney nodded.

"Nine, but three were oral. You?"

"I lost count," she confessed. "I'd guess at least twenty, but who knows? You did things to me that made my mind go numb. I didn't know who I was, where I was, or if I were even still alive. If I hadn't experienced it, I would never have believed it."

"Are you okay that we started the day in such an intense way? I certainly don't expect it to be this way every time. I don't think either of us would survive that."

"I'm more than okay with what we did," Laney assured him. "And I can honestly say that you're the first man who ever made me enjoy having sex. But why did you continue after you made me squirt the first time?"

"You brought out the towels, so I assumed you wanted me to give you the full treatment. Was I wrong?"

Laney put her head on his shoulder. "No, you weren't wrong. I wanted it. I just didn't know that it would... Anyway, I should recover after breakfast."

As she moved closer to him, she asked, "What if you keep doing that to me and I can't walk afterwards?"

"I'd push you around in a wheelchair," Alex replied. "And I'd look for ways to build up your stamina."

Laney giggled. "What other surprises do you have for me?"

"Not that many. We jumped right to the grand finale

this morning. Now it's more a matter of finding the things we like the most and the ways we want to please each other."

Laney's stomach rumbled.

"Before I order us breakfast, we need to discuss a few things," Alex said, facing her. "You need to make a phone call and leave Dwight a voice mail, we need to check you out of your room and move you up here, I need to let the front desk know to extend my stay, and I need to let my security detail and flight crew know about our new departure date."

"Why don't I go back to my room, pack, and make my phone call while you call the front desk and alert your people. Then you can come to my room to get me and bring me back here once all that's done. We can order breakfast, and I can unpack while we're waiting for the food to arrive."

"That sounds like a very good idea," Alex said.

Laney looked at her clothes on the floor where they had been left the night before, and she started getting dressed. Alex grabbed his clothes and took them into the bedroom. When he emerged, he was dressed, and so was Laney.

Laney gave Alex a kiss. "Call me when you're ready to come get me."

Alex walked her to the door. He kissed her, and then she stepped outside and headed for the elevator.

Mike was standing just outside the door, looking confused. "What's going on, Boss," he whispered, watching Laney disappear around the corner.

"She stayed with me last night, and now she's moving into my suite. We're staying here for another two weeks."

Mike stared at Alex, and then he smiled. "Is this going to be like Charlotte?"

"Well, apart from it being unplanned and without matchmaker involvement, it's a lot like Charlotte."

Mike nodded, looking happy. "I'll let the guys know."

"The same rules as Charlotte, Mike," Alex said, grinning. "Ignore loud noises, and I'll let you know when our plans have us leaving the room."

"Thanks, Boss, and congratulations. She's lovely."

"She is that," Alex confirmed. "You let the guys know, I need to let the front desk and the flight crew know, and then I need to go to Laney's room and help her move her things."

"I'll be ready to go with you, Boss," Mike promised.

"Thanks, Mike."

Alex went back inside his suite and called the front desk to extend his stay. Then he called housekeeping and told them he needed the bed remade and lots of fresh towels delivered to the room. Then he called Henry, his pilot, and told him that their departure had been moved back two weeks to Saturday, February 8th, and that there would be an additional passenger on the flight home. Henry promised to inform the rest of the crew.

Alex then called Laney and told her that he was on his way to her room.

When Alex and Mike reached the lobby, Alex made a detour to the front desk. "I called a few minutes ago about getting an additional key for the Franklin Suite. The name is Barclay," he said to the front desk manager.

"I have it right here," the front desk manager confirmed. "I just need to see your ID, please."

Alex showed his ID, and the front desk manager

102

handed over the key. Alex thanked him, and then Alex and Mike took the elevator to Laney's floor.

When Alex knocked on her door, Laney opened it. She had changed clothes, and her bags were lined up neatly just inside. Alex helped move the bags into the hallway while she made one more search of the room to make certain that nothing had been left behind. Satisfied that she had everything, she stepped into the hall.

Alex and Mike had already moved the bags to the elevator. She joined them, and they rode down to the lobby. It was strange to see the lobby so empty, after the chaos of the past several days caused by the weather.

She dropped her room key at the front desk, and then Alex handed Laney her key to the suite. "This is a good time to make sure the key works," he said, gesturing for her to use her key to summon the elevator. The key worked, and soon they were on the top floor.

Mike and Alex carried the bags, and Laney opened the door to the suite with her key. Then she helped Alex and Mike bring in the bags and put them in the bedroom.

Alex walked Mike to the door while Laney put her things away in the closet and the bathroom.

"Housekeeping is heading up to make the bed and deliver towels," Alex whispered to Mike. "Room service should be along in the next thirty minutes or so."

"Got it, Boss. I'll be on the lookout for them."

"Thanks, Mike."

Alex walked back to the bedroom in time to see Laney walking out of the bathroom.

"Everything is put away," she said.

"Good. Let's order breakfast." Alex grabbed the room service menu, which they practically had memorized by that time. After Laney selected what she wanted, Alex called room service and ordered their breakfast.

Housekeeping and room service arrived at almost the same time. Housekeeping brought lots of extra towels, remade the bed with fresh sheets, and emptied the trashcans before leaving.

Once breakfast was done, the dishes had been removed, and Laney and Alex were sitting on the couch, he asked, "What do you want to do today?"

"I'd like to do some sightseeing while I'm in DC," she replied. "Most of the crowds have left by now. Maybe we could take one of those sightseeing tours that take you around to see everything."

Alex nodded. "I think the hotel should be able to recommend one." He called the front desk, and the front desk manager provided him with contact information for the better tours of the DC area.

Alex enjoyed being a tourist again, even though he had been to DC dozens of times on business. Mike, Ray, and Travis stayed close to Alex and Laney, but they also gave them space for privacy. They had lunch and dinner away from the hotel, returning to the Waldorf Astoria after dark.

When Alex and Laney returned to Alex's suite and were sitting on the couch, Laney discovered that she wanted Alex inside of her. Without a word, she walked into the bathroom, grabbed a couple of washcloths, undressed, and put her bathrobe back on. Then she walked out and joined him on the couch.

Alex watched as she opened her robe, revealing her beautiful body. Then she helped Alex undress.

She stood, allowing her robe to fall off, and knelt down in front of him. After stimulating him with her mouth for a while, she moved on top of him, forcing him to penetrate her. She clutched the back of the couch as she moved up and down, allowing him to penetrate her deeply.

She felt his first release, and she loved the sensation of the hot liquid shooting deep inside of her. She kept moving up and down on him, and soon she felt the second release. She stood, turned around, and sat on him again, facing away from him. She used her strong legs to rise up and down on him until he climaxed again.

Alex grabbed one of the washcloths, placed it between Laney's legs to keep the liquid from running down her inner thighs and getting on the furniture, and lifted her off of him. He stood and maneuvered her onto the couch so she was on her knees and leaning on the armrest. He removed the washcloth and penetrated her deeply. He put his hands on her hips and moved her forward and backward, stimulating him to two more climaxes. He put the washcloth back between her legs and turned her around so she was sitting on the couch. He stood in front of her, and she put his erection in her mouth, using her lips to stimulate him to another climax... and then another. The liquid was dripping down her chin and neck as he finished and pulled out.

Without a word, they went to the bathroom to clean off, and then they came back to the living area. Alex was now wearing his robe, and Laney put her robe back on. Then they sat together on the couch.

"Still having fun?" he asked.

Laney laughed. "More than I ever thought possible. You?"

"Absolutely. As long as you're not too sore, I guess we're okay. But the moment it stops feeling good and starts hurting, we stop. No arguments."

Alex and Laney made love several times over the next two weeks. They tried every position, used nearly every piece of furniture, and tried multiple combinations of techniques until they found what they liked and how to give the most pleasure to the other.

They also managed to have several dates and outings, including eating at the Mount Vernon Inn and several restaurants specializing in Maryland-style seafood, which was Alex's favorite.

On the Friday evening before they were to fly back to Fort Worth, they sat at the dining table, enjoying their last room service supper of the trip.

"It's time for us to discuss the checkpoint and decide if we're moving forward or ending things now," Alex said. "We've certainly learned quite a bit about each other's bodies, pleasure points, thresholds, and preferences, so we've met the terms of the first checkpoint as Bethany defined it. Would you like to go first?"

"Sure," Laney said. "Put simply, making love with you is the most incredible thing I've ever experienced. You've taken me places I didn't know existed, and you've done things to me I didn't know were possible. But it's not enough. I want more. I want us to move forward and see if we can build a true relationship—a true partnership—together. You've touched my body; now I'm ready for you to touch my mind, my heart, and my soul."

"Beautifully stated," Alex said, "and it's everything that I wanted to say. As a lover, you are unequaled, and I think we fit together very well. You bring out the best in me, and I hope I do the same with you. It's a good start, but it's not enough. I want to see if we can become life partners, and if you can be happy living on a horse ranch. It's a great life, but there are conditions. The ranch has a large security force to protect the property and everyone living on the property. Just like I have a security detail, you'll have one, too, for as long as we're together. That includes a driver and at least one bodyguard. And if we get married, you'll need to consider having a GPS tracker placed underneath your skin. I have two myself. But that's just administrative things. The ranch is an amazing place, and we help a lot of people. I hope you'll want to be part of that, but it's up to you. All that being said, do you want to continue with me?"

Laney nodded. "I do. Do you want to continue with me?"

"I do," Alex replied. They hugged each other for several minutes.

There was a knock on the door, and when Alex opened it, Mike was standing there. "You wanted to review the plans for tomorrow. Is this still a good time, Boss?"

Alex nodded. The three of them sat at the dining table, and Mike reviewed the plans and the procedures for Laney. Once the briefing was finished, Mike left the room.

Alex turned to Laney and asked, "Are you okay with what we discussed? This is what it's going to be like from now on, and once you get your own security detail, you'll be having conversations like this every time you leave the ranch. It may seem like a lot, but they know what they're doing, and security is a fact of life for as long as we're together."

Laney nodded. "It's going to take a bit of getting used to, but I'll manage. If this is what's required to be with you, then I'll put up with the extra burden, although I can't imagine I'll find it too much of an inconvenience."

Laney looked around the living area. "If you'll excuse me, I think I'll get ready for bed."

"Don't forget... you need to let your boss know that you're taking a leave of absence."

Laney groaned. "I know. I'm dreading that conversation. I'll call him in the morning."

"You can always call him from the plane tomorrow," Alex suggested. "Hopefully the call will go to voice mail, and you won't have to deal with him until sometime next week."

"That's a great idea. Want to hear another one?"

"Sure."

Laney had a mischievous twinkle in her eye as she held out her hand to him. "Come to bed with me."

THE RANCH

CHAPTER 9

The next morning, Laney and Alex packed and had a quick breakfast. The final bill for the two suites, covering the three weeks Alex and his security detail were in DC, had been slipped under his door that morning. Alex reviewed them, placed them in his briefcase, and used the online system through the television to check out of both suites.

"Ready to go home?" Alex asked as Laney brought her luggage out into the living area. Alex was wearing jeans, casual shoes, and two long-sleeve shirts—a cream pullover underneath, and a hunter green button-up outside. It was still cold outside, and North Texas was expected to be cold when they landed.

Laney was wearing her black leggings with black riding boots and a blue and red ski sweater. Her coat was draped over her luggage, and she placed it on the coat rack next to Alex's. She turned around to look at the Franklin

Suite one last time. "I was starting to think of this as home." She looked at Alex. "There are a lot of memories in this place."

Alex smiled. "And we have even more memories to make when we get to the ranch. Speaking of which, did you talk to Dwight yet? I thought I heard you leaving him a voice mail."

Laney nodded. "We traded voice mails this morning. He approved my leave of absence but is demanding to know the reason I'm taking it. Anyway, I'll call him from the plane, like you suggested, and tell him something vague." Laney looked at Alex. "You don't suppose that Elizabeth has talked to him and told him about us at the ball, do you?"

Alex snorted. "Knowing her, she has."

There was a knock on the door. Alex answered it, and Mike entered, followed by a bellhop. The bellhop gathered the luggage and placed it on the luggage caddy, which already had the security detail's luggage on it. Then he left the suite, followed by Ray.

"All set to go?" Mike asked. "Travis went to bring the car around, and Ray is staying with our luggage until it's loaded in the SUV."

Alex handed Laney her coat, and then he put on his coat and cowboy hat. He looked at her, and she nodded. "All set," Alex confirmed to Mike.

They left the suite and headed downstairs. Ray and the bellhop and already loaded the luggage when Alex, Laney, and Mike reached the car. Ray got into the front seat, and Laney, Alex, and Mike got into the back seat.

As they rode to Reagan-Washington National Airport, Laney reached over and took Alex's hand. He squeezed it gently and smiled at her.

"I've never ridden on a private jet before," she admitted. "Are they as nice as I hear?"

"Mine is, but that's because it's still new. If you don't maintain them, inside and out, they can get ratty after a while. I hate that."

As they turned into the airport entrance that led to the hangars, Mike leaned over and whispered, "The guys and I will take the forward seating areas, so you and Miss Connor can have the back two to yourselves."

Alex nodded. "Thanks, Mike."

When they pulled into the hangar, Laney exclaimed, "Holy crap! That thing is huge!" She had never seen a private jet that big before that hadn't started out as a passenger jet.

"You have a choice," Alex said. "You can sit next to me, or you can sit facing me. Do you have a preference?"

"Next to you," Laney answered without hesitating.

The SUV came to a stop. Mike and Ray got out and began their security sweep. Travis remained with Alex and Laney. Laney expected this procedure, after spending almost three weeks with Alex and his security detail, and after being briefed by Mike the evening before.

When Mike signaled that it was safe for Alex and Laney to exit the SUV, Travis opened Laney's door and helped her out before helping Alex out. Alex introduced Laney to the flight crew, and then Ray, Travis, and Keith started unloading the luggage from the SUV and placing it in the jet. Jenny led Alex and Laney to the rear two sitting areas, showing Laney the locations of the lavatories and the bed in the living area behind their seats.

"You have a bed on your plane?" Laney asked.

"Actually, the jet sleeps up to nine, and can seat up to eighteen," Jenny said. Then she took their coats and Alex's hat, and she returned to the front of the jet to get ready for take-off.

Mike, Ray, and Travis took their seats in the forward sitting areas. Jenny and Keith retracted the stairs and closed the hatch before taking their seats. The Jet pressurized and then began rolling out of the hangar toward the taxiway. Within minutes, they were airborne and heading west back to Texas.

Alex glanced at his watch. It was 10:05 AM Eastern Time. "We'll be landing just before noon Texas time," he whispered to Laney.

He had to repeat himself because Laney was too busy looking all around the jet to hear him. She grinned like a schoolgirl when she realized he had been saying something to her. "Sorry about that, Alex. I'm just... trying to process the whole experience."

"I understand," Alex said. "After I bought my first jet, I was the same way. I don't know what's more surreal... the thrill of flying in your own aircraft, or the moment when it becomes so commonplace that you barely notice it anymore."

Laney was amazed at how little time it took for them to be airborne. "No curb-side check-in? No airline counter lines? No security checkpoint delays? No departure lounge crowds? No flight delays or cancellations? No cheap, uncomfortable seats? Just pull up in your car, get onboard, and take off? I could get used to this!"

Jenny brought drinks, and Laney started peppering Alex with questions about the ranch and the residence. Alex took out his notebook from his briefcase and started sketching a diagram of the ranch's layout, explaining the difference between the residence, the equestrian center, the meadow, the community, and the buffer zone.

"So the ranch itself is five miles by eight miles, but the entire property is ten miles by ten miles?"

"That's right," Alex said, pointing to the diagram. "We call the entire property 'The Estate,' and I have an estate manager who manages all of that except for the equestrian center. I have a ranch manager who is responsible for that, including the barns, bunkhouses, dining hall, and training facilities. Then I have the trainers, who are the real value of the ranch. The rodeo trainers and the hunter-jumper trainers are the best in the country, and they're why so many great riders and riding teams use the ranch to prepare for competitions."

"You have a charitable program, too, don't you?" Laney asked.

Alex nodded. "The Equine Therapy practice. I started it as a way to help vets suffering from PTSD, then it expanded to anyone with PTSD, and now it includes adults and children with all sorts of physical, mental, and emotional challenges who can benefit from the practice. It was the reason I created the ranch in the first place. The other training was added later as a way to help the ranch bring in revenue. So was the breeding program."

"Is the ranch profitable?" Laney asked.

"Not really. It could be, potentially, but there are some businesses I either haven't or won't get into. For instance, we don't train dressage, and I won't have anything to do with horse racing. It costs us revenue, but it also keeps our costs and liabilities down considerably."

"Why stay away from racing?" Laney asked. "I understand there's big money in that. The firm has several clients who breed and compete racehorses."

"It's just too corrupt for me," Alex replied. "I've always prided myself on being honest, ethical, and trustworthy, but if I got involved in that business, I'd either end up broke, or I'd end up becoming a real scumbag. In my opinion, any time you get involved with an activity that's popular with gamblers, you have trouble. That's why I don't own sports teams and why I won't get involved with racing. And the minute I find that hunter-jumper events are becoming popular with gamblers, I'll drop that program in a heartbeat. I don't need the aggravation, I don't need the liability, and I don't need the risk. The cost for a decent racing horse is astronomical, as is the insurance and the litigation potential if something happens to the horse when it's in your possession, and I've found that the owners are the worst kind of people. I just can't stand dealing with spoiled, pampered, overrated, obnoxious, expensive, *beasts*... or their horses."

Laney laughed at Alex's description of racehorse owners.

Jenny served Alex and Laney a light meal and then cleared their dishes when they were finished. Laney looked at her watch and changed it back to Central Time.

Glancing at Alex, and knowing what was behind her, she suddenly felt very horny. *"I can honestly say that I've never done it in an airplane before. Car? Yes. Plane? No. Why pass up the opportunity when it presents itself? It can't hurt to ask."*

"We don't land for another ninety minutes," she whispered. "Want to lie down for a bit?"

Alex looked at her. "Anxious to join the mile high club?"

"How often does a girl get the chance?" she purred, running her fingers along his arm.

Alex looked around. "We can't make too much noise. There are too many ears that can hear, and I have to be able to trust these guys to protect me, which they can't do if they're snickering behind my back."

"I'll be quiet," Laney assured him, "but that means none of the messy-messy stuff."

Alex nodded in agreement. They stood and went back to the last living area, which had a bed. Alex closed the door, and then Laney put her arms around his neck and started kissing him.

After a minute, Laney sank to her knees, unbuckled and unzipped Alex's pants, and pulled them down. She reached for his already swollen member and stroked it until it was hard. Then she put it in her mouth, using her lips to stimulate him. She continued doing this for several minutes. Then, with her hand clutching him tightly, she stood and pulled down her leggings and panties. She got on her hands and knees on the bed, facing the window so Alex could penetrate her from a standing position behind her.

Alex reached down to make certain she was wet, and he stimulated her clit with his fingers. Then he penetrated her deeply, thrusting slowly to give her a slower buildup of pleasure.

Laney gasped when he penetrated her, and the view outside the window made her feel like she was having sex on a cloud. The longer he thrust, the more intense her gasps came. At one point, her legs began shaking so hard that he had to clutch her hips tightly to keep her from going flat on the bed. When she finally stopped shaking and spasming, he began thrusting harder, building up to his own release. He climaxed a moment later, shooting his hot sticky liquid deep inside of her.

Laney gave a soft squeal of delight as she felt him release inside of her. Alex was the first man she had ever allowed to do that to her, and now she was addicted. She wanted it all the time, no matter how messy it was. The sensation of feeling him shooting his liquid inside her pussy was the most wonderful feeling to her. She couldn't explain it, but she couldn't deny it either.

There was a basket of washcloths and hand towels on the ledge underneath the window, and without pulling out, he reached forward and grabbed one of each. He placed the hand towel between Laney's legs as he pulled out, and he used the washcloth to clean himself off.

Laney turned around and sat on the edge of the bed, facing Alex. "Best quickie ever!" she said softly.

"And now I can officially welcome you to the mile high club," Alex said with a smile. "It's a select membership, but you've earned your place among us."

Laney stood and gave Alex a kiss. "Thanks for handling my initiation," she said. Then, with the washcloth between her legs and her leggings still pulled down, she waddled to the lavatory to finish cleaning herself off.

When she reemerged, her clothes were all back where they belonged, as if nothing had happened. Alex entered the lavatory next, and when he exited, Laney was lying back on the bed. She patted the mattress, and he sat down next to her.

They just stared at each other for a while, and then Laney said, "If we stay here, I'm going to want more, and I don't think we have time. Besides, I want to save my strength for when we get to the ranch."

Alex nodded, stood, and held out his hand. She took it, and he helped her up. Then he put both arms around her and kissed her, holding her tightly.

When he finally pulled back, Laney's face was flushed, but she was smiling. "Me, too," she whispered.

Alex opened the door, and they returned to their seats.

They landed at Alliance Airport ahead of schedule. When they pulled into the hangar, there were two vehicles waiting for them. Gordon Hopkins was driving one SUV, and Terry Vance, who was also part of the security detail team, was driving the other.

Alex and Laney put their coats on while the security sweep was underway. Once it was finished, Alex thanked the flight crew, put on his cowboy hat, and escorted Laney off the plane to the first SUV. Alex introduced Laney to Gordon, and they waited for the luggage to be sorted. Gordon was taking Alex and Laney's luggage to the Residence. Terry was taking the security detail's luggage to the security center.

Ray and Travis got into Terry's SUV, and Mike got into Gordon's SUV. Then the two vehicles left the hangar, exited the airport, and headed for the ranch.

Nearly thirty minutes later, the two SUVs turned off at

the Justin, Texas exit. Ten minutes after that, they turned onto Barclay Ranch Road. The sign in front of them said AMB Ranch.

"We're here," Alex said as they approached the first gatehouse. The guard came out, recognized Alex, Mike, and Gordon, and quickly inspected the vehicles before allowing them to enter the property.

"All this is yours?" Laney asked.

"Yes, it's all part of the estate," Alex told her.

Laney looked at all the grassy areas on either side of the road. "I bet bluebonnets would look great along here."

"They would," Alex acknowledged, "but you can't grow bluebonnets around horses. They're toxic, and if any got mixed in with the hay, or started blooming where we let the horses graze, we'd have a lot of very sick animals around here."

"I had no idea," Laney said. "I have a lot to learn about ranching, don't I?"

Alex smiled. "And we have the best teachers you could ever want working here. Don't worry. You'll get the hang of it soon."

A couple of miles later, Laney saw two large gatehouses like the one she saw at the main entrance. One was on the right, and one was on the left.

"The right gatehouse leads to the community," Alex explained. "The left one goes to the ranch."

The SUVs turned left. Once they were through that gate, Gordon took another left to a smaller gatehouse while Terry drove straight to the security center parking area. The guards waved Gordon through the gate and through a cut in a ridge that seemed to go on for miles.

"There's a man-made ridge that surrounds the

residence, called a berm," Alex explained. "And there are groves of trees like the one we're driving through now lining the inside of that berm. You can't see the residence unless you're inside the berm's perimeter, or from the air. The estate is a no-fly zone, which includes drones, and I'm the only one who can fly over the property or authorize drones over the property."

"You really like your privacy, don't you?" Laney asked.

"I do. I built the residence as a sanctuary. The equestrian center is a constant hubbub of activity. I needed somewhere on property to get away from it all, to get away from all the pressures of my work." The SUV drove out of the grove, and Alex's home appeared in the distance. "And there it is."

Laney's jaw dropped as she looked out the window at the house. Even from that distance, she could tell that it was gigantic. The center part of the house appeared to be three stories, and the two wings appeared to be two stories. It was all stone with white trim, and there was a large cupola on the center roof that reminded her of the one at Mount Vernon in Virginia.

They passed a road on the right with a sign that said, "Office" and "Pool House." They kept driving forward, and then the road turned right and headed straight for the house. The ground sloped upward as they approached Alex's home, and Laney saw the huge porte-cochère covering the front entrance and part of the circular drive that led to it.

In the center of the circular drive were three flagpoles and two antique-looking cannons. The flagpoles were flying flags that Laney recognized immediately: the US flag, the Texas flag, and the Gonzales flag from the Texas

Revolution.

The SUV pulled around the circular drive and stopped in front of the main entrance, which consisted of a massive wrought iron and leaded glass set of French doors with the Texas Star worked into the design on each side.

Alex jumped out of the SUV before anyone else, came around to Laney's door, opened it, and helped her out. "Welcome home, Laney."

CHAPTER 10

Laney just stared at the front of Alex's home. It was grander than she imagined, and she couldn't wait to see the inside.

Mike and Gordon exited the SUV and began unloading the luggage. "Where do you want your bags, Boss?" Mike asked.

Alex thought about it for a moment. "If you don't mind, just take them up the elevator and put them outside the den. We can take it from there."

"Are you sure, Boss? We don't mind taking them just inside the bedroom."

Alex smiled. "I'm sure. Thanks, Mike. Thanks, Gordon. Oh, and remember, we're going to Laney's townhouse tomorrow morning to pick up her clothes and anything else she'll need while she's here, so please be here at seven."

A blast of icy wind blew through the porte-cochère,

and Alex escorted Laney into the house.

Laney thought the foyer was amazing. Two semi-circular staircases came downstairs from the second floor. A huge chandelier was hanging between them, and in the center of the marble floor below the chandelier was the Texas Star surrounded by laurels. The wooden stairs were covered by a deep red runner rug, held in place on each step by brass rods.

As Laney turned around, she saw the crown molding all had the Texas Star worked into the design, as did the sconces along the walls.

On either side of her, there were four huge rooms, but rather than walls, they had pillars holding up connected arches. Deep red and gold curtains hung from the top of the arches with semi-circular valances filling the space between the curtains and the top of the arches. The curtains were swagged back and tied with velvet ropes to the pillars, allowing the rooms to be opened to the rest of the house or closed off.

"Shall I give you the full tour?" Alex asked.

Laney could only nod. She had no words for what she was seeing.

Alex pointed to the right. "To your right, facing the front of the house, is the downstairs living room. The dining room faces the rear of the house. Beyond that is the guest wing. There are five large guest suites on this floor, and there's a sliding door that closes off the wing from the rest of this floor."

Alex pointed to the left. "To your left, facing the front of the house, is the lounge. Facing the rear of the house is the card room, although we also use it for party seating and for playing board games. Beyond that is the master wing, where the library and study takes up the entire wing on this floor. It, too, has a sliding door that can close it off from the rest of the house."

Alex took her to the living room on her right. It was large enough for four separate seating areas, and it had two fireplaces. The dining room had a massive table that seated twenty-four guests, and a butler's pantry led from the dining room to the kitchen in the back-center of the house.

Alex then showed her the guest wing before leading her across the first floor to the lounge and card room. "Every bedroom has a fireplace," Alex explained as they walked. "All gas logs, so we don't have to keep firewood in the bedrooms. Also, the entire residence is steel framed, not wood framed, so structurally, it's almost indestructible, and it should last for at least a century."

The marble floor extended from the foyer to the guest wing and the library and study, but the guest wing itself had all hardwood floors with burgundy Persian rugs. The four rooms surrounding the foyer had the same hardwood floors and rugs.

The lounge, which looked like an upscale western saloon, also had two fireplaces. The stools and chairs were covered in saddle leather, the Texas Star was visible on almost every piece of furniture, and western art covered the walls that didn't have the arches and curtains. The card room looked like a continuation of the lounge, with almost identical furnishings.

Alex led Laney into the library and study. There were two massive fireplaces on opposite ends of the largest home library Laney had ever seen before. The wall across from the entrance was filled with bookcases, each having a rolling ladder to reach the higher shelves. There were a number of sitting areas around the room for reading, and there were tables and desks for studying. Western bronze sculptures were visible on several of the bookshelves, end tables, and desks around the room.

On the same wall as the entrance were a number of alcoves containing suits of armor. Between these alcoves were glassed cases containing antique weapons from the French and Indian War, American Revolution, War of 1812, Texas War for Independence, Mexican War, Spanish-American War, War Between the States, and the Old West.

Alex then led Laney to the kitchen, where the cook—Fran Burrows—and her two sous chefs—Jerry Dubois and Cindy Frederick—oversaw all of the cooking. The chef's kitchen was beautiful, and looked like a top-of-the-line restaurant kitchen. The flooring was hardwood with no rugs to trip on, and the breakfast nook was decorated like an extension of the lounge and card room.

After Alex introduced the culinary team to Laney, he promised to be back after they had finished the tour.

Alex led Laney to the second floor. The layout leading to the guest wing looked similar to the first floor, except that the flooring was all hardwood. There was another living room facing the front of the house, but instead of a dining room, there was a third living room facing the rear of the house. The curtains swagged between the columns were a deep blue and gold color.

"The guest suites on this floor are identical to the ones on the first floor," Alex explained, showing her the front and rear balconies.

"Why make all the guest suites so large?" Laney asked. "You could easily make two rooms out of each of them, doubling the number of guests you can have staying here."

"The architect and I went back and forth about that for weeks," Alex confessed. "At one point, we thought about having five suites on the first floor and ten on the second floor as a compromise, but that created some plumbing challenges and issues with the fireplaces and the windows. To keep from having ten chimneys in the guest wing, the fireplaces have to be in a straight line on both floors, and it really does help if all water and drainpipes can run together. An uneven configuration between floors wouldn't allow for that. Besides, I realized that there'd be few occasions where I'd be having more than twenty guests in the house at the same time."

"What's over there?" Laney asked, pointing to a wall on the other side of the stairs with a sliding door in the center. Her luggage and Alex's luggage were just outside the sliding door.

"That's the den. I'll show you that after I show you the third floor."

Alex led Laney up a staircase next to the rear balcony. This went to the upstairs game room, which was a large open space with windows all around. From the game room, you could see the entire grounds of the Residence part of the estate.

The room was filled with pool tables, ping-pong tables, and clusters of sofas and chairs for playing video games.

Looking out the rear windows, Laney pointed to the pool area and the buildings surrounding it. "What's out there?"

"The building on the right is the pool house. It has two locker rooms complete with showers and bathrooms for pool parties. The building on the left is the garage. It has six bays, including one that has a lift system leading to the underground equipment areas. I'll show you that when I show you the basement. The building on the far side of the pool is the office. My office and a currently empty office are both out there, along with two bathrooms and two conference rooms."

As Alex led Laney downstairs, she asked, "Did you design the house?"

Alex nodded. "Yes. I had an architect take my designs and make them complete—you know, up to code, electrical wiring, plumbing, security systems, etc. But the layout, the trim, the colors, the art... it was all my design. I had a team of decorators finding what I wanted, but I picked it all out. You know, originally the house was going to be dark red brick—colonial style. In fact the name of the house was going to be 'Williamsburg'."

"Why did you change it?"

"I was visiting a ranch out in the panhandle, to get inspiration, and I saw that the owner was using light colored stone instead of brick. When I asked him about it, he told me that it was to keep the buildings cooler, and the colors blended with the landscape better than brick would. He was right. You'll find every building on the ranch has the same look and was constructed the same way."

"What did you end up naming the house?"

"Barclay Manor," Alex replied.

Alex led her into the den on the second floor. "This room is for us. It's family only. It has the only television on this side of the house."

Laney looked surprised.

Alex explained. "All of the guest suites have televisions, and the master bathroom has two TV monitors so I can watch the weather and the news as I'm getting ready, but I don't like having a television in the bedroom. For me, the bedroom is a quiet place. I don't even like phones in the bedroom, but I understand the necessity. Anyway, that's why the den is just outside the master bedroom. This is where I watch television or movies when I don't want to go downstairs to the theatres."

"Theatres? Plural?" Laney asked.

"There are two theatres in the basement, underneath the library. I'll show you that in a while. Anyway, this is part of our private space, which is why it can be closed off from the rest of the house."

While Laney looked around, Alex took their luggage and placed it inside the bedroom. The den was also western themed, with leather chairs and couches facing a massive wall-mounted television, and bookcases filled with art and movies. There were also two desks. On the wall—either side of the sliding doors—were several gun cases, holding a variety of modern pistols, lever-action rifles, shotguns, and tactical rifles.

"That's a lot of guns," Laney noted.

"Those are the ones I actually use," Alex said. "The ammo is in the drawers down below, as are the holsters. I carry one of the lever-action rifles whenever I ride, in case I encounter any critters that don't belong around here, and I carry at least one pistol whenever I leave the house. Even though we're close to Fort Worth and Dallas, it's more like the wild west out here, and we have to be prepared."

Alex pointed to the French doors on the opposite side of the den. "On a happier note, that leads to the grand master suite. You might want to brace yourself. It's as big as the library."

"Just how big *is* this house?" Laney asked.

"Not counting the basement, it's just over seventy-five thousand square feet. With the basement, it's just over a hundred and eight thousand square feet."

"That's almost twice the size of The White House!" Laney exclaimed. "This isn't a house, it's a castle."

"I think of it as a western chateau," Alex said, walking toward the Grand Master suite.

"Or palace." Laney entered the master bedroom, which had a vaulted ceiling with exposed beams, a fireplace at the far end, a sitting area in front of the fireplace, two more seating areas on each side, and the largest, grandest bed Laney had ever seen. "And I thought your suite at the Waldorf Astoria was huge!"

There were two openings in the wall behind the bed, which led to a hallway that ran between two combination walk-in closets and dressing rooms. At the end of the hallway was the master bath, which looked more like a spa. Like the bedroom, it had a vaulted ceiling with exposed beams. The closets and dressing rooms didn't have vaulted ceilings, so the up above space could be used for storage.

There were two of everything in the bathroom, except one side had an oversized soaker tub that could hold two people comfortably, and the other side had a two person, glass enclosed shower. In the middle of the far wall was another fireplace.

Laney walked back into the bedroom and stared at the bed. Then she sat down on it, testing how soft the mattress was.

"What are you thinking?" Alex asked as he sat next to her.

"How much I'd like to test out the bed," she replied.

Alex smiled at her. "I think lunch and the rest of the

tour can wait until later."

Laney cocked her head to one side. "Will anyone hear us? You know, in case one of us gets... noisy?"

Alex laughed. "You mean in case *you* get noisy? Trust me; you have nothing to worry about. The subfloor underneath all of the flooring on each level is three-inch thick oak, and the space between every floor and ceiling, and between every wall in this house, is filled with fire-retardant, mold-resistant, and sound-proofing spray foam. That's how I could place two theatres underneath the library and not disturb anyone in there reading."

Alex stood and closed the Den's sliding doors and the bedroom's French doors. "Now there's no way anyone will hear us."

Alex pushed a button on the panel next to the door, and all of the plantation blinds in the room closed. He pushed another button, and the fireplace opposite the bed turned on, providing a warm glow around the massive room.

Laney stood and walked over to Alex. She put her arms around his neck, and he leaned in for a kiss.

"How many other women have you had here?" she whispered.

"You're the only one who matters to me," Alex replied.

Laney liked that answer and pulled him closer. Alex held her tight as they kissed, and then he began moving her back toward the bed. When they reached the tufted bench at the foot of the bed, he gently lowered her so she was sitting. Then he knelt and removed her boots. He ran his hands up her legs to her waist, and he pulled her leggings off and laid them on the bench next to her. Then he removed her sweater, leaving her wearing just a t-shirt and her bra and panties.

The t-shirt was the next to come off, and then the bra. Last of all, the panties came off. Alex began kissing and caressing her inner thighs. He pushed her legs wider apart and began licking her clit. She shuddered from the sensation, but her hands held his head in place so he couldn't stop.

Laney started moaning, and when Alex inserted two fingers into her wet pussy and began gently stimulating her internal pleasure spots, she let go of his head, leaned back, and her legs began shaking as her stomach spasmed uncontrollably.

"We're going to need towels," she whispered between her gasps and moans of pleasure.

"They're in the night table cabinets," Alex said, letting his fingers brush across her clit rapidly, causing her to shake even harder.

All at once, Alex stopped. He stood, picked up Laney, and carried her to the bed. He pulled back the covers with one hand and carefully lay her down on the sheets. He undressed in record time, grabbing the back of his shirt to pull it off over his head. Then he reached for the lower cabinet door of the closest night table. He extracted several washcloths and hand towels, along with two bath towels. He tossed them onto the far side of Laney and then joined her on the bed. He moved down so his head was between her legs, slid his hands underneath her butt, and began licking her clit as her moans increased in volume.

Laney pushed his head away and moved her hand to cover her pussy. "Your turn," she purred.

She pushed Alex onto his back and immediately put his erection into her mouth. He was already hard, and her tongue stimulated him as her lips clamped down and moved up and down on his swollen shaft.

"I'm going to cum," he moaned after a few minutes.

She didn't stop. She just increased speed and kept going until she tasted his release shooting into her mouth and down her throat.

When he was done, she licked him off, and then she got on top, straddling him. His erection was still rock-hard, and without allowing him to penetrate her, she used her pussy lips to stimulate him and lubricate herself on his shaft as she moved her hips forward and backward.

After a few minutes, she was quite wet again, and she whispered, "I need you inside of me."

She lifted up, guided him inside of her, and lowered herself until the shaft was all the way in. Then she began moving up and down on him and he caressed her breasts. She leaned forward and kissed him as she continued moving him in and out of her pussy. He licked and nuzzled her breasts. Then she leaned back, using her hips to move him in and out even faster, bringing both of them to a climax. Her legs began to shake and her stomach muscles clenched and unclenched as he released inside of her. She felt the hot liquid shooting deep into her body, and that made her climax even harder.

Alex pulled her forward so they were kissing. His hands held her hips in place as he thrust in and out until he climaxed again. He rolled her over, without breaking the connection, so he was on top of her, and he began thrusting again. He was lubricated by his own cum, which frothed as it leaked out of her and clung to him. He reached for a hand towel and stuffed it between her legs so they wouldn't mess up the sheets.

Laney wrapped her legs around him and used her arms to pull him closer to her. He began kissing her as he felt his next release building. She didn't let go of him, and feeling their bodies so close together as he thrust brought them both to another climax.

Laney's orgasm was more powerful than any she had shared with Alex before, with the exception of when he made her squirt. In spite of that, she still didn't release him. Feeling him pressed against her and inside of her at the same time gave her a feeling that went beyond the sexual. It was a oneness she had never experienced with another person. Even during the two weeks in Alex's suite, she had never felt such an inseparable connection that touched her body, her mind, and her soul to such a degree.

Suddenly, Laney started crying—not from sorrow or emotional confusion, but from the power of that sense of oneness she was sharing with the man she was falling for. It went beyond the mere physical and the emotional. It struck her very core.

Alex looked at her. "Are you all right?" he whispered, sounding confused.

Laney nodded. "Happy tears," she said softly. She let go of him so she could wipe her eyes. "Something about the way we connected overwhelmed me. I didn't mean to break the mood."

"Don't worry about that," Alex said. "All I want is to make you happy. As long as you're not upset about anything, then I'm good. Do you want more, or are you satisfied with what we've done."

Laney giggled. "You're the only man who's ever asked me that question. Even after the last two weeks, I'm still getting used to someone who can keep making love longer than I can. I'm not used to it yet. I love it, but I'm not used to it."

Alex was still erect and inside of her. "I'll do whatever you want. You know that."

Laney looked at him, and then she kissed him. "We should probably take a shower and then eat lunch. I still want to see the rest of the house and the ranch before sundown."

Alex reached for another hand towel and a washcloth. He pulled out of Laney and put the fresh hand towel between her legs. Using the washcloth to clean himself with one hand, he grabbed the hand towel he had placed underneath Laney with his other hand.

Laney moved to the edge of the bed and stood. Alex put away the clean towels, made sure that the sheets hadn't gotten too soiled, and pulled the covers back the way they were. Then he led her to the bathroom and showed her how the shower worked.

As they stepped into the glass enclosure, feeling the water jets spraying them from all around, Laney suddenly realized that she wasn't quite finished with Alex after all. She reached for him, stroking the object of her desire until it began to stiffen again. She looked at him and grinned. "I need a little more."

"Whatever you want," Alex said.

She sank to her knees and put the head of his erection in her mouth. Her hair was wet, and her body tingled from the spray jets all around her. Alex released quickly, shooting his hot liquid down her throat. Then he lifted her up and pressed her against the side wall. Placing his hands underneath her butt, he lifted her and guided himself inside. He pressed her against the wall and began thrusting. She wrapped her legs around his waist and her arms around his neck. He moved away from the wall so all of the water jets were spraying on them as he lifted her up and down on his shaft.

After a few minutes, he sat down on the wide bench that ran along the wall next to the one where he had first penetrated her. She was on her knees and began moving up and down on him.

"Turn around," he whispered.

Laney stood, turned around, and sat on him, like she had on so many of the chairs in their DC hotel suite. She put her hands on his knees and lifted herself on and off of him. Then he placed his hands underneath her butt to hold her in place as he started thrusting. Two minutes later, he climaxed so hard that his cum ran out of her and swirled down the shower drain while he was still inside of her.

Laney leaned back and kissed him as he moved his hands and wrapped his arms around her stomach and breasts.

"Had enough?" she asked.

"Only if you have."

"I'm completely satisfied," she purred.

"Then let's get cleaned up and eat. I'm starving."

After they showered and dressed, Alex turned off the fireplace and opened the blinds. Then he opened the French doors, and the two of them left the bedroom.

CHAPTER 11

I t was just after 1:30 PM when they passed through the den on their way downstairs to the kitchen. Laney looked at Alex's modern gun collection. She was fascinated by the western theme of most of them, and she started to understand the different environment Alex lived in when he was at the ranch. Being a native of Fort Worth, she loved all things western, but this was the first time she found herself so immersed in it.

"What did you mean by this place being more like the wild west?" she asked as Alex opened the sliding doors.

"We're a working ranch," Alex explained, "out in the middle nowhere. We're at the southern end of the county, there's a cattle ranch at the north end, and hay farms to the west. Apart from that, there's not much of a population out here. We have a sheriff, but most of his deputies are my security team and the cattle rancher's guys. There are still cattle thieves and horse thieves who prey on remote ranches like ours, so we have to be vigilant to protect our animals and our people, since just about all of them live here on the estate. We also have to protect our equipment and anything else that could be stolen and sold."

Alex and Laney entered the kitchen. Fran, Jerry, and Cindy were busy putting away the supplies that had just been delivered.

"Are you ready for lunch, Mr. Alex?" Fran asked pleasantly.

"Yes, we are," Alex replied.

As he and Laney sat at the island counter, Fran asked, "What would you like to eat?"

Alex looked at Laney. "Any preferences? There's nothing Fran and her team can't make."

"I'd love a fried chicken club sandwich," Laney replied. It was her favorite sandwich.

"Can you make two of those?" Alex asked.

Fran just nodded. Jerry and Cindy began making lunch while Fran talked to Laney about what she liked and didn't like to eat.

"Do you want fries or chips, Miss Laney?" Jerry asked as he took the chicken breasts out of the fryer.

"Fries, if you have them," Laney replied. Alex nodded in agreement.

Cindy took the bacon out of the oven and began assembling the sandwiches on a freshly baked bun. Then she added the condiments, lettuce, and tomatoes. Jerry took the fries out of the fryer and placed them on both plates. Fran then placed each plate in front of Laney and Alex.

Laney took a bite and rolled her eyes. "This is delicious! Thank you."

Everything except for the condiments and vegetables had been made from scratch right in front of her, and yet the meal was completed faster than in a restaurant. Laney was impressed.

As the two sous chefs cleaned the kitchen, Fran discussed dinner for that night and breakfast for the next morning. A few minutes later, someone Laney had not yet met entered the kitchen.

"Laney, allow me to introduce Kelly Fernandez, my head of housekeeping. She and her staff are responsible for keeping the main house—apart from the kitchen—the pool house, and the office space clean. With all the floor space, you can imagine how big a job that is. She and her staff also handle laundry twice a week. Kelly, meet Laney Connor."

"My pleasure," Kelly said politely. Turning to Alex, she said, "Mr. Alex, I need to let you know that one of the dryers is misbehaving. Maintenance has been called, but it won't be fixed until at least Tuesday if new parts have to be ordered."

"Does that put you behind schedule?" Alex asked.

Kelly shook her head. "Mondays are usually small laundry days, so we should be good... depending on what you brought back from DC."

"Not all that much," Alex confirmed, "Although Laney will be adding to that."

"We'll make it work," Kelly assured him.

"I know you will. If the dryer can't get fixed quickly, or if the parts needed are too costly, let me know, and we'll replace the machine. I don't want any equipment out of service for an extended period."

"I'll let you know what maintenance says."

"Thanks, Kelly."

When Kelly left the kitchen, Alex explained how large the housekeeping staff was. In addition to the Residence, they cleaned the estate manager's office, the ranch manager's office, and the security center. It was a large staff, but Laney was learning that Alex liked everything kept clean.

After lunch, Alex and Laney completed the tour of the house. He showed her the basement, including the theatres, and the entrance to the equipment area underneath the pool, where all of the water, power, and gas entered the residence.

When he led her to the patio, which was glass enclosed, Alex pointed out that the glass panels could turn and be pushed back to make the patio open to the pool area.

The water for the pool, which was heated, was fed from two water features on the far side of the pool from the house. Both were waterfalls, and each one had a waterslide built in that, from a distance, looked like part of the waterfall's rock formation.

Laney noticed that there was a glass-enclosed corridor surrounding the pool area. When she mentioned it, Alex said, "I don't normally like detached garages, especially with the rain we get here sometimes, so I had all four buildings connected by a temperature controlled walkway. There are doors that open onto the pool area and the parking lot outside the garage, and there are doors leading to the garage, the pool house, the office, and the patio."

He showed her the pool house first, and then the garage. Then he took her to the office.

When she entered Alex's office, she was impressed

with the layout. The wall across from the windows facing the pool was filled with bookshelves, and there was a conference table by the windows. Alex's desk and credenza were on the far wall. The office was "L" shaped, and to the right of Alex's desk was a sitting area with two couches facing each other, and a fireplace at the far end.

"This is beautiful, Alex," Laney said. "What do you do here?"

"I still run my companies from here," Alex replied, "but mostly I write and take care of any ranch business that requires me to get personally involved."

Alex then showed her the two bathrooms and conference rooms. Lastly, he showed her the empty office.

"What's this used for?" she asked.

"Nothing, at the moment. I had planned for this to be my personal assistant's office, but I realized her place is at the consulting company headquarters, which is thirty minutes south of here in the Alliance Business Park."

It was identical to Alex's office, but everything was a mirror image. There was no furniture, no rugs, and no curtains. In addition, the bookcases were white, whereas Alex's bookcases were stained wood.

As Laney looked around, she said, "You know, this would make a great law office."

"And the office of one of the State Party's leaders, if you accept Elizabeth's offer," Alex added.

Laney nodded. "I guess that depends on what happens between us at the next two checkpoints."

Alex chuckled. "You know... I had already forgotten that this was a trial period. I've started thinking of you as a permanent part of my life."

"Is that what you want?" Laney turned to face him.

Alex nodded. "It's what I'm hoping for, but there's a lot we both need to still learn about each other before we're completely convinced that it's the right thing."

"True. Shall we take a look around the equestrian center?"

"Good idea," Alex said. He led her to the garage, where one of the ranch pickup trucks was parked. He grabbed the keys as she climbed into the truck. He joined her, and soon they were driving towards the gatehouse leading to the equestrian center.

When Alex passed through the gate, he turned left. "These are the estate, ranch, and security offices," he said, pointing to the buildings on the left. Pointing forward he said, "On the left up there is the employee parking deck, and the warehouses where we keep the horse trailers, the trucks that pull the trailers, and the grounds equipment."

Pointing to the right, he said, "The long building there is the dining hall for the equestrian center. In front of that are the four bunkhouses, and on either side of the bunkhouses are two large pools with their own pool houses."

"How many people can sleep in each bunkhouse?" Laney asked as they drove past the dining hall.

"Seventy-two," Alex replied. "Two hundred and eighty-eight total. We have slightly less than that at the moment, but just the single staff sleep in the bunkhouses. The married staff, senior staff, department heads, and the staff for the residence, all live in the community across the street. The estate employs close to four hundred people. We're the largest employer in the county."

"That's unbelievable," Laney said.

"It takes a lot to run a working ranch, and it takes a lot

to run world-class training centers for junior rodeo, hunter-jumper, and equine therapy, and we do all three. Plus we allow locals to board their horses here, and the teams we train keep their horses here as well. Those horses have to be protected, fed, and cared for, just like the horses I own. We have our own veterinary team with a surgical center about ten minutes down the road. He also helps out the cattle ranch north of here, but the practice technically works for me."

As Alex followed the road around the bunkhouses, Laney saw that they all had the same stone exterior as the residence. "All these buildings are steel framed?"

"Steel framed, metal roofed, stone walled, and spray foamed... just like the residence." Alex pointed to the left. "Just like the barns and stables."

There were four midsized barns, and past them were eight huge stables that were each almost the size of a football field.

"The four barns are for storing hay and feed. We store the hay away from the stables in case of a hay fire, which happens more than you think. There's one barn for every two stables, and we have room to build up to four more stables, two more barns, and four more bunkhouses here."

Alex drove around to the front of the stables and stopped the truck. "I'll show you the inside."

They got out of the truck and entered the stable. The foreman called out a greeting to Alex, and he introduced Laney to the ranch hands working inside. Several were women.

"How many female ranch hands do you have?" Laney asked.

"Somewhere between a quarter and a third," Alex

answered. "One bunkhouse is all female, and one floor of the bunkhouse next to it is all female. There are also several females living in the apartments across the street who work here, both with the horses and with the ground crew. The security team has several women, too. I hire the best people for the job, no matter if they're men or women. As long as they can do what has to be done and can keep up with their team members, that's all I care about."

Alex led Laney to one stall. Inside was a magnificent-looking dark brown horse with a black mane and tail. The horse let out a loud whinny when it saw Alex approach. "This is Duke," Alex said, stroking the horse's nose. "This is my personal horse. He's a thoroughbred. I think he misses our daily rides, although the guys keep him well exercised when I'm not around."

Laney rubbed Duke's nose, and Alex handed her an apple he took from the barrel near the stable entrance. "Give him this, and he'll love you for life."

Laney put the apple on her flat palm, and Duke took it and ate it happily. He nodded his head several times and whinnied again.

Alex showed Laney the tack room, where the saddles and other equipment were kept, the restrooms, the shower stall for washing the horses, and the other amenities that the stable had.

"It's a rubber coated concrete floor, and fresh hay and feed are distributed first thing every morning, so it's ready once the stalls are cleaned. The stalls are all oak, as are the columns, although the columns are decorative since the building is steel framed with I-beams that don't need any extra support. Each stable is temperature controlled and well ventilated for the comfort of the horses."

After saying goodbye to Duke and the foreman, Alex and Laney got back in the truck and drove around the equestrian center. Alex pointed out the indoor and outdoor training facilities. He parked in front of the equine therapy building and took her inside. After touring the building, they walked around the building so Laney could see the meadow.

"That's two-and-a-half miles wide by eight miles long?" she asked, looking at the beauty of the land—its rolling hills, the trees, the grasses, the ponds, and the streams.

"It is," Alex confirmed, "and it will never be developed. I've seen to that. It's just for the horses to run around and for riders to enjoy the unspoiled land."

She ran her hands along the fence, feeling the black steel sections. The fence was at least ten feet high. "Is all of the fencing like this?"

Alex nodded. "One fence line surrounding the entire estate, one fence line on either side of the road that runs between the buffer zone and the ranch, one that separates the meadow from the rest of the ranch, and one that separates the residence from the ranch. In all, there's over 100 miles of fencing on the property. The fences on either side of the buffer zone have razor wire coiled at the top."

"Isn't that much fencing expensive to maintain?"

"Yes, but it's a small price to pay to keep the people who live here, the horses, and the facilities safe."

Laney looked at Alex as he viewed his property. He had a look of joy on his face that she hadn't seen in the three weeks they'd spent together. "I'm just now starting to understand how much you love this place."

"This ranch—the entire estate—is everything I ever

144

wanted," Alex said. "I built it to last at least 150 years... long after I'm gone. That's what those contracts you prepared for me were all about. I wanted to make sure the ranch would survive without me. I don't want it broken into pieces and sold off to people who can't or won't appreciate its beauty and all it does to help the people who train here, work here, and live here."

They got back in the truck, and Alex drove out the gate and across the street to the community. Laney didn't realize just how large it was or how many people lived there.

Alex stopped at a large stone building that looked similar to the buildings on the ranch. "This is the community center," he explained as they got out of the truck. "This is where the after school programs are held, the athletic programs are held, and where the two community pools are located."

Alex led her inside the building. "There are programs here for people of all ages. Book clubs, training for homeschoolers, adult education... a wide variety of options for the folks who live here."

They walked around the community center for several minutes. As they were leaving, Laney saw a medium-sized building across the parking lot, where a number of refrigerated trucks were making deliveries. "What's that building over there?" she asked.

"Ah, that's the commissary," Alex said. "It's like a convenience store for the folks who live here in the community. Wes Blalock runs the commissary operations for the entire estate."

"I don't understand," Laney said.

Alex stopped next to the truck and faced her. "As you

can imagine, there aren't a lot of grocery store options out here. All the food used at the dining hall is delivered by trucks like those. We get farm-direct and ranch-direct deliveries several times a week, so we can ensure the freshest food possible for the staff. Bo Perkins and his staff put in regular orders for the supplies they need, and it gets delivered a day or two later. Fran and Kelly do the same thing for the food and supplies at the residence. It comes in with Bo's order, and then Wes Blalock's staff separate what goes to the dining hall and what goes to the residence."

"And that building there?" Laney pressed.

"That's for the people who live here in the community, but don't eat at the dining hall. They can put in orders for food and supplies online, and it gets delivered with Bo's orders. Just like the residence supplies are separated and delivered to Fran and Kelly, the food and supplies for the community residents is brought here, separated by the address of who placed the order, and the folks who placed the order are notified to come pick it up. The commissary also carries incidentals and ranch-specific items for sale. There's a smaller commissary at one end of the dining hall for the ranch hands, where they can purchase ranch-specific items, and pick up incidentals and other items they've ordered."

"Sounds like a huge operation," Laney said as she and Alex got into the truck.

"Not as big as you think, but it does take some coordination to get the right orders to the right people. The good news for the folks who order items through the commissary is that they get it for what we paid for it, which is usually wholesale or less. We don't mark up any items that they order. That's another perk of living here."

"And you just eat the cost?"

Alex nodded. "Just like I eat the cost of having local physicians come out on a regular basis to perform health checks on the staff and their families. It's a benefit I offer to keep people wanting to work and live out here. I'm trying to make their lives easier, not harder."

"Wow," Laney said as they drove past the commissary, admiring all that Alex was willing to do for his people.

"And all these houses and buildings are built the same way as the ranch buildings and the residence?" Laney asked.

"That's right," Alex confirmed. "The community center has the same stone exterior as the ranch buildings. So does the commissary, the training dorms, and the apartment buildings. The individual houses have a variety of exterior façades for visual appeal, but the construction is identical. Steel framed, steel roofed, thick oak subfloors, and spray foam insulated and protected."

"Why steel roofs?" Laney asked.

"Have you seen the hail that North Texas gets in the spring and fall? We'd be replacing roofing all the time if I didn't have this kind of roofing installed. The steel is coated, which has to be touched up periodically to prevent rust, but apart from that, the roofs are practically indestructible."

"And do the people who live here own the houses?"

Alex shook his head. "I own all of this. Instead of rent and house payments, living space is deducted from their paychecks—well below market value—as another one of the perks of working for me. Utilities and insurance is included, as is landscaping. All they have to do is keep their place neat and clean, and they're responsible for any damage. The same goes for the bunkhouses. Living quarters are part of their pay, as are three meals a day. In fact, the dining hall serves three meals a day at no charge for everyone who works on the ranch. If the people who live in the community prefer to cook their own breakfast, lunch, or dinner, they're welcome to, but the dining hall is always an option for the staff."

"How can you afford all of this?" Laney asked, shocked.

"How can I afford not to?" Alex countered. "We're here in the middle of nowhere. I don't want people commuting miles away after a hard day's work. I want them close by. I make it affordable for them and desirable for them to want to live and work here. All kids are homeschooled, since this county doesn't really have a school system to speak of, and the community center provides everything apart from the core basics, so the children can build social skills. We also use the ranch for educational purposes, in case any of the kids want to grow up to be vets, or ranch hands, or anything else involving animals. We offer scholarships to the kids who do well on their college entry exams. I've tried to build a true community among those who live here, but the only way to live here is to work here. If they leave, or if their employment is terminated, they have to vacate. That's the only way all this works."

"And the ranch doesn't break even every year?"

"No," Alex confirmed as he drove back to the residence. "It'll never recoup the initial investment I made to build everything. Our revenue from breeding, horse sales, and training does offset some of the operational expenses, but the trust I set up—with your help—covers the rest. Honestly, I never set up the ranch to break even or be profitable, I set it up to preserve horse ranching, to preserve the land, and to provide employment opportunities for people who needed good jobs and a safe place to live. Doing that brings me joy."

"What about social lives?" Laney asked. "It's not like there's any nightlife around here."

"Those who want to go out and have a good time are welcome to. Denton and North Fort Worth aren't that far away. I only have three rules. First, don't drive drunk. Call the ranch, and someone will come pick you up. Second, if you're going to be late for your shift, because you're... sleeping elsewhere, call the ranch and let someone know. And third, I don't tolerate the use of or the possession of illegal drugs. There is random testing, and anyone caught using or possessing drugs on my property will be dismissed immediately. There's too much risk in tolerating that sort of behavior."

As they drove, Laney thought about what Alex had shared with her. She was fascinated at how different he was here from how he was in DC. But in DC, he was a mega-donor who owned several very successful businesses. Here, he was a rancher who loved horses, loved the land, and did his best to take care of the people who worked for him.

"No wonder his employees at his consulting company are so loyal to him," she thought. *"If this is how he treats all of his employees, I can't imagine anyone attracting and retaining better talent. No wonder I'm falling for him. He has found a way to be both tough and gentle. I think I could be happy here for the rest of my life, but we'll see what the next few months bring."*

CHAPTER 12

After dinner, once all the staff had gone home, Alex turned on the security system, and he and Laney sat in the den, talking in depth about their pasts and their plans for the future. In spite of the age gap, it was still surprising to both of them how much they had in common.

They easily could have talked all night, but since they were driving to Laney's townhouse in the morning to pick up her things, they decided to go to bed early.

As Laney got ready for bed, she was processing everything that she had seen and heard that day. *"This is a man who cares deeply for people, and he has the means to see to it that everything is done the right way. He doesn't have to compromise, unless it's the right thing to do for all parties. I'm beginning to understand why his matchmaker doesn't want money discussed until there's a commitment in place. I know Alex is a billionaire, and I know he's the forth richest man in Texas, but knowing and seeing it all around you are two different things. And yet he doesn't carry himself like most of the oil and cattle barons I've met over the years. He's grounded, he puts others first, and he cares deeply about people and the land. I think he'd be that way if he were penniless, but he's rich. He can go wherever he wants, do whatever he wants, buy whatever he wants, and this is what he does. Yes, this palace he built and lives in is amazing and incredible, but with all he spends for the horses and the employees, he deserves to spend money on himself. He's generous, he's kind, and he's exactly the type of man I always wanted to be with. I have a chance to be part of his life. I just hope he wants the same, because I have totally fallen for him."*

When she finally entered the bedroom, the lights were off, the fireplace was on low, and Alex was already in bed. Laney crawled into bed next to him, and he looked like he was already asleep. She gave him a kiss on his cheek, but he didn't stir.

"Goodnight, Alex," she whispered. "I love you."

She curled up next to him and closed her eyes. Then she heard him say, "Goodnight, Laney. I love you, too."

The next morning—Sunday—Alex and Laney woke just before six and started getting ready. As they were dressing, Laney just had to ask, "Were you serious last night?"

"About what?" Alex asked, sticking his head into her closet.

"What you said when I came to bed."

Alex grinned. "Were *you* serious about what *you* said

when you came to bed?"

"I asked first."

"I asked second," Alex replied.

Laney crossed her arms in a huff. "Fine. We answer at the same time... on three. One... two... three!"

"Yes," they both said together.

Laney smiled, and Alex entered the closet and put his arms around her. "I'm sure of it, and I'm glad to know that you feel the same way." He gave her a kiss, and then he said, "Let's finish getting ready. Mike and Gordon will be here shortly."

Mike and Gordon were waiting in the foyer when Alex and Laney came downstairs ten minutes later. Fran had made breakfast sandwiches for the four of them to eat on the road, along with four travel mugs of hot coffee. She had also made sandwiches and coffee for Ray, Travis, and Terry, who were riding in the second SUV.

It took over an hour to reach Laney's townhouse, and once there, they wasted no time helping Laney pack the things she wanted to bring back to the ranch.

After most of her things had been loaded into the two SUVs, Alex noticed Mike talking to Gordon and Terry. When he walked over to them, he asked, "What's going on?"

"Terry clocked someone following us from the ranch, Boss," Mike said quietly so Laney wouldn't overhear.

"Could you see who it was?" Alex asked.

Terry showed Alex his tablet. "Here's what the rear camera on the SUV caught." He played the video, and he saw an average vehicle following them at a distance. When Terry zoomed in on the video, Alex saw two Hispanic males in the front seat.

"Where are they now?" Mike asked.

Terry glanced east. "About two blocks from here. I spotted them when I was walking the perimeter ten minutes ago."

"Were there any other cars with them?" Alex asked.

"Not that I could tell, but it's possible," Terry replied.

Alex instinctively felt for his pistol, which was in a hip holster underneath his jacket. "How do you want to play this?" he asked Mike.

"I've alerted the security center. We'll be intercepted by additional units as we head back to the ranch. They'll fall back and engage that car, giving us time to get home safely while they find out what that other car is doing."

Alex nodded. "Let's get Laney's things loaded and get back on the road quickly. We're sitting ducks out here if that car has friends nearby."

"Right, Boss," Mike said.

Alex went back inside Laney's townhouse. "All done?" he asked.

Laney pointed to the stack of boxes next to her front door. "Yes, finally. All I need to do is put these in one of the cars, and we can head back."

The guys each picked up a box and headed for the SUVs while Laney locked up. Then she joined Alex and Mike in Gordon's SUV.

In less than a minute, the rear hatches on both SUVs were closed, and everyone was ready to leave. Gordon pulled out of Laney's parking lot first, followed by Terry.

Laney didn't know about the car following them, but she heard Gordon talking with someone else over his earpiece, and she saw Mike constantly checking the rearview mirrors and the rear camera images on the dashboard monitor. She knew something was wrong.

"What's going on?" she demanded.

"What do you mean—" Alex began before Laney interrupted.

"I've been a lawyer for nearly a decade. I know when there's something going on that people are trying to keep from me. What is it?"

Alex nodded. "We're being followed. The same car was behind us from the ranch to your place, and now it's following us again. We have security teams coming to intercept it, so we can get back to the ranch safely while the teams find out what that car is doing."

"Are we in any danger?" she asked.

"There are only two of them in the car," Mike said. "We're more than enough to deal with that, unless there are other cars with them. That's why we called for additional teams. We'll be safe."

"Who are they?" Laney asked.

"No clue," Alex said. "We've received reports that foreign nationals are landing charter flights at Alliance Airport and heading north. They're using back roads to keep from being spotted by the State Police, and evidently some of those roads run through our county. In fact, at least one of the roads runs right past the ranch. We've been monitoring the increase in traffic along that road, and it matches the times when these charter flights land at Alliance. This is the first time they appear to be monitoring us, though."

"Is the ranch safe?" Laney asked.

Alex nodded. "I expect so. Like I mentioned yesterday, the entire estate is fenced, the perimeter road that runs between the buffer zone and the ranch has the same fencing on either side, and the community is fenced. It's not easy to sneak or break onto the ranch, and we've increased camera and drone surveillance over the property. No one is getting in without a fight."

Laney leaned back in her seat and crossed her arms. "Wild west indeed."

"I told you it could be like this sometimes," Alex said, putting his hand on her knee.

"First team is five minutes from intercept, Boss," Gordon informed Alex. "Second team is three minutes after that, and the third team is ten minutes out. When they've all joined us, the teams will intercept the car following us."

"And what if that car has friends tailing us or waiting for us up ahead?" Alex asked.

"There are two more teams joining us just north of Alliance Airport, and they'll provide support for us all the way to the ranch," Gordon answered.

Alex nodded. "Good. Mike, I want a briefing on this situation later today. I especially want to know what the occupants of that car are up to, and if they have any friends about who could continue following or harassing people coming to or leaving the ranch."

"Yes, Boss."

Ten minutes later, the three teams coming to intercept Alex and Laney had arrived. Gordon listened to the drivers of the other vehicles, then he said, "Boss? The three intercept teams report that our tail is not alone. There are two other cars with him."

"Three team surveillance?" Alex commented. "That's more efficient... for them. Bad for us. What's the plan?"

"I recommend we don't confront the three tails until the other two security SUVs join us just north of Alliance

Airport," Gordon answered. "They can escort us back to the ranch, while the three teams that already joined us take care of the tails."

"I agree," Mike said.

Alex glanced at Laney, who was watching him. "I agree," he said after a moment.

Gordon nodded. "We're about fifteen minutes from the airport. I'll alert the other teams."

"And I'll notify the security center," Mike said.

Laney felt anxious as they headed north. When two SUVs pulled up alongside, Gordon notified the three teams following them to intercept the tailing cars.

Laney turned around and watched the three SUVs slam on their brakes and turn sideways, blocking the road. Then she saw the occupants jump out.

"What are they going to do?" she asked as she lost sight of the three teams behind them.

"Photograph the occupants," Gordon replied. "We can't detain them in Tarrant County, but we can keep them from following us to the ranch. And once we have their photos, ICE should be able to tell us who they are."

"Why can't we detain them?" she inquired.

"Because they haven't broken any laws," Mike said. "It's not illegal to follow us... just annoying."

Gordon kept in contact with the two SUVs alongside, as well as with the three SUVs detaining the tails.

"We have photographs of all six occupants of the tailing cars, Boss," Gordon said as they passed Argyll. "The occupants tried to intimidate our guys by trying to ram and sideswipe the SUVs, but our guys pulled their weapons and motioned for all three cars to pull over. They complied, and our SUVs boxed them in on the side of the road, keeping the tails from being able to get back on the road and follow us."

As they approached their exit, the two additional SUVs changed positions. One SUV took the lead in front of Gordon, and the other SUV took the rear behind Terry. A short while later, they reached the ranch without spotting any additional cars following them.

Gordon, Terry, Travis, and Ray helped bring Laney's things into the residence and up the stairs to the second floor. Alex then helped Laney move her things into her closet and unpack, while the guys returned to the security center.

"That was an interesting outing," Laney commented as she and Alex put away her clothing. "Has that ever happened before?"

"It was a first for me," Alex responded. "I've always known that competitors would want to watch the people who train here, but gangs operating in this area are new. It's all tied to whoever is landing at Alliance Airport and then disappearing. We'll keep the State Police and ICE informed. Maybe they can do something about it. It's not really something we should be involved with unless they try to breach the estate."

"Why would they want to do that, if they're just passing by on their way somewhere else?"

"Anyone who drives past the fence knows that this isn't an ordinary ranch. Given its size and security, it's clearly protecting something valuable, and if these people are part of a gang of criminals, then we're a tempting target. There are tens of millions of dollars in horses and equipment in the equestrian center, not to mention the personal items in the community and here in the residence."

Laney nodded. "I hadn't thought about it that way."

Alex watched her for a while. Then he asked, "Does that impact your decision to live here? I understand if it does."

"No... it doesn't make me want to reconsider. I feel safe here, in spite of this incident. Your security teams handled the situation professionally and quickly. Hell, I never really felt safe as a single woman living and working in Fort Worth, even though I was always armed. And Fort Worth is a fairly safe city. But there are always threats, and you know what traffic is like down there. As long and you and your staff keep me safe, then I'll always feel good about living up here."

"I promise I'll do all I can to keep you safe," Alex said.

Two hours later, shortly after noon, Alex and Laney were in the kitchen eating lunch. Fran and her team had grilled steaks and served them with au gratin potatoes, grilled vegetables, and freshly baked bread. The meal was fantastic.

Alex and Laney had just finished eating, and were heading toward the stairs, when Alex received a phone call. He listened to the caller, and then ended the call.

"Mike and Chuck Washington will be coming up here at 2:00 PM to brief us on what they learned about our tail this morning," Alex said as he and Laney went upstairs to the den.

"Who's Chuck?" Laney asked.

"My head of security," Alex answered. "He's also bringing my security detail, and he's bringing your security detail with him so you can meet them. Remember, if you don't like the team he selected for you, we can replace any of the members—no questions asked."

"How does a security detail work?" she asked as they sat on the larger couch.

"They won't be with you when you're on the estate, but if you go anywhere off-site—meetings for instance—they'll be with you, like my detail in DC was with me. You'll have a driver, a team leader, and two team members. You have to remember to let them know in advance if you're leaving the property and where you're going."

"What if I'm going somewhere with you?"

"Then we'll share the driver, and depending on where we're going and what we're doing, either one or two of your detail will go with us to guard you while my detail is guarding me."

"I can see why your ex-girlfriend complained about how complicated your security measures were," Laney said, smiling.

"Do *you* find my security measures complicated?"

"A little," Laney admitted, "But that's because I'm not used to it yet. Once I am, it won't be a problem. Unlike your ex, I appreciate having security around—especially after this morning."

"Good," Alex said, looking relieved. "I don't want to lose you, too, just because I believe that security is necessary."

Laney laughed. "If you ever lose me, it definitely won't be because of your security measures."

At two o'clock, Alex and Laney met with Chuck Washington and his teams in the dining room. Chuck, a handsome older black man, had the appearance of being ex-military, and he had a commanding presence.

Gordon, Mike, Travis, and Ray sat on one side of the table. Laney's detail sat on the other side. In addition to Terry Vance, who would be Laney's driver, her team consisted of Ken Dover, Paul Phillips, and Hans Jürgen. Ken was her detail leader, like Mike was Alex's detail leader. All of her team members were ex-military with years of experience in protection services.

Chuck started by showing Alex and Laney the photographs taken that morning of the occupants of the three cars that tailed Alex and Laney to and from her townhouse. They were all Hispanic.

"Any idea who they are?" Alex asked.

Chuck nodded. "My contacts at ICE confirmed that they're TDA members currently operating in the Dallas area."

"TDA?" Laney asked.

"Tren de Aragua, a criminal organization from Venezuela," Chuck replied. "They've been operating in a number of cities around the country. They're violent, and they don't seem to be afraid of anything. They have cells in Dallas and Houston, and ICE thinks the new arrivals are setting up operations in Wichita Falls, Texas, and Lawton,

Oklahoma. Evidently, the route they're taking from Alliance Airport brings them along the south edge of the estate. ICE thinks they're curious about us, given that they drive past our location every time a new planeload of gang members arrive. The State Police, however, think that they may be looking to raid the estate, steal what they can, sell it, and use the money to fund their operations. They may even have kidnapping for ransom in mind, although I hope that's not the case. No one that they've kidnapped in the United States has been recovered alive. They extort the money, and then kill their captive—women, children, babies, it doesn't matter to them."

"We should increase security immediately," Alex said.

"In the works already, Boss," Chuck said. "We've increased the number of drones flying over the estate, and we've increased patrols along the buffer zone road and the four outer perimeter roads that run along the fence line. I'd suggest having the sheriff come out and deputize all the ranch hands, in case we need to call on them as reserves. The bunkhouses all have pistols, rifles, and ammunition. I'd suggest that, as soon as they're deputized, the ranch hands carry a sidearm with them at all times, and anyone riding on a horse or in a vehicle, also carry a rifle with them."

Alex nodded. "I agree. Can you contact the sheriff to arrange deputizing the ranch hands? Also, we'll need to notify the bunkhouse department head so he can notify the ranch hands about what's happening."

"I'll take care of it, Boss."

They talked for a few more minutes, and then the security staff left the residence.

Alex and Laney remained in the dining room. "Any

thoughts about what was discussed?" he asked. "I want you to feel free to participate in these meetings, but even if you don't, I want to hear your thoughts."

"It all makes sense," Laney said, hesitating, "but it's interesting that you're turning your employees into an army."

Alex shrugged. "It's not like I'm trying to recreate the Regulators that John Chisum, Henry Tunstall, and Alexander McSween created to fight in the Lincoln Country War against Murphy & Dolan's gang of thugs, but I did tell you that this can be like the wild west sometimes. I just never thought we'd potentially be going up against a bunch of Venezuelan invaders. But if we are, I want to be prepared, and I want whatever we do to be legal."

Laney looked at the photos again, and then she handed them to Alex. "So, apart from preparing for a war, what's the plan for this week?"

"I have meetings over breakfast every day, and I hope you'll participate in them with me. It's the best way to immerse yourself in what it takes to run this ranch. On Mondays, I meet with the heads of security, ranch operations, and estate operations. Tuesday, I meet with the ranch department heads. Wednesday I meet with the security department heads. Thursday, I meet with the estate department heads. Friday, I meet with Kelly Fernandez, the head of housekeeping, and Fran Burrows, who leads the residence's culinary team. There's also a monthly poker night here at the residence with all the department heads and senior staff. Not for money," Alex added quickly. "Just for fun and so we can all interact socially."

"You really want me to sit in on your staff meetings?"

Laney sounded surprised.

"Of course. Why not?"

"Well, we're... we haven't... we're not official yet, as a couple I mean. Do you want an outsider knowing the details of what goes on around here?"

Alex grinned. "You're not an outsider, your my attorney. Client privilege, remember?"

"You're not serious, are you? You don't just think of me as your attorney, right?"

"Of course not. I imagine by now that most of the staff knows I brought a girlfriend back from DC, and they'll want to meet you. One mistake I made last time was not involving your... predecessor in ranch and estate operations. I thought she was too young, but it could have helped her make her decision sooner. I want to immerse you in this place, so you'll know exactly what you're getting into if you and I stay together. I also hope you come to love it here as much as I do, and since I'm looking for a true life partner, I want you and I to eventually run this place together."

Laney smiled, but her eyes teared up. She nodded, wiped her eyes, and then asked, "How many department heads and senior staff do you have here?" Laney asked.

"Thirty-four men and women," Alex answered.

"That many?"

Alex nodded. "And that's not counting all the foremen who oversee specific work around the property. It takes a lot of personnel and leaders to run a ranch like this."

Alex stood. "Getting back to your original question, apart from the standing meetings, there are no specific plans for the week. I figured I'd take you around and let you see the breeding and training operations. We have both indoor and outdoor training, depending on weather, and since it's still early February, everything is currently being done indoors. It might warm up by the weekend, and I'm hoping we can go riding so you can truly experience the beauty of the ranch."

"I'd love that," Laney said. "And I'd love to see the training, especially equine therapy. Since that's your charitable operation, I think I'd like to get a lot more familiar with what it involves."

"We'll make that a priority for this week," Alex said. "Is there anything you'd like to do this afternoon? It'll be dark soon, but there's still time to explore the property some more."

Laney was silent for a minute. "Honestly, I think I'd like to relax today and then dive into everything tomorrow. Can we go upstairs and watch a movie? Suddenly, I'm in the mood for a western."

CHAPTER 13

𝒜t breakfast the next morning, Alex and Laney met with the three people who oversaw the operations of AMB Ranch and Equestrian Center: Rick Jackson, the estate manager, Pete Reynolds, the ranch manager, and Chuck Washington, the head of security.

After Rick and Pete brought Alex up-to-speed on what was happening on the property over the previous three weeks, Chuck talked about the incident involving the TDA members following Alex's SUV to and from Laney's townhouse. All three managers promised to make certain that their staff kept a close watch for anything unusual happening around the ranch and to report any drone sightings or incursions to security immediately.

After breakfast, Alex took Laney to the equine therapy building to meet with Bradley Hays, the head of that department. Hays gave Laney a complete tour of the facilities and allowed her to watch several of the therapy sessions.

"Most of the horses used here are dedicated to our various equine therapy practices," Hays explained. "What we do here is allow our patients and clients to interact with horses, under the guidance of a therapist, to address various conditions and challenges. There are four types of therapy that we do here: equine-assisted psychotherapy or EAP, hippotherapy, equine-assisted learning or EAL, and therapeutic horsemanship or TH. Equine therapy fosters self-awareness, confidence, and emotional regulation. Interactions with horses improve communication and social interaction skills, and the presence of horses has a calming effect, reducing stress and anxiety."

He led her to the EAP area. "Here, we focus on emotional and psychological well-being, using the horse's presence and behavior as a tool to explore personal challenges. EAP helps patients and clients manage anxiety, depression, trauma, and other mental health concerns."

"What does the equine-assisted learning do?" Laney asked as they approached that practice area.

"The EAL approach uses horses to enhance learning and development in areas like communication, problem-solving, and social skills." Hayes explained.

Pointing to the therapeutic horsemanship practice area, Hays said, "And TH involves teaching horsemanship skills and using horses to promote physical and emotional healing."

Laney saw several staff members working with young people. "What are they doing over there?" she asked.

"Ah, that's Special Equestrians. It's part of our hippotherapy program. We offer therapeutic riding lessons for individuals with multiple diagnoses, including autism spectrum disorder, intellectual disability, development disability, ADHD, cerebral palsy, genetic disorders, and brain injuries. Hippotherapy uses the movement of the horse to achieve therapy treatment goals for children and adults with neuromotor, cognitive, and sensory dysfunction. A therapist guides the session, focusing on improving physical abilities like balance, coordination, strength, and muscle control. It's one of our most successful programs, and the one that Mr. Barclay is the most passionate about. We're always looking for volunteers to help, if you're interested."

At the end of the tour, Hays said, "As you've seen, patients and clients engage in activities with horses, such as grooming, leading, or riding, depending on the type of therapy. Our therapists observe and provide guidance to help individuals understand their behavior and emotions in relation to the horse. The horse's nonjudgmental nature and unique ability to mirror human emotions provide opportunities for emotional processing and growth. Do you have any questions?"

"Just one," Laney said. "How does equine therapy help people suffering from PTSD?"

Hays smiled. "Ah, that's part of our equine-assisted psychotherapy practice. EAP utilizes the unique bond between humans and horses to help individuals with PTSD process trauma, develop coping skills, and build trust. It's a powerful tool for building self-awareness, emotional regulation, and social support."

Hays led Laney and Alex back to the EAP practice area. Seeing one of the therapists concluding a session, he called her over. "This is Angela Parker, one of our EAP therapists. Angela, can you explain how EAP helps with PTSD patients?"

"Of course," Angela said pleasantly. "PTSD assistance is one of the reasons this practice exists here on the ranch, and we've had a lot of success with our approach. Horses are highly sensitive to human emotions and behaviors, providing a mirror for individuals to observe and understand their own reactions. This non-verbal exchange is particularly helpful for individuals who struggle to express their feelings verbally. The process of bonding with a horse, earning its trust and learning to communicate with it, builds self-confidence and trust in oneself and others. Activities like grooming, leading, and interacting with horses help our patients develop new coping mechanisms for managing stress, anxiety, and other common PTSD symptoms. Focusing on the present moment when interacting with a horse helps individuals ground themselves and reduces the impact of intrusive thoughts, memories, and triggers associated with their trauma."

"Thanks, Angela," Hays said. "Our EAP practice provides a sense of community and social support, which can be crucial for patients with PTSD who often experience isolation and disconnection. The process of interacting with and taking care of a large animal is empowering for patients who feel powerless or overwhelmed by their trauma. Through the horse-human interaction, patients gain a deeper understanding of themselves, their feelings, and their behaviors, which can be a crucial step in the healing process."

When she and Alex left the building, she felt she had a much better understanding of the services provided and why the practice was so important to Alex, but she also knew she had barely scratched the surface of understanding all that Hays' people provided to their patients and clients.

"I'm amazed at all they do," she said as she got into the truck.

"They're a great group of folks," Alex said. "And they've helped hundreds and hundreds of people. Several former clients now work here on the ranch, as do members of their families. Nate Gierson, the lead horse groom, is a former client of the equine therapy team. He personally takes care of my horse, Duke." Alex started the truck and headed for the stables. "Speaking of which, we need to pick a horse for you. Nate is something of a horse whisperer, and he has a gift for picking the perfect horse for any rider. He picked your predecessor's horse in less than three minutes, and it proved to be the perfect horse for her."

Laney giggled. "It's funny to hear you call Penny my 'predecessor,' rather than calling her by name or calling her your 'ex'."

"It's easier that way," Alex said. "After being with you these past three weeks, I no longer really think about her that much. She doesn't feel like an ex-girlfriend, she was just someone here before you."

"So you don't feel like I've taken her place around here?"

Alex snorted. "It was always *your* place. I just didn't know it until a couple of weeks ago. There's nothing for you to take from her, because nothing here was hers."

Laney didn't respond, but the smile on her face said volumes.

When they arrived at the stables, Nate greeted Alex.

"Nate, my friend, this is Laney Connor." Alex introduced Laney to Nate. "I need you to work your magic and pick her a horse."

Nate gave Laney an appraising look for a minute. "You've ridden before?" he asked.

"When I was much younger," Laney replied. "Not in the last fifteen years."

"You remember how?"

Laney nodded. "For the most part."

Nate rubbed his chin for another minute. "English or western?"

"Western," Laney stated.

Nate nodded and looked at Alex. "Max."

"Seriously?" Alex asked, surprised.

Nate nodded. "You want her to be able to keep up with you and Duke, right? Max is the right horse for her *and* for you and Duke."

"Who's Max?" Laney asked.

"Max is an American Quarter Horse with Draft Horse, Spanish, Arabian, and Thoroughbred ancestry," Nate answered. "He's a spotted bay Appaloosa with a black mane and tail. His narrow build will be a more comfortable ride for you, and his height will allow him to keep up with Duke's gait. Duke, like most Thoroughbreds, is spirited and bold, whereas Max is fast and energetic, but he's also gentle and patient with inexperienced riders. If you want a horse for the long term, Max is it."

"He's also one of our breeding horses for the ranch," Alex added. "We don't sell his stud services, but he's sired a number of ranch horses here."

"May I see him?" Laney asked.

Nate led them inside the barn to a stall about six past

Duke's stall. Alex stopped to see Duke and give him an apple, while Nate took Laney to get acquainted with Max.

When Laney saw Max, she fell in love. He was a beautiful horse, with a slightly lighter coat than Duke's, and spotted, rather than a single color all over. She and Max locked eyes, and Laney felt an immediate connection. Max walked forward, and Laney stroked his head. Then she fed him an apple she had grabbed from the barrel at the building's entrance. Max ate the apple quickly, and then he placed his head on Laney's shoulder.

"I told you Max was perfect," Nate said to Alex when he joined them.

"Right as usual," Alex conceded. "Shall we let her saddle him up and see how he feels to ride?"

Nate looked outside and then at the temperature gauge over the main doors. "It's too cold to ride outside, but she can ride here inside the building, as long as she doesn't go fast."

Laney turned to look at Alex and Nate. "Please?"

Nate nodded. "I'll take her to the tack room and help her pick out a saddle."

"Who grooms Max?" Alex asked.

"Tommy Butterfield, and as much as I'd like to handle Max for Miss Laney, like I do with Duke for you, I wouldn't advise changing Max's groom. Tommy has been with him since Max was born, and you never want to upset a breeding horse by changing handlers."

"Okay," Alex decided. "Can you have Tommy let us know Max's routine, so we know when he's unavailable to ride, and make sure that Duke's schedule and Max's schedule match as much as possible. Laney and I will be riding together most days."

"I'll take care of it, Boss."

Nate led Alex and Laney to the tack room. Laney hated tearing herself away from Max, but the horse seemed to know that she'd be coming back shortly.

She tried several saddles before she found one that was comfortable to sit on.

"It'll take a while before you get completely comfortable riding," Nate said as he wrote Laney's name and Max's name on a card and placed it above the saddle. "The stiffness will eventually go away, and riding will feel just like walking."

Nate selected the rest of the gear that Laney would need. Then they carried the saddle and gear back to Max's stall.

There was someone standing outside Max's stall as they approached. "That's Tommy," Nate said.

Tommy looked at them and recognized Alex. "Good afternoon, Boss," he said pleasantly.

"Good afternoon, Tommy," Alex replied. "We're here to see Max."

Nate explained that Laney would be riding Max, and Tommy nodded. "Do you want me to help her saddle Max?" Tommy asked Nate.

"Yes," Nate replied.

Alex and Nate watched as Tommy showed Laney what to do, starting with making sure there was nothing caught in Max's fur that could irritate the skin once the saddle was in place. Then he showed her how to place the bit in Max's mouth, how to put the saddle on, how to tighten the straps, and how to adjust the stirrups. "We'll make the final adjustment once you're seated on Max, to make sure the length is correct," Tommy told her.

Laney looked up at the saddle. "I forgot how high the back of a horse can be. What if I can't get my leg in the stirrup?"

"We have portable steps to make it easier for you," Tommy assured her. "Let's give it a try, and if he's too tall, I'll get the steps."

Laney leaned back, lifted her leg, and managed to get it in the stirrup. Then she grabbed the saddle horn and pulled herself up. She swung her other leg over Max's back, and sat on the saddle.

"Well done, Laney," Alex said, smiling.

Tommy checked the straps and adjusted the stirrups, lengthening them slightly to make riding more comfortable for Laney. Then he removed Max's tether and handed Laney the reins.

Laney coaxed Max out of the stall and down the center aisle between the stalls. Then she turned around and headed to the front of the building. She turned around again, leaned down to grab another apple from the barrel, and brought Max back to his stall.

"The saddle is perfect," she said to Nate and Tommy. "He's a dream to ride. I can't wait to take him out to the meadow!"

"It should be warm enough this weekend," Nate said. "Saturday should be a great day for riding."

Laney dismounted and held the reins to Tommy. He shook his head. "No, ma'am. You brought him out, you take him back in and remove the saddle and the rest of the tack."

"That's ranch rules," Alex said. "I should have told you that when we arrived. Sorry about that."

"That's fine with me," Laney said. She led Max back

into his stall, connected the tether, and began to remove the tack under Tommy's watchful eyes. Once all of the gear had been removed, she rubbed Max's head again, fed him the apple she grabbed from the barrel, picked up the gear, and headed for the tack room as Tommy closed the stall gate.

"You removed the gear like a pro," Tommy said as he followed Laney to the tack room.

"Thanks, Tommy."

"We'll be coming down here every day," Alex said to Laney. "The horses get used to seeing us, and it's important to keep a routine with them. Obviously we can't come down when we're away, but as long as we're here, then we spend time with our horses."

Laney beamed. "Perfect."

Once all the gear had been put away, Alex and Laney thanked Nate and Tommy, and then they headed for the truck.

"Hungry?" Alex asked once he had the engine running.

"Starving," Laney answered.

"I'll take us back to the house. I don't know what Fran has in store for us, but I should warn you that the lunch menu on Thursdays is always the same every week."

"What's special about Thursdays?" she asked.

"Bo Perkins, the chuck wagon cook who runs the dining hall, is a former pit master from a restaurant in Grapevine. When the restaurant he worked at closed, I hired him and his entire team to manage the food service here on the ranch. On Wednesday evenings, he fires up the pit, and by Thursday mornings, you can smell beef brisket and ribs over much of the property. He delivers a half brisket to the residence, along with the sides his team

174

makes, and we have the best barbecue sandwiches you've ever eaten. If there's ever any leftovers, which is rare, Fran puts the meat into either enchiladas or chili. It's delicious! Which reminds me, I need to tell him to send up a larger brisket from now on."

Alex stopped the truck and looked at Laney. "Unless you're one of those weirdoes who doesn't like barbeque beef brisket."

Laney laughed. "I'm a native Texan. Of course I love barbeque beef brisket!"

Alex started driving again. "Good. I'd hate to have to end things with you here and now. Barbeque is a deal breaker in my book."

They both laughed as they headed back to the residence.

After lunch, Alex took Laney to the hunter-jumper training center and the junior rodeo training center, so Laney could tour the facilities and see what kind of training they offered. Since teams were in their winter training at the ranch, Laney couldn't meet any of the staff, but she watched with great interest.

Tuesday morning, Alex and Laney met with Pete Reynolds and the ranch department heads over breakfast. It was the first time Laney had met any of Pete's staff, apart from Bradley Hays, who ran the equine therapy operations.

She had heard of Elizabeth Harrison and Sam Stewart, who headed up training for hunter-jumper and junior rodeo. Both were famous competitors, and they had a reputation for being among the best trainers in their field.

She also met Miles Brody, who handled the ranch's breeding operations. She had no idea how big a business horse breeding was, and even though Alex didn't raise or train racehorses, managing the bloodlines of his herd was a full-time job.

She also met Bo Perkins. "I understand you're a pit master," she said when they were introduced. "I'm looking forward to Thursdays around here."

"I think you'll be pleased with the food," he said with pride. "Good beef, good wood smoke, a secret recipe of rubs and sauce, and patience, always makes for great barbeque."

Laney quietly listened to the reports from the head trainers, the stables manager, the hay and feed manager, the bunkhouse foreman who oversaw all of the ranch hands, the breeder, and the food service manager.

"I never realized how many departments it takes to operate a horse ranch," she thought as she listened. *"This is a bigger operation than I ever imagined."*

After breakfast, Alex and Laney visited their horses before visiting the training operations again.

On Wednesday morning, Alex and Laney met with Chuck Washington and the Security Department Heads. She already knew Mike Billingsley, who headed up the security details, and she was introduced to the camera and drone surveillance leads, the perimeter security leads, the head of the horse stables patrols, and the head of the rapid response unit, which took care of emergencies requiring a team of well-trained operatives.

On Thursday morning, Alex and Laney meet with Rick Jackson and his estate department heads. This was the group that provided administrative support, including HR and accounting; management of the commissary operations, maintenance for vehicles, buildings, and equipment; grounds keeping for the entire property; and the upkeep for all roads, sidewalks, and fences on the property.

One of the responsibilities of the meadow and buffer zone grounds keepers was keeping the grazing grasses planted and weed-free for the horses. Both areas were planted with alfalfa for foraging by the horses, but the bulk of their feed and hay was handled at the horse barns and came from nearby suppliers.

When Alex and Laney returned to the residence after visiting their horses, Bo's barbeque was waiting, and it didn't disappoint. It was the best brisket Laney had ever eaten, and the potato salad, coleslaw, and baked beans were outstanding.

"I can't believe how good this is," Laney said when she finished her plate. "And you get this every Thursday?"

"Every week of the year except Thanksgiving," Alex confirmed. "Personally, I could eat it every day, but variety is good, and Fran and her staff are terrific cooks."

On Friday morning, Alex and Laney met with Fran and Kelly Fernandez. Laney learned that Kelly's housekeeping staff took care of the residence and all of the offices on the property. They also took care of cleaning the three security gatehouses.

Fran reminded Alex that the monthly card night was that evening. She and her staff were making finger foods to serve to the thirty-four people coming.

"How does card night work?" Laney asked. She knew they played poker, but she also knew that Alex hated gambling.

"Everyone draws for their table," Alex began. "That way there should be a good mix of people at each table. We use poker chips instead of cash, and we keep it a friendly game. It's only draw and stud poker, since black-jack and Texas Hold 'Em requires one player to be the dealer and the bank. Each table plays until there is a winner. Once all tables have a winner, those winners all play against each other until there is a final winner. The table winners each get a small prize, and the overall winner gets a prize— usually ranch related or something I brought back from my travels."

"What happens if *you* win?" Laney asked.

"That can't happen," Alex said.

"Why not?"

Alex looked at Fran and Kelly. "Not to leave this table, but if it looks like I'm about to win at my table, I throw the hand and lose. For me, it's not about winning, it's about spending time with the managers who work for me. Let them think I'm a lousy poker player. I don't care. Besides, I have another poker club that meets quarterly, and *they* know I'm not a lousy player."

"Mr. Alex usually wins those games," Fran said. "It's a good thing he doesn't play for money, or he'd put them in bankruptcy."

"So you love the games, but not gambling?" Laney asked Alex.

Alex nodded. "I don't like throwing away money. I have a ranch, horses, and an airplane for that. But I do love card games, and not just poker. I'm trying to get a bridge club going, but too few people know how to play it. I hope you'll participate tonight. I think you'll have fun."

"I wouldn't miss it!"

After reviewing the menus for the next week, Alex and Laney headed to the ranch to visit their horses and then the training centers. Laney was just starting to understand the ins and outs of hunter-jumper competitions and junior rodeo competitions, and she wanted to learn all she could.

As they watched one of the junior rodeo trainees performing the barrel race, Alex asked, "So I forgot to ask. How did the conversation with Dwight go about your leave of absence?"

Laney chuckled quietly. "You remember we wondered if Elizabeth mentioned to him that you and I danced all night at the ball?"

Alex nodded.

"Well, she did. The first words out of his mouth were, 'Are you sleeping with Alexander Barclay?'"

"How did you respond?"

"I told him I was sleeping with you every night, and had been for the past three weeks," Laney responded, grinning. "He flipped out. He told me that it was unethical to sleep with a client, and I was jeopardizing my partnership promotion."

"And what did you tell him?"

"That if you and I stayed together, I'd be walking away from more than just the partnership. That left him speechless. I think it was his greatest fear, and suddenly he saw it as a real possibility. I told him that I'm taking this time to see if you and I can make our relationship work long-term, and depending on what we decide, I'll either be returning to the firm or leaving it altogether. He reminded me of all I'd be giving up, and I reminded him of all I'd be gaining that a law firm could never give me."

"You actually told him that?"

Laney nodded. "I don't like lying to him. He has been too good to me. But he needed to know that I'm making plans for the rest of my life, and only one of two scenarios can happen where my career is concerned; I'll either stay with the firm or leave the firm, and I won't know which until later in the spring."

Alex put his arm around her and pulled her close. "I think you handled that conversation well." He kissed her cheek. "We should head back to the house and get ready for tonight. It should be a fun evening."

UNWELCOME VISITORS

CHAPTER 14

The managers and department heads of the ranch arrived at six o'clock on Friday evening. It was a casual affair, and Laney enjoyed interacting in a social setting with the leaders she had met that week.

Several people wanted to know how Laney and Alex had met, and she had to repeat the story a number of times throughout the evening.

Fran and her staff had prepared finger foods for the evening, and Alex served as the bartender, fixing alcoholic and non-alcoholic beverages for the guests.

Once everyone had eaten, they drew for tables, which consisted of reaching into a leather pouch and drawing out a poker chip. There were thirty-six chips in the bag, and the chips were one of six colors. Everyone who drew the same colored chip sat at the same table.

The poker chips for each player were quickly distributed, along with the card decks. Alex gave a review of the house rules, and then each table selected who would deal the first hand. Once that was done, the card games began.

Laney sat at the same table as Bradley Hayes, the equine therapy head, Elizabeth Harrison, the hunter-jumper lead, Kate Fleming, the drone surveillance lead, Pasqual Lopez, the residence maintenance lead, and Alan Rowe, the head of human resources. Elizabeth proved to be a true card shark, and in less than an hour, she had taken all of Bradley's, Pasqual's, and Alan's chips. Only Laney and Kate were still in the game against Elizabeth, who seemed unbeatable.

Laney was the next player at her table to lose all of her chips. She looked over at Alex, who had lost all his chips first at his table. He was busy refilling drinks, and he winked at Laney when he saw her looking at him.

Kate and Elizabeth continued the card battle for another hour, but just as it seemed that Elizabeth was going to win it all, Kate proved to be the superior card player and wiped Elizabeth out of chips.

When the table winners began playing each other to see who was going to be the overall winner, Kate proved to be unstoppable. She cleaned out the chips of all the other players in thirty minutes.

Once Alex presented the table winners and Kate with prizes he had picked up in Washington, DC, the managers and department heads left the residence. The kitchen staff had already cleaned the dishes before they left for the night. Alex gathered the glasses and other empty beverage containers. He washed the glasses and returned them to the lounge, and the bottles, cans, and cups were rinsed out and put in the recycle bin.

"Did you have fun?" Alex said as they headed upstairs.

"It was a blast, getting to see everyone away from work," Laney responded. "Now I understand why you do this."

"I'd do it weekly if I could, but with everyone's schedules, monthly is the only way I could arrange for everyone to be here at the same time."

"Schedules?" Laney asked, confused. "Isn't it after working hours?"

"This ranch is a 24 hour a day operation," Alex answered. "Many of the departments work three shifts a day, and the department heads do shift work. Kate, for instance, takes the second shift quite a bit because she's our best night drone operator. She'll be taking third shift tonight, which is why she wasn't drinking anything except water."

As they relaxed in the den, Laney asked, "Are we still riding tomorrow?"

Alex nodded. "The weather looks like it'll be perfect. We can head down after breakfast, if you want to get an early start."

"Perfect," Laney said, snuggling closer to him.

The next morning was crisp, but the air was slightly humid, and there was a warm breeze blowing from the south. The high was expected to reach the upper 50s, and it was in the low 50s when Alex and Laney headed for the stables.

Laney noticed that Alex had two lever-action rifles in leather scabbards with him, and he was wearing his favorite pistols openly for a change. Laney was also wearing a pistol, but her holster was tucked into her waistline and was out of sight underneath her jacket.

When they arrived at the stable, they wasted no time getting Duke and Max saddled. Alex attached one of the two rifles to Laney's saddle, and the other one he attached to his own saddle. Once the horses were ready to go, Alex handed Laney a communications device that consisted of an earpiece, a microphone, and a transmitter that attached to her belt.

"This is in case something happens to you," Alex said, attaching his own transmitter to his belt and putting the earpiece in his right ear. "It's connected with security, and it's so they can contact you, too. The meadow is 20 square miles, and that's a large area to search for someone if something goes wrong."

Laney attached her communication's device as Alex did, and then they mounted their horses. As soon as they were outside the barn, Duke and Max began getting excited. It had been a while since they had been ridden outdoors, and they wanted to run.

It was over a mile to the gate that led to the meadow. When they reached it, Alex contacted security to open the gate and close it behind them.

Once inside the meadow part of the ranch, Alex motioned for Laney to turn north, and they rode to the north end of the meadow side-by-side. Max had no problem keeping up with Duke, and Laney found being on a horse again exhilarating.

The rolling hills of the meadow were beautiful, and the horses loved running up and down the slopes. After showing Laney the northern part of the meadow, Alex turned south, and they rode along the ridges that lined the eastern edge of the meadow.

When they reached the highest point in the meadow, Alex stopped so Laney could enjoy the view.

"When I stood on this spot for the first time, and I saw all the land to the west, north, and south, I knew this is where I wanted to build my ranch," he said. "I wanted this ridge in the center of the property, but the land east of here wasn't for sale, and there was a state road running right between that property and this one. It wouldn't have worked. So I made this ridge the edge of the meadow, and put everything else to the west. I still get the view, and I only have to look in one direction to see most of what's mine."

Laney looked at the rest of the ranch, stretching out from where their horses were standing. The residence was hidden behind the berms and the groves, but she saw the ranch's buildings perfectly.

"What grows here?" she asked, looking down at the brown grass. "Is this alfalfa?"

"Yes," Alex answered. "The meadow and the buffer zone are both alfalfa. We let the horses graze here, and we bale it every five to six weeks to keep it low, reduce the water demands, and bring the hay to the barns. It's only part of what the horses eat, but it allows them to forage when we let them out here to run and exercise."

"I'm getting a crash course in what it takes to operate a ranch like this," Laney said, sounding overwhelmed.

"It's a lot of work, which is why I hired the best people to operate it for me. A lot of ranchers said I was crazy when they saw how many different operations we have here. Raising and breeding horses is hard enough, but boarding horses, operating four training centers, maintaining a residence, and managing an entire community as large as many subdivisions or planned communities? It's like eight ranches all occupying the same land. But it's the legacy I wanted to build and leave to future generations, and I personally think it's a much better way of spending my money than seeing how many silly things I can buy. I don't need five homes, I don't need a fleet of jets, I don't need nightclubs or restaurants or sports teams, I have no interest in casinos or gambling, and money just sitting in the bank isn't doing anyone any good except for the bank. I employ over four hundred people here, I'm keeping several other local farms and ranches afloat, I'm ensuring that the children who live here get a superior education, and I'm helping people who need specialized assistance. What could be a better use of my money?"

Laney looked at Alex. "I can't think of a single thing. What you've built here is amazing, and I'm happy just being a small part of it."

"Hopefully a large part of it soon," Alex said, smiling.

"Hopefully," Laney agreed.

They looked around the property for a few more minutes, and then they headed southwest.

Just before they were about to turn north again, Alex heard a strange buzzing sound.

"What's that?" Laney asked.

"I don't know." Alex removed the binoculars from his saddlebag. Then he scanned the skies above them. There was a dark spot moving south toward them.

Laney saw it and pointed. "It looks like a drone. Is it one of yours?"

"No, it's not," Alex said, darkly.

"I thought this was a no-fly zone and no one could fly drones here except for security."

"This is a no fly zone." Alex reached for the microphone. "Security, this is Barclay. There's an unauthorized drone over the meadow, heading for this position."

"Rodger, Boss. We see and are tracking the drone. Can you see any vehicles on the path of the drone?"

"Security, there are too many trees along the buffer zone's outer perimeter to see who or what's on the public road."

"Rodger, Boss. Do you wish to bring it down?"

"Security, once it passes our position, I'll see if I can drop it in the buffer zone."

"Rodger, Boss. Alert us after the attempt."

Alex drew his lever-action rifle from the scabbard underneath his leg. He put a round in the chamber, hooked a strange device to the side of the rifle, and began aiming.

"What's that you added to the side of the rifle?" Laney asked.

"It catches the cartridges when they eject," Alex explained. "I don't want spent casings littering the ground."

"What are you shooting?"

".45 Long Colts," replied. "I prefer rounds with full metal jackets, but there's nothing smoother than the .45 Long Colt. The exposed lead slug is why I don't like shooting it in the meadow, but if I can drop that drone in the buffer zone, then the lead won't affect the horses. And the larger slug should damage or destroy that drone nicely."

The drone flew overhead, and Alex turned his horse

around and began aiming. Laney took the binoculars and watched the drone. A minute later, Alex whispered, "Fire in the hole." The rifle fired, making a loud crack that echoed around the nearby hills.

"Miss," Laney said, seeing no damage to the drone.

Alex fired a second time. This time, Laney saw the drone lurch and then drop from the sky.

"Perfect hit!" Laney exclaimed.

"And it landed in the buffer zone," Alex said. "That means it's still on my property and I can recover it legally."

Alex called security and told them where the drone landed. He and Laney waited until they saw two four-wheelers racing along the buffer zone toward the downed drone.

After a few minutes of searching, Alex heard from his earpiece, "Boss, we found it, and the bullet it still inside the control casing. We'll take it back to the security center."

"I'll meet you there," Alex responded.

The two four-wheelers took off, and Alex and Laney rode back to the stables. They heard several other drones overhead, but Alex recognized them as belonging to the ranch. "Security must be looking for whoever was flying that drone," Alex told Laney.

As they rode back to the gate that went from the meadow to the equestrian center, Laney saw dozens of horses running or grazing around the meadow, along with a number of ranch hands on horseback, keeping an eye on the other horses.

"What's going on," she asked, pointing to the horses.

"We let the horses that belong to me, as well as some of the boarded horses, come out here on most days to exercise and forage. There's a lot of room here, and they love to run and play. The ranch hands lead the horses out here, make sure that nothing happens to them, and then take them back to the stables, where they get brushed down."

"Every day?"

"Weather permitting," Alex replied. He waved to two ranch hands who were watching several of the horses. They waved back, and then they moved with the horses, who were heading southeast.

When Alex and Laney reached the stable, all of the stalls were empty. They removed their saddles and gear, and they returned it to the tack room. Then they brushed their horses to remove any alfalfa flowers that may have gotten caught in their hair.

"We'll go riding again tomorrow," Alex promised Laney. "This is just the first of many riding days here. It's probably best that we don't overdo things, given that neither of us has ridden for a while."

Laney nodded, and they walked back to the truck and drove to the security center.

When they arrived, Kate was taking apart the drone that Alex had shot down.

"It was a clean shot, Boss," she said. "Right through the radio controller. The camera is undamaged. If there's a memory card in it, we'll see everything that the operator saw."

She continued taking apart the components until she had the camera separated from the drone. She opened the memory card slot and extracted a card that looked undamaged. She inserted the card into a reader attached to her tablet and began scrolling through the images.

"Wow," she said softly. "This thing has been flying

over the estate for a while, Boss. Someone has been spying on us for weeks. Most of these clips look like they're from outside the buffer zone. Today's video seems to the be first time they flew into the interior of the property.

She held up her tablet so everyone could see. "It started from the southwest and flew north over the training center, the stables, the barns, the bunkhouses, the dining hall... Then it flew over the residence, turned around, and flew south over the meadow. That's when it saw you."

The image began gyrating after the drone passed over Alex and Laney. "That's when you shot it, and it fell. Without the radio controller, it couldn't receive commands, and it couldn't send any images."

"Can you trace the serial number of that drone?" Alex asked.

"I'll see what I can do," Kate replied. "If there's a way to track who bought it, I'll find it."

"Thanks, Kate," Alex said.

"Anytime, Boss. In the meantime, I'll keep our drones flying more often so we can spot another incursion. I doubt this is the last time someone will be sending cameras over the property."

Over the next two weeks, Alex and Laney settled into a comfortable routine on the ranch. They had their standing meetings in the mornings, and then they went riding. The weather was getting warmer every day, and Laney loved the feeling of a horse beneath her. There was very little soreness that she had to deal with, which made her happy since she didn't want anything interfering with her and Alex's love life.

At the beginning of Laney's fourth week on the ranch, Chuck Washington and Kate Fleming met with Alex and Laney at the residence to give them an update. Art Torino, the head of ground camera surveillance also attended.

"Remember those six TDA members who followed you from Miss Laney's townhouse, Boss?" Chuck asked.

Alex nodded.

"Well, they're watching the property."

Kate and Art showed drone and camera footage of four cars watching the property—one on each of the public roads that bordered the buffer zone. Close-ups of the occupants showed that six of the people were the ones photographed by the security teams that intercepted the TDA members following Alex when he moved Laney to the ranch. There were several other people photographed as well.

"We sent the images to ICE, and they're all known TDA members from Dallas," Chuck said. "We also traced that drone you shot down. It was stolen from a hobby store back in January. Since you shot it down, we've had six other drone incursions over the property. All of the drones were shot down and recovered, and the images show close-ups of every building on the ranch and the community, as well as several flyovers of the residence. There are detailed images of the main gates, interior gates, and fencing. Someone is casing the estate, Boss. Whether it's curiosity, security for the TDA members heading north from Alliance Airport, or they're planning a manned incursion is anyone's guess at this point. We've increased drone patrols, as well as vehicle patrols, both inside the buffer zone and along the roads bordering the property. We've chased off the watchers a few times, but they always come back once the patrols have left."

Chuck looked at Alex, who had a strange look on his face. "What are you thinking, Boss?"

Alex snorted. "Part of me wants to button up the ranch tight, but I don't want to panic our residents, our patients and clients, or our staff. The other part of me wants to let them in—somewhere that we control. And once they step foot on the property, then we capture them or..."

"That's risky, Boss. These guys don't mess around. They're incredibly violent, they're depraved in ways that can't easily be described... If they get past our trap and make it to the female bunkhouses—or worse, make it to the community—the women and children will be subject to unspeakable acts before they're killed. The men will be killed outright. They'll get the horses, they'll get the equipment, they'll loot the community, they'll loot the arsenal in the security center, and they'll loot your house."

Alex leaned back and scratched the back of his head. Laney had seen him do this enough times to know that he was thinking through a variety of scenarios in his mind.

Alex leaned forward. "What if we... fail to patrol a particular section of the meadow. Say... just south-east of the highest ridge. If they think that this is a vulnerable spot, there's a likelihood that they might attempt an incursion there. We can hide an army on the other side of that ridge, not to mention cameras. If we're ready for them, but they don't think we are, we could catch them in a trap."

"And if we capture the men they send, what do we do if they come back for revenge?" Chuck asked.

"Catch them in another trap, hopefully," Alex replied.

He leaned back and scratched his head again. "But to make them want revenge bad enough to send all of their people here, we need to do more than just take out an incursion team. We need to hit them where it hurts the most. We need to damage their reputation, not just their numbers."

"And how do we do that, Boss?" Chuck asked, sounding skeptical.

"We know the Dallas TDA members are providing transportation and security for their compadres arriving at Alliance Airport and heading north, right?"

"We're fairly certain of that," Chuck confirmed.

"Same vehicles every time?" Alex asked.

"No, different ones," Chuck said.

"Always past the ranch?"

"As far as we know, Boss. ICE isn't aware of any other routes they take."

Alex nodded. "And what if the Dallas TDA members prove to be unable to adequately protect the new members heading north?"

"TDA doesn't tolerate failure, Boss. If Dallas can't protect them, they'll have to find another way into the U.S."

"And the Dallas bunch should do anything to keep that from happening, right?"

Chuck's eyes opened wide, as did Kate's and Art's. "You're going to take out the TDA members heading north to provoke the Dallas members?"

"Not us," Alex assured him. "ICE and the State Police."

"They haven't been much help so far." Chuck sounded dubious.

"That's because I haven't made a couple of phone calls yet," Alex said.

194

"Who are you going to call?" Laney asked.

"The governor, and our newly inaugurated Vice President. Vice President Glass should be able to connect me with the Secretary of Homeland Security, and the governor should be able to connect me with the head of the State Police. Then I just need to get those people talking so we can coordinate several arrests of the new arrivals and confiscations of the chartered aircraft. That should make the Dallas members angry."

Chuck shook his head. "Boss, when you kick a hornet's nest, you really kick a hornet's nest."

Alex shrugged. "Look, as long as those thugs are using Alliance Airport, this ranch is vulnerable. I have an obligation to protect this ranch and everyone on it. To do that, TDA must go, and if we get all of the north Texas TDA members out at the same time, I'm good with that."

Alex looked around the table. "If any of you has a better idea, please tell me. I want to hear it. But in the absence of another suggestion, we have to take action. Doing nothing leaves us all at risk. Doing too little leaves us all at risk. Leaving TDA in Dallas leaves us all at risk. Allowing TDA to continue using the roads that pass this ranch on their way to threaten other cities leaves us all at risk. We need to stop the Alliance pipeline, and we need to stop the Dallas TDA from threatening the region."

"And what about the Wichita Falls and Lawton TDA Members?" Chuck asked.

"We never let them find out what happened. No press, no publicity, just silence and a mystery that—hopefully—they'll be too busy to come and solve."

Chuck leaned back and stared at the ceiling. Then he looked at Kate and Art. "Your thoughts?" he asked his surveillance leads.

"It's bold and daring, but it's dangerous," Kate said. "It'll have to be well planned to prevent loss of personnel and damage to property."

Art looked troubled. "I don't see an alternative, and that worries me. I agree something needs to be done and soon. If this works, it could benefit a lot of people who'll never know what we did to help them."

Alex looked at Laney. "Laney? Thoughts?"

Laney cocked her head to one side. "I'm going to put my lawyer hat on for a moment. If you leave a door open, and someone walks inside, you can't capture them and claim they broke in. It's called entrapment."

"I'm not going to leave a door open, or a fence open, I'm just going to leave a section of the fence seemingly unguarded. If I'm right, they're going to break in anyway. I'm just trying to give them a reason to break in at a spot of my choosing so I can have a trap waiting for them."

"Do you have enough men for this operation?" Laney asked.

"That was my next question," Chuck stated. "We don't have enough security staff for an operation this large, especially if TDA decides to breach in multiple places."

"What about the ranch hands?" Alex asked. "They've all been deputized by the sheriff, haven't they?"

Chuck nodded slowly. "Two weeks ago. I had already forgotten about that. With them serving as reinforcements, protecting our flanks and guarding against multiple incursions, we should have enough people. But just remember, TDA is well armed, and most of what the ranch hands have are lever-action rifles and handguns."

"The weapons that won the west," Alex noted.

"But not the weapons we'll be going up against," Chuck reminded him. "TDA will have military-grade weapons and ammo. We're no match for that."

"Then we'll have to use the terrain and our knowledge of the land to even the odds."

"And *that* might just be our biggest asset," Chuck said.

Alex looked around the table again. "Does anyone have any other suggestions?"

No one responded.

Alex put both palms flat on the table. "Okay. I need to call the Vice President and the governor, and get the ball rolling with them. After I have those conversations, we'll reconvene. Chuck, we'll inform the managers and the department heads at our morning meetings, including your department heads at our Wednesday meeting. In the meantime, it might be a good idea to start rotating the ranch hands to do security patrols on their off-hours— volunteers first, and then we'll draft additional ranch hands if we need more men. Earl Crawford should be able to help you with that, since he's the ranch hand foreman."

"I'll get right on that, Boss."

After Chuck, Kate, and Art left the residence, Alex looked at Laney. "I imagine you have questions or comments you didn't want to say in front of the others."

Laney smiled. "Not really, although a whole lot of old western theme songs were running through my head as you outlined your plan."

Alex laughed. "I told you it could be like the wild west out here."

"Yes, but you're planning on going to war with the scariest bunch of thugs to ever appear this side of the border. That terrifies me."

"It terrifies me, too. I'm a business man and a rancher, not a soldier. But I truly believe that it's just a matter of time before they attack us, and for no other reason than the fact that the ranch lies along their smuggling route. If their reputation for ruthlessness is well-earned, then we're all in danger if they manage to breach the fences. We have to stop them, and it has to be done before they can get reinforcements, or we'll be overrun eventually. We're on our own out here, but if we succeed, we can end this, and no one will dare attempt to breach the perimeter ever again."

"You believe that?" Laney asked.

"Yes, I do."

Laney nodded and stared at Alex for a minute. "Then I believe it, too. We're in this together... for better or worse, even though we haven't taken any vows to each other... yet."

"You know this weekend is our one month checkpoint, don't you?"

Laney nodded with a wide smile. "Oh, yes. And I'm looking forward to it."

"Me, too."

"Speaking of looking forward to things, I have a meeting with Elizabeth Talbot and some of the other Tarrant County Party Leaders this week. She called me earlier, but I forgot to tell you."

"When's the meeting?"

"Day after tomorrow—Wednesday. It's a lunch meeting, so I'll be heading down there late morning."

Alex nodded. "Okay. You need to inform the leader of your security detail, so everything can be planned."

"I'll take care of it," Laney promised.

Alex stood and held out his hand to Laney. "What do you want to do for the rest of the afternoon? It's more than two hours until supper."

Laney had a wicked smile on her face. "Let's go upstairs. Planning battles suddenly has me very horny."

She and Alex ran up the stairs, pausing only long enough to close the doors to the den and the bedroom.

CHAPTER 15

Tuesday morning, right after the regular breakfast meeting with the ranch department heads, Alex walked to his office. He sat down at his desk, reached for his phone, and placed a call.

The first call was to the governor's private number, which only a few people were ever given. Alex was one of those people. When the governor came on the line, Alex gave him an overview of what was happening with TDA.

"I hope the State Police and ICE can work together to stop the smuggling of new TDA members that flows past my ranch from Alliance Airport to Wichita Falls and Lawton," Alex said. "It's a dangerous situation up here."

"I'll be happy to have the State Police work with ICE, Alex," the governor said, "but ICE seems so busy lately that I don't know if I can get them to help with your problem."

"My next call is to someone who might be able to help with that," Alex said. "If that call goes well, I'll have the director of ICE get in touch with the State Police Commander. If it doesn't go well, then we'll have to come up with a plan B."

The governor chuckled. "Are you going to call the President?"

"No, the Vice President. He's a friend."

"Well, good luck with that, Alex. Let me know what happens, and I'll talk to the State Police Commander in the meantime."

"Thanks, Governor."

Alex ended the call, and then he called Vice President Glass. He had to go through several secretaries and assistants, but finally, the Vice President came on the line.

"Alex! To what do I owe the pleasure of this call?" he asked.

"Good morning, Mr. Vice President. This is a business call, or I'd never call during office hours. Are you familiar with Tren de Aragua?"

The Vice President confirmed that he was well acquainted with TDA, and Alex explained about the problems he was having lately with the Dallas TDA members and the new members arriving at Alliance Airport and passing by the ranch on the way north.

Alex then outlined what he wanted from ICE and the Texas State Police.

"It sounds like you'll need the FAA looped in," the Vice President said. "They'll be able to identify when a charter is arriving that fits the pattern of TDA arrivals."

"I'd like that. We need the TDA members picked up, but we also need the planes seized. If we can stop their human smuggling operations into North Texas, they'll have to regroup and find a new point of entry. Meanwhile, we can take down the TDA members already here. The good citizens of the area will applaud that."

"All right, Alex. Let me meet with some folks and make a call or two. I'll call you by the end of the week and let you know what I've accomplished. Talk to you then."

"Thank you, Mr. Vice President."

On Wednesday morning, shortly after 11:00 AM, Laney left the ranch with her security detail. Terry Vance was driving the SUV. Ken Dover, the head of Laney's detail, was in the back seat next to her. Paul Phillips was in the rear seat, and Hans Jürgen was in the front passenger seat.

This was Laney's first outing with her security detail, and only the second time she had left the ranch since she moved in with Alex. It felt good to be doing something she loved, but she hated leaving Alex and the ranch, even for a few hours.

They arrived at the downtown Fort Worth hotel, where the meeting was being held. Laney loved this hotel because of the western décor. Terry pulled up to the front entrance, and Ken got out of the vehicle with Hans. After seeing nothing suspicious, Ken motioned for Laney to get out, followed by Paul. They entered the hotel, and Terry drove to the parking area, where he'd remain with the car.

They rode up the escalator, and Laney found the meeting room quickly. Elizabeth was at the entrance, greeting the attendees. Paul and Hans began their patrols around the meeting rooms, while Ken remained with Laney.

"Delaney, my dear," Elizabeth said when Laney approached her. "I'm so glad you came. How's ranch life treating you?"

"Better than I ever thought possible," Laney said.

"Do you think it will leave you time to accept my offer?" Elizabeth pressed.

"If nothing changes, then yes, it will. However, should anything change, then no, it won't."

Elizabeth nodded. "I'm sure Dwight will probably be happy if something changes, but I think being with Alexander suits you. You certainly seem happier than I've ever seen you before."

"It's because I'm not working myself to death in a law office six days a week," Laney responded as she stepped inside the meeting room to find her seat. She didn't want to think about returning to the law firm. Ever.

The meeting went well, and it felt good to be surrounded by people she had worked with during the previous election. There was still work to be done, and Elizabeth outlined a bold plan to keep the Party energized between elections so the victories they won wouldn't be lost due to inattentiveness.

The lunch wasn't bad, but it couldn't compare to Fran's cooking. She and her team made the best food Laney had ever eaten. *"Another reason I don't want to return to the law firm. It means leaving Fran's cooking, and I've grown accustomed to eating fantastic food every meal."* She knew this was a small thing compared to being with Alex, but it was part of the equation for remaining at the ranch instead of returning to her townhouse.

When the meeting was over, Ken and Laney walked out of the meeting room and joined Paul and Hans at the escalator.

"Just out of curiosity, has anyone checked on my townhouse lately?" Laney asked as they rode down to the first floor. "We know those six TDA thugs followed us there, and I'd hate to find out that they trashed the place. I may be selling it soon."

"Your place is safe and sound," Ken assured her. "We have someone check on it at least twice a week."

"Thanks, Ken," Laney said. "I keep meaning to ask, but I never seem to do it."

Looking around the lobby, she asked, "Are we sure no one followed us down here?"

"We didn't *see* anyone following us," Ken said. "That doesn't mean that they haven't gotten smarter about tailing since the last incident. Believe me, we're watching for that closely."

They remained in the lobby until Terry brought the car around. Ken and Hans checked the car and then motioned for Laney to exit the hotel. She and Paul walked to the SUV and got inside. Once Ken and Hans were inside, Terry pulled away and headed back to the ranch.

As they left downtown, Laney thought about the checkpoint meeting she and Alex were having on Saturday morning. This meeting would decide if Laney was staying at the ranch for another three months, or if the relationship was going to come to an end. Laney felt sure that Alex would want to continue, and she knew she did. She just needed to hear it said out loud. *"Things are good between us,"* she thought. *"I can't imagine he'll want it to end, but you never know."*

There was light traffic as they drove north, and the trip was uneventful... until they passed I-820. That's when Paul spotted a vehicle that seemed to be following them.

"That's the third time I've seen that SUV," he told Ken. "It stays two-to-three cars behind us, but when we change lanes, it does, too."

"You're sure?" Ken asked.

"I'm sure," Paul replied.

Ken contacted the security center and told them that someone was tailing them back to the ranch.

Two miles later, Hans said, "We've got a second tail. Same make and model, staying right next to the other vehicle."

Laney was nervous, but Ken was calm about the situation, and that helped her remain calm.

Ken called the security center with the updated information.

They approached Tarrant County Parkway, and suddenly a third SUV—identical to the other two—merged onto the interstate right in front of them and pulled over to the lane on their left. The other two vehicles tailing them moved up, boxing them in.

Ken looked at the SUV beside them and saw the rear window rolling down. The occupant had a fully automatic short-barrel firearm. He started pointing it at the tires of the ranch's SUV.

"Gun!" he cried. He made Laney drop to the floor, and then he lowered his window as he drew his weapon. The person inside the other SUV raised his firearm, but Ken fired first. The person fell backwards, and Ken fired at the driver. The other SUV swerved erratically, hit a K-rail being used to block one of the lanes under construction, and flipped over.

Ken rolled up his window as Terry increased speed.

The other two SUVs increased speed and followed them. Ken saw the Golden Triangle exit sign. "Get off at this exit," he yelled.

Terry waited until the last second, and then he jerked the wheel and raced down the off-ramp. The SUV immediately behind them managed to follow, but it hit the exit sign, which shattered its windshield. The second SUV slammed on its brakes and was rear-ended by an 18-wheeler, knocking it off the road and down the embankment into the intersection in front of the ranch's SUV.

The SUV in the intersection rolled onto its side and was promptly hit by a dump truck that was too close to slow down or stop. The SUV was smashed by the dump truck.

Terry saw an opening and raced through the intersection while the other drivers were too busy watching what was happening with the dump truck. The one surviving SUV tailing them stayed close behind, in spite of its damaged windshield.

Paul, who was watching the tailing SUV, saw someone kick out the windshield. Then automatic gunfire came from the tailing SUV. The bulletproof glass of the SUV held, but no bulletproof glass could hold out forever, and there was more than one weapon firing.

"We're going to lose the rear window in a minute," he shouted from the rear seat.

"If I pop the rear hatch, do you think you can hit the shooters?" Terry called.

"Possibly, but you might get hit," Paul shouted back.

"I'll get hit anyway if that window shatters," Terry said.

"Do it," Ken yelled.

Terry pushed a button, and the rear window swung up. Paul emptied the magazine in his pistol into the tailing SUV. Then he ejected the spent magazine, loaded another one, and emptied the pistol a second time.

The tailing SUV rammed the ranch's SUV in a desperate attempt to get Paul to stop firing. Ken turned around and yelled for Paul to duck. Ken then emptied his pistol into the SUV, which ran off the road and flipped over.

"Is everyone okay?" Ken yelled.

"I am," Paul responded.

"I am," Terry said.

"I am," Hans stated.

Laney didn't respond. Ken looked down on the floor at her. There was blood on her forehead.

"Laney's down," Ken shouted.

Terry spun the SUV around and headed south on the northbound access road, weaving through the oncoming traffic. Traffic at the Golden Triangle intersection was still backed up from the wreck with the dump truck, but Terry maneuvered through the cars, turned east on Golden Triangle, and then turned south into the parking lot of Texas Health Harris Methodist Hospital Alliance. He raced to the Emergency Room entrance, squealing to a stop.

Ken notified the security center that Laney was down and had been taken to the hospital, while Hans raced inside for assistance. A moment later, two orderlies with a rolling stretcher ran out of the hospital to the SUV. An ER nurse was close behind.

"What happened?" the nurse asked.

"We were rear-ended," Ken said. "She went down on

the floor. I don't know if she hit her head, but I saw blood, knew we were next to the hospital, and headed here."

The nurse carefully checked Laney's neck and shoulders. Seeing no neck trauma, and motioned for the orderlies to carefully remove her from the car and put her on the stretcher. Once Laney was strapped down, the nurse examined her. All she found was a deep cut on Laney's forehead.

"It doesn't look life threatening, but we'll check her out anyway." The nurse told the orderlies to take her inside.

Ken followed. She pointed to the waiting room, but Ken said, "My orders are to never leave her side. As long as she's not going into surgery, I'm staying with her."

The nurse stared at him, saw his earpiece, and immediately realized that he was her bodyguard. She nodded. "All right. Just stay out of the way."

Ken nodded and followed her to the examination room.

Mike Billingsley rang the doorbell and then entered the residence. Alex came out of the library, looking confused.

"Mike, what's going on?" he demanded.

"TDA attempted to either kill or kidnap Laney. Her detail thwarted the attempt, but Laney was hurt. She's at Harris Methodist Alliance, since the attack happened close to there. The cars and your detail are waiting outside. Let's go."

Alex was in shock, but the training kicked in. "Give me

a minute." He ran upstairs, armed himself, grabbed a jacket with the ranch logo on it, and ran down the stairs. He and Mike got into the center of three SUVs, and the motorcade raced down the hill toward the residence gate.

The motorcade arrived at the hospital forty-five minutes later. Warned about the back-up caused by the incident with the dump truck, Gordon took a different route, and they entered the hospital parking lot from the northbound service road south of Golden Triangle.

When Alex and Mike raced through the Emergency Room entrance, Paul and Hans met them.

"She's okay, Boss," Paul said to Alex. "She was on the floor when we were rear-ended in the chase, and she hit her head on that metal strip that reinforces the seats. It knocked her out, and she has a cut on her forehead, but it only required a couple of stitches. She's awake and waiting for you."

"Where?" Alex asked.

"I'll take you," Hans said.

Hans led Mike and Alex down the hallway to Examination Room 6. Mike waited outside, as did Hans. Ken, who was inside the room, saw Alex enter the room. Ken nodded and stepped outside so Alex and Laney could be alone.

Alex rushed forward and hugged Laney.

"I'm okay, Alex. Really. They're keeping me for observation, but it was a clean cut, and it's going to heal nicely. There's nothing to worry about. The team did a great job protecting me and taking care of the bad guys."

Alex nodded, and Laney noticed that there were tears in his eyes. "Hey," she said gently. "I'm *okay*."

"When Mike came to get me, I was so scared." Alex wiped his eyes. "I kept thinking, 'Did I put you in harm's way? Am I the reason they've come after you twice?' I couldn't live with myself if I were the reason you were hurt."

"It's not your fault," Laney assured him. "You know you can't see who's inside those SUVs. They followed me because they knew where the SUV was from, not because of who was inside. And the team kept me safe, except from my own clumsiness when we got rear-ended. I was trying to get up when it happened. I should have stayed down until the last SUV was stopped, and then I wouldn't have hit my head."

"*Last* SUV? Just how many vehicles were there?"

Laney told Alex the story as Ken told it to her while they were waiting for Alex to arrive.

"A high speed chase, a gun battle with two vehicles, and a wreck that still hasn't been cleaned up? I hope Elizabeth appreciates what you're willing to do for the Party."

Laney laughed. "I almost forgot that's why I was on the road today."

Ken stuck his head inside the room. "Miss Laney? The police are here. They want a statement from you. We've already given ours."

The local police entered the room, glanced at Alex, and then started asking Laney questions. When they were done with her, Alex asked, "What's going to happen to my men, Officer, and what's going to happen to the occupants of the

SUVs who tried to capture or kill my people?"

"And just who are you?" the police officer demanded.

"Alexander Barclay," Alex replied.

The police officer noticed the logo on Alex's jacket, and his eyes bugged out. "Mr. Barclay! Yes... um... as for your men, I doubt any charges will be filed. They were defending themselves and their passenger, and they did everything possible to prevent any collateral damage. We don't condone gunfire from moving vehicles, but under the circumstances... As for the men in the SUVs, they're all dead. Nine altogether—three in each SUV. There were no survivors. Some were killed by your men, the rest from the two wrecks."

"Thank you, Officer."

"You're welcome, Mr. Barclay."

The police left the room, and Laney chuckled. "Nice to know the Barclay name carries some weight around here."

"It should," Alex said. "I funded the local police force, I paid for most of this hospital, and I used to own all of the land between here and Tarrant County Parkway. This was one of my real estate investments that did rather well."

A nurse came in to check on Laney. "When can I take her home?" Alex asked.

The nurse recognized Alex immediately. "Mr. Barclay! I didn't realize she was with you. She's free to leave at any time. All of her vital signs look good. As long as she doesn't experience any headaches, dizziness, or other problems like that, she should be fine. But if she does have headaches or dizziness, bring her back as quickly as possible."

"I will," Alex promised.

Alex checked Laney out while she got dressed. Then Alex escorted her to the SUVs waiting outside.

"What happened to your SUV?" Alex asked Ken.

"It's scratched and the rear window needs to be replaced, but it'll be easy to repair," Ken replied.

"Have Terry, Paul, and Hans bring your SUV back to the ranch," Mike said. "They're to take the number three position. Ken, you'll ride with me, the Boss, and Miss Laney in number two. Travis and Ray will ride in Number one. I have another team in the SUV bringing up the rear."

Everyone got into his or her assigned SUVs, and the motorcade headed back to the ranch. There were no tails spotted, and no incidents on the drive.

Alex was grateful that Laney was all right, and he held her tight all the way home. Deep down, though, he was seething. *"TDA has come after her twice. It's time to end their reign of terror. It's time to put them down like the dogs they are."*

CHAPTER 16

It was suppertime when Alex and Laney were dropped off at the residence. Fran and her staff had made a delicious meal of crab cakes, shrimp tortellini in a lemon butter sauce, and a Greek salad. In spite of her ordeal, Laney was starving, and she ate everything on her plate.

Later, after Laney had changed clothes, Alex made her comfortable on the couch in the den.

"You don't have to fuss over me," she said, reaching out and holding his hand.

"I like fussing over you," he replied. "I hope to do it for a long time to come."

She looked in his eyes and saw the pain there. "Alex, what's wrong? You've been in a mood ever since we got home."

Alex was silent for a moment. "I never thought bringing you here would put you in danger," he said finally.

"I've always known that security was a fact of life for me, but I never wanted this for you. It's one thing to be prepared. It's another thing altogether to experience that preparation while under fire."

Alex took her hand and gave it a gentle squeeze. "Look, I don't want to lose you, but I don't want to see you get hurt because you're with me. I can't let that happen."

Laney smiled. "You haven't lost me, and as good as my security detail is, I doubt you ever will. But even if you sent me away for my own safety, you can't guarantee I'll be safe somewhere else. I could get hit by a car while crossing the street. I could get t-boned at an intersection and have my car explode. I could fall down the stairs of my townhouse. I could slip in the shower and crack my head open. There are no guarantees. You want to keep me safe? Carry out your plan for TDA and make sure it works. Accidents will always happen, but at least we can end the one immediate threat to all of us here on the ranch."

Alex stared at her. "You want me to proceed with taking down the TDA member's smuggling pipeline, and taking out the Dallas TDA members?"

Laney nodded. "I had a lot of time to think waiting for you to arrive at the hospital. I'd hate to see the ranch become an armed camp with the ranch hands becoming a private army like the Regulators, but this threat will never go away as long as TDA members are running around here free. You have a plan, and you have the determination—and the manpower—to carry it out. So carry it out and end the TDA threat, so we can return to normal."

"With you at my side, or with you sent somewhere for your safety?"

"At your side," Laney stated flatly. "This is where we

214

prove that we're meant for each other... as lovers, as fighters, as partners in all things. We either stand together now, here, or there's no sense in continuing."

Alex leaned back and crossed his arms. "Sounds like were having our checkpoint meeting right now, instead of waiting until Saturday."

"Why wait for Saturday when we both know what we want right now?" Laney pressed. "I'll go first. I want this to continue. I want to stay here with you for at least another three months. I'm prepared to call Dwight tomorrow morning and extend my leave of absence. All I need to know is if you want me to stay... if you want this to continue, too."

Alex nodded. "More than anything, I want you here with me. I want this to continue. But your safety is important to me, so don't be surprised if I worry about you. If anything ever happened to you here, I'd be devastated."

"And I love you for that," she said. "If anything happened to you, I'd be devastated, too. But as long as we're working together, whether it's side by side or back to back, whether it's in the trenches or on the hills and ridges, whether it's with the rest of the ranch staff or by ourselves, as long as we're one, and our fate is intertwined as one, then I'll be satisfied with whatever happens."

Alex smiled. "When did you become such a warrior?"

"When I decided I wanted to be a lawyer. This is just the first time you're getting to see that side of me."

"Well, I like that side of you." Alex slid his arm around her shoulder and pulled her close. "Are there any other sides I haven't seen yet?"

Laney snuggled close to him. "I'm a woman, Alex. There will always be sides you haven't seen. Welcome to adult relationships."

Alex kissed her passionately. Then he whispered, "How are you feeling?"

"Like we should rock each other's worlds," she replied.

Alex stood, gently picked her up, and carried her into the bedroom.

By Friday morning, Laney was back to her old self, apart from the bandage on her forehead. After breakfast, Alex went into his office. He had been notified the day before that the Vice President would be calling with the Secretary of Homeland Security and the Director of ICE.

Laney joined him in his office to listen in on the call.

When the call began, the Vice President asked Alex to bring everyone up-to-speed on what was happening in North Texas with TDA. Alex explained about the charter flights landing at Alliance Airport, where fifty to a hundred TDA members would be picked up by the Dallas TDA members, and then they'd be driven on the back roads to Wichita Falls and Lawton, Oklahoma.

"They pass right by my ranch," Alex told the government officials. "And now the Dallas TDA members are watching my ranch and molesting vehicles coming from and returning to the ranch."

"I heard about the attack on your girlfriend," the Director of ICE said. "I'm sorry that happened. We had no idea TDA had gotten so bold and so organized down there. How often do these planes arrive? Do you know?"

"Judging by the traffic patterns that our security

cameras record, about once every two to three weeks. There's no set pattern for their arrivals, but their route past my ranch seems consistent. I've checked with Alliance Airport, and they confirm that an hour before I see a line of vehicles passing my ranch, they have a charter flight landing with a flight plan that says the flight originated in Phoenix, but radar shows the flight originating south of the border. The flight is met by the same number of vehicles that pass my ranch. The planes always arrive mid-morning, and take off again as soon as they refuel. The airport also confirms that the amount of fuel the planes take on is more than double what's required for a return trip to Phoenix."

"Sounds like we have enough to go on to intercept the TDA members either at the airport, or en route on the North Texas back roads," the Secretary of Homeland Security noted. "I don't want to risk a shootout at an airport, but I do want these people caught, and I want that plane impounded."

They talked for a while longer, and Alex reminded them that the governor had committed the cooperation of the Texas State Troopers. He was just waiting for a point of contact.

"I'll call him this morning," the Secretary of Homeland Security promised.

They talked for a while longer, and before the call ended, Alex asked, "Is there any way I can be notified when you intercept the TDA members and impound their airplane? With their interest in my ranch, I want to be prepared against any potential retaliation."

"Certainly," the Director of ICE stated. "You'll hear from me directly."

When the Director of ICE and the Secretary of

Homeland Security dropped off the call, Alex and the Vice President remained on the line.

"I had no idea your girlfriend was attacked," the Vice President said. "I had no idea you *had* a girlfriend. Gina will be thrilled to know about that. Who is she?"

"Do you remember that stunning woman sitting next to me at The Starlight Ball?" Alex asked. He looked over at Laney, who blushed.

"The brunette in the dark blue dress?" the Vice President asked. Charley Glass had a phenomenal memory.

"That's her. Laney Connor. Turns out she's one of my attorneys. We danced all night, and we've been inseparable ever since. She's sitting next to me right now, by the way."

"Hello, Laney," the Vice President said. "I have some stories for you about Alex when we were younger, but those will have to wait for another time. I do hope the two of you will be our guests in DC sometime soon."

"I'd love that, Mr. Vice President," Laney said.

"So would I," Alex echoed.

"Good. We'll figure out a time later in the year. Things are a bit hectic right now, as you can imagine."

"I understand. Thanks again for looping in ICE and DHS to help with our problem down here."

"Thank the President. He's the one who authorized it."

"I will," Alex promised.

When the call was over, Alex looked at Laney. "That went well," he said.

She nodded. "Don't forget, you promised to call the governor."

Alex nodded and dialed the governor's number. When he answered, Alex told him about the call with ICE and DHS. "You can expect a call from the Secretary of

Homeland Security later this morning," Alex told him. "I think they're anxious to move on this quickly."

"Outstanding, Alex. Thank you for your help."

"My pleasure, Governor. I hope you'll be able to attend the fundraiser later in the spring."

"At your ranch? I'd love to. We'll talk more about it later."

The call ended.

Laney stood. "Can we go into the other office for a minute?"

Alex nodded and followed her out of his office.

Laney walked around the empty space for a while. Then she said, "This would make a great law office and office of a State Party Leader. It needs a bit of decorating, but it should work nicely."

"You've made up your mind about your career?" Alex inquired.

"Let's just say that I have a proposal to make." Laney said coyly.

"And what is this proposal?" Alex asked.

"This ranch needs a contracts attorney. You have dozens and dozens of contracts active at any one time, you have multiple people negotiating and approving contracts, and you have even more people managing those contracts. That's understandable, but you need someone reviewing them before they're signed, and someone overseeing negotiations, approvals, and managing the contracts on your behalf. I want to be that person. I want to work for the ranch, and I want this to be my office."

"So, you'd be my corporate attorney?" Alex asked.

Laney nodded. "I don't know how to run a ranch like you do, but I know how to be a lawyer better than you do.

Contracts are my specialty, although I know more law than just that. If I'm to be *your* partner—God willing—this is how I can support you the best."

Alex nodded. "I love the idea. We can talk more about it closer to the next checkpoint, just in case Dwight makes a counter-offer you can't refuse. By the way, how did that conversation with him go yesterday?"

Laney rolled her eyes. "Awful. He's livid that I'm extending my leave of absence, and he made it clear that he's rethinking the partnership offer. I told him to do what he needs to do, and I'm going to do what I need to do. Then I hung up on him. He's being a big baby about this, and I'm tired of dealing with him as an employer. I think no matter what happens between you and me, I'm never going back to the law firm. I'll either work for you, or I'll go into private practice. I want a life, and now that I've seen how good life can be, I'll never be satisfied with anything less."

Alex smiled. "I think that's the right decision. Anytime you want to clean out your office, you let me know, and we'll help you pack your things."

"Let's wait until things settle down around here first," Laney suggested. "Crush TDA, then make major career decisions."

Alex put his arms around her. "I love you, Laney."

"I love you, Alex. But before we do something messy that we'll both enjoy immensely, I'd really love to go see Max and ride him for a while. We can show each other how much we love each other when we get back from riding."

Less than a week later, Alex got a call from the Director of ICE.

"Mr. Barclay? I promised to call you and let you know what's happening. We intercepted the first planeload of TDA members arriving at Alliance Airport this morning. We took them at the charter hangar, captured the Dallas TDA members driving the vehicles, and impounded the vehicles and the aircraft. According to the FAA, there have been three aircraft used in the past, based on the tail numbers on each plane. That means two more planeloads could be arriving over the next five to six weeks. We'll be ready for them when they arrive."

"Outstanding, Director," Alex said. "Will all of the takedowns happen at the airport?"

"For now, yes. We're concerned that, once off airport property, they could scatter, and we'd never find them again. This way they're contained."

"Fantastic, Director. I imagine the Dallas TDA members will be scrounging for more vehicles in the next couple of days. Do you think they know that their vehicles and men were captured?"

"I doubt it. We jammed all cellular and radio signals once the aircraft was at the hangar. Then we moved in to take them. There's no way they should have been able to get the word out to their superiors. Also, we're keeping this quiet. No press, no announcements. The TDA members that we captured are already on their way to Gitmo, and they'll have no way to tell anyone where they are or what happened. The aircraft was flown to another state, where it will be thoroughly searched and analyzed. We don't want any traces left of what happened today."

"I think that's for the best, Director. Anything else I

need to know?"

"I don't think so. I'll call you when the next plane is intercepted, and you'll get a call from me each time until the planes stop coming."

"Thanks, Director!" Alex said.

When the call ended, Alex looked at Laney. "I imagine the Dallas TDA members will start paying more attention to the ranch when their vehicles don't return or check in."

"We should alert the security center to step up patrols and surveillance," Laney suggested.

Alex nodded, and then he called the security center to talk to Chuck Washington.

CHAPTER 17

Two weeks later, Alex woke up early and found that Laney wasn't in bed with him.

"Laney?" he called out softly.

Laney stepped out of her walk-in closet. "I'm here."

Alex sat up. "Can't sleep?"

Laney shook her head. "I know it's early, but I really want to go riding. I've done just about everything on this ranch except see a sunrise from horseback."

"Want some company?"

"Of course I want company!" Laney said.

Alex got out of bed, dressed, and joined Laney in the den. He put on his gun belt and holstered his favorite pistol, along with five extra magazines. Laney did the same, now that all of the ranch hands were armed whenever they were working.

Alex then selected two lever-action rifles. One was a blued-barrel rifle that shot .45 Long Colts. The other was a chrome-barrel rifle that shot 30-30 rifle rounds. He placed both rifles into separate leather scabbards, grabbed two leather pouches of rifle ammo, and went downstairs with Laney to get their coats and hats.

"Have I told you how sexy you look in that cowboy hat?" Alex asked.

"Only every time I wear it," Laney said, laughing. "But don't stop. I love hearing it."

"I won't stop," Alex assured her. "It makes you look like you belong here."

When they arrived at the stables, some of the ranch hands and grooms were already working. The outside lights on each of the stables were lit, allowing the staff to move around without tripping or bumping into anything. Once inside the stable, they saw the stalls being cleaned, and hay and feed being distributed.

Alex and Laney grabbed their gear, and saddled their horses. Alex attached the two rifles to their saddles, and then they mounted up.

They headed for the gate that led to the meadow. Alex contacted the security center to open the gate and close it behind them. Soon they were away from the stables, and the first morning light was visible on the horizon. It was nothing more than a pale orange glow at first, but as they rode, more colors appeared, and the light became slightly brighter.

It was a brisk morning, but Laney felt exhilarated being on her horse, riding in the near-darkness. She could see Alex riding next to her and some of the terrain, but the rest of the meadow was shrouded in darkness.

They rode to the top of a hill near the center of the meadow. The sun was still below the horizon, but the light was getting brighter. Laney looked up and watched as the stars began to fade—replaced with the rays of sun streaming from the east.

"This is so beautiful," she said, watching the steam from her breath as she talked. "I forgot how beautiful dawn could be out in the country."

"It's always here for you," Alex said.

They rode for the ridges along the eastern edge of the meadow, so Laney could see the ranch as the sunlight first touched the building roofs.

As they approached the ridges, a call came in from the security center. "Boss? Miss Laney? Can you hear me?" It was Kate.

"Yes, Kate," Alex replied. "We hear you."

"I'm here with Art, Boss. Are you near the eastern ridge?"

"Yes."

"Okay, we have a GPS fix on your position. Just outside the buffer zone fence, a little southeast of you, there's a pickup truck that's parked on the side of the road. Twelve guys are getting out."

Alex looked at Laney. "Did the truck break down?"

"Negative, Boss. It pulled over and parked. The guys getting out aren't looking at tires or underneath the hood. They're unloading something from the back of the truck." There was a pause, then Kate added, "They're armed, boss. Pistols on their hips, and rifles slung over their backs."

"Okay. We'll investigate. Open the meadow and buffer zone gates east of our current position and close them when you see us go through."

"Rodger that, Boss. We have a team heading in your direction on the outer roads, but they're at least ten minutes out."

Alex looked at Laney. "There's another ridge that runs through the eastern buffer zone. We can stay behind it, and the occupants of that truck will never see us."

Laney nodded, and they headed for the meadow's east gate.

Once they were through the gates and in the buffer zone, they rode southeast toward the ridges silhouetted in front of them.

"Kate, where are they from our position?" Alex asked when they reached the base of the ridge.

"Thirty yards south and just outside the fence, Boss," came the reply.

Alex dismounted and grabbed his rifle. He also grabbed a pair of binoculars from his saddlebag. Laney dismounted and grabbed her rifle. They tied the reins of their horses to the branch of a nearby tree, and then they climbed up the back of the ridge.

When they reached the top, they heard the voices of men speaking Spanish drifting over the edge of Alex's property. They lay down on the grass, and Alex looked through his binoculars.

After a couple of minutes, he muttered. "Oxy-acetylene. Those are oxy-acetylene tanks they're unloading, and that looks like an acetylene torch attached to the regulators on the top of the tanks."

He looked at the back of the pickup truck, which was parked a few feet away. The bed was covered in blankets and quilts—probably to make it more comfortable for the men riding back there—but next to the cab was a line of flat metal cans standing in a row.

Alex handed Laney the binoculars. She watched the

men struggling with the two tanks for a while. "They don't seem to know what they're doing," she noted.

"Amateurs. Not good when messing with oxy-acetylene. It's cold, they have the tanks lying on the ground instead of upright, and the guy trying to light the torch looks like he's never worked with a gas torch before." Alex nudged her arm. "Look at the back of the truck."

Laney looked. "That's a lot of blankets back there. I guess riding in the back of an open air pickup in this weather isn't too comfortable."

"Look just behind the cab. What do those cans look like to you?"

Laney looked for a minute. "Gasoline cans?"

"That's what I thought."

"Why do they have gasoline cans in the back of the truck?" Laney asked.

"I don't know. Maybe they don't like to take their vehicles into gas stations, where security cameras might see them."

Laney handed the binoculars back to Alex. He looked at the guy trying to unsuccessfully light the torch.

"If he ever gets that torch lit and gets the right mix of oxygen and acetylene, they could cut through the fence and possibly reach the security road that goes around the ranch. They could access any part of the property from there."

He watched for a while longer, and then an idea came to him. "A 30-30 round can pierce the oxygen and acetylene tanks from this distance. If I can put a hole in both tanks, the gas will leak out into the air, and then that torch won't work at all."

"They'll just get into the truck and go get more tanks,"

Laney said.

"Not if you puncture those gasoline cans in the back of the pickup. Alex rolled onto his side and faced Laney. "Look, the minute I fire my rifle, they're going to hear the shot. 30-30 rounds are loud. Plus, the impact with the oxygen and acetylene tanks will ring like a bell. Their first instinct will be to drop to the ground and return fire. If you can puncture the gasoline cans quickly, they might not have enough fuel to get back to their base. That, plus not having a working oxy-acetylene rig, could give them a long walk home, and give us enough time to prepare for when they return, which they undoubtedly will."

Alex tapped her rifle. "You have a .45 Long Colt. It's one of the smoothest firing rifle rounds you'll ever shoot. That rifle is amazingly accurate, and even though it's a lever-action, you should be able to puncture the gasoline cans in the time it takes me to puncture the oxygen and acetylene tanks, and then fire a few rounds to keep them from shooting at us until we can get back to the horses. Security can handle it from there."

He looked at Laney, and she grinned at him. "Shoulder to shoulder. That's what I said I wanted. I guess we put it to the test today. But won't the tanks explode when you shoot them?"

"No, a bullet can't make those tanks explode. The gasses need to mix with air to become flammable. Now if there's an open flame right above the gas leak, the gas could ignite, and then there could be a flashback, which would cause the tank to explode. We're far enough away to be safe if that happens, but I don't see any open flames anywhere nearby, so it's highly unlikely. The gas will just escape into the air, and they won't have any way to breach

228

the fence."

Laney nodded.

"Ready?" Alex asked.

"Yes."

"Okay. When you hear my rifle fire, you start shooting."

"Right."

Laney chambered a round in her rifle and aimed for the rear of the pickup. Alex chambered a round and aimed for the closest of the two tanks on the ground.

"Boss? This is Kate. Can you hear me?"

"Rodger, Kate."

"The team is about five minutes out."

"Rodger that."

"And we've confirmed that three of the men were involved in the first time TDA tried to intercept your SUV, and they're part of the teams that have been watching the ranch."

"Rodger that."

Alex aimed carefully at the tank closest to him.

The TDA member holding the torch continued trying to get it lit.

"Fire in the hole," Alex whispered.

The same moment that Alex fired, the TDA member trying to light the torch finally got it lit. But he was standing right next to the tanks, and the torch was directly over the tank where Alex was aiming.

Laney began shooting at the gasoline cans.

The TDA members heard the shots, and they heard the ringing sound from the 30-30 round that pierced the first tank. A second round pierced the other tank a heartbeat later.

The TDA members dropped to the ground. Alex watched them, aiming for the one closest to him. Suddenly, there was a flash as the leaking gas from the tanks was ignited from the flame of the now lit torch.

"Oh, shit!" Alex grabbed Laney's arm and pulled her back down the ridge away from the TDA members.

A moment later, there was a massive explosion, sending a fireball high into the air.

"Flashback," Alex said.

A second explosion sounded as the gas from the other tank ignited and caused a flashback. Then there was a third explosion.

"Three explosions?" Alex looked confused. He carefully crawled back to the top of the ridge and looked to the southeast. Laney crawled up next to him and gasped at the scene below them.

The TDA members were still on the ground, but they weren't moving. Three looked like they had been burned to death. Both tanks had exploded. One tank was lying next to the fence, the other was just below the pickup truck. The gasoline leaking from the cans in the back of the truck had ignited and exploded, setting the truck on fire and causing the truck's fuel to explode.

"I thought you said that a bullet couldn't ignite the gas," Laney hissed.

"It didn't. The guy trying to light the torch got it lit as soon as I fired. The gas hit his flame and exploded."

"Boss, this is Kate. The team saw several explosions. Are you all right?"

"We're all right, Kate. The oxygen and acetylene tanks exploded, causing the pickup to explode. The TDA members are down. I don't know if they're dead, but they're down."

Alex saw the headlights of a truck approaching from the north. It stopped about twenty yards from the TDA pickup.

Alex stood and waved to the team as they got out of their truck. They waved back, and then they carefully moved forward, guns at the ready.

Alex and Laney watched as the team searched the carnage the exploding gasses unleashed. The TDA members were all disarmed as the team looked for survivors.

"The shoulder of the road there is gravel," Alex said as they watched from the top of the ridge. "If the tanks exploded close to all that rock, it could have acted like shrapnel and killed them all."

Several minutes later, Kate contacted them. "Boss, the team says there were no survivors. Three were burned to a crisp, four look like their necks snapped, and the rest looked like some kind of shrapnel hit them. The tanks look intact, so they don't know what it could be."

"Probably the gravel on the shoulder of the road," Alex said. "Notify the State Police to send a team out to process the scene, collect the bodies, and haul away what's left of their truck. I don't want the press to find out about this. Have the team secure the scene until the police arrive. If the police need a statement from us, we'll be at the residence."

"Rodger, Boss."

Alex and Laney headed back to the horses. They secured the rifles, mounted, and then rode back to the meadow.

"Are you all right?" Alex asked, concerned at how

quiet Laney was being.

"Yes," she replied, staring back at the sunrise. "I was just thinking that this started out to be such a beautiful morning."

"It *is* a beautiful morning," Alex stated. "Focus on that. Look at the colors of the sky. Look at the way the rooftops of the stables and barns are glowing in the sunrise. Look at the hills and trees around us. It's beautiful!"

"But I just killed twelve people," Laney insisted.

"No, you didn't! They were killed by the gas tanks exploding. You were shooting at the truck. *I* punctured the tanks, and the TDA guy trying to get the torch lit is the one who put an open flame directly above the tanks. *He* killed twelve people, including himself. All you did was help the truck catch fire."

"Are you sure?" Laney asked, wiping her eyes.

"Yes, I'm sure. All you were trying to do was cause them to run out of gas. All I was trying to do was keep that torch from damaging my fence. If the guy with the torch had known what he was doing, that flame would never have been near the tanks, and all twelve men would still be alive. This was caused by their own stupidity, not by what we did. It was just one of those unforeseen sequence of events, which they set in motion by coming here and trying to breach my property."

Laney nodded. "But we shot at their tanks and their truck *outside* the fence. They hadn't breached the fence yet. Technically, they weren't on your property, and we had no right to shoot at them."

"Not quite," Alex said. "I own everything up to the road. I had to keep the fence ten feet back from the property line since my property line is the road itself. Plus I needed room for fence maintenance without crossing outside my property. The minute they pulled over, they were on my land, and I had every right to run them off. When they started trying to light an oxy-acetylene torch on my property next to my fence, I had every right to defend myself and my property. The only laws broken here today were broken by them, not by you and not by me."

Laney looked at him. "So, the explosions were just an accident, and we broke no laws?"

"That's right."

Laney was clearly relieved, but she still felt sad that she had contributed to the death of twelve people, even if her involvement was unintentional. The beauty of the meadow all around her, and the sight of the morning sun casting its glow on the grass, trees, and buildings, didn't lift her spirits. "I'm not ready to take Max back to the barn. Let's ride some more. I need to clear my head before breakfast."

Laney and Max took off at a gallop. Alex and Duke followed her as the sun rose over the eastern ridges of the ranch, heralding the start of another beautiful day.

CHAPTER 18

As March progressed, the days grew longer and the weather grew warmer. Laney went riding with Max every day—weather permitting—and Alex and Duke rode with her, unless Alex had a meeting he needed to attend.

Alex and the ranch hands showed Laney how to help out with the horses in the stables. She learned how to clean the stalls in the morning, spread the hay around, feed the horses, brush the horses, wash the horses, check their hooves, and a dozen other chores that had to be performed on a regular basis. The more she participated, the more she learned, and the more she loved doing the mundane things that had to be done around a working horse ranch. It made her love the place even more. Some days she would spend hours in the stables, working with the grooms and the ranch hands and learning all she could. Alex joined her whenever he could.

New security procedures were put in place whenever Alex or Laney left the ranch. Rather than one SUV, security now used three to provide additional protection in case there should be a repeat of TDA's two attempts to intercept Laney on her way back to the ranch.

Laney learned a great deal about the ranch by sitting in on the daily leader's meetings, and she began to participate in those meetings, asking questions and making suggestions. She also started volunteering with the equine therapy practice—particularly the Special Equestrians program. She was fascinated by the successes they had, and she wanted to be part of it, even if just a small part.

Laney also started helping Alex by reviewing all of the ranch's contracts, organizing them, standardizing them, and monitoring the compliance of both parties. She found several ways to improve contract pricing by comparing what was estimated in the contracts with what was actually spent or received. She loved applying her attorney skills to help the ranch, and Alex appreciated her efforts.

At the end of March, Alex received a phone call from the Director of ICE. "Mr. Barclay? We took down another charter plane bringing in TDA members through Alliance Airport. We captured everyone on the plane, including the pilots and the drivers, and they're all on their way to Gitmo. We impounded the vehicles and the aircraft. That just leaves one more aircraft that we know of, but we'll keep monitoring the situation to see if they find a different charter service for their infiltrations."

"Thank you, Director," Alex said. "I appreciate the call. I'd love to be a fly on the wall while the Dallas TDA members try to figure out why their drivers never return."

"And what happened to the dozen they sent to your

ranch," the director added. "At some point, they'll probably come looking for answers."

"We'll be ready if that happens."

"Good. I'll give you a call after the next aircraft is taken down. Until then, Mr. Barclay."

In early April, Laney accompanied Alex to the quarterly board meeting of Barclay Aerospace. While Alex was in the closed-door meetings, she had the opportunity to tour the plant. For the first time, she understood exactly what the company did.

"Barclay Aerospace makes components for jet engines and liquid fuel rocket engines," her tour guide informed her. "Perfect components. Mr. Barclay's grandfather discovered a metallurgical process for creating parts that are virtually indestructible and that never fail. He started the company, and three generations of Barclay's have led the company to greater and greater heights. The components we make are so strong, that the examination of crash sites show our components are the only parts of the aircraft completely undamaged. In fact, they *could* be used in other aircrafts for many more years. We're the only company in the world that makes some of these components, and we have the patents on them. There are a handful of companies who make the other components we make, but you'd be a fool to use anyone's but ours. Competitors and foreign governments keep trying to discover the secrets of why our components are the best, but they never succeed. We sell these components to aircraft manufacturers and engine manufacturers all over the world."

Laney watched the workers crafting the components for a while. "Does the U.S. Government ever try to steal those secrets?"

The tour guide laughed. "Oh, yes. We find their agents poking around all the time. The government has also tried to control or interfere with our foreign export contracts, but the Barclay family manages to put a stop to that every time. The company will never be sold to, controlled by, or reveal its secrets to outsiders."

Once the meetings were concluded, and Alex was comfortable that the company was exceeding all quality and profit projections, Alex and Laney flew to DC to have dinner at The White House with the President and Vice President.

After spending a couple of days in DC, they flew to the U.S. Virgin Islands to relax in the sun for a few days before returning to North Texas.

Laney had never been to a Caribbean island before, and she found the experience delightful. The resort was beautiful, and the private bungalow that Alex reserved gave them plenty of privacy. The four days they spent there were like a mini-version of the two weeks Laney spent with Alex in his hotel suite at the Waldorf Astoria, except that there was no snow or icy winds, just sandy beaches and tropical breezes. They did find time to swim in the ocean and work on their tans, but much of their time was spent in bed, making love like their lives depended on it.

One evening, after experiencing more orgasms, and squirting more than she ever had in her life, Laney curled up next to Alex, watching the moonlight through the window and listening to the waves crashing on the bungalow's private beach.

"If I didn't love riding horses and helping out around the ranch, I'd never want to get out of bed with you," she purred. "The things you do to me, with me... it's incredible. I love everything about you—your gentleness, your strength, your compassion, your decisiveness, your brilliance, your modesty, the way you treat the staff, the way you interact with your partners and associates, the way you make me feel every single day... I never knew I'd find a man so... perfect, and now that I have, you're all I want."

Alex kissed her and held her tight, waiting until she was done. He knew there was something else on her mind.

"But am I doing enough to keep you happy with me?" she asked finally. "I'm trying, but it seems so... little compared to all that you do for me."

"Laney, I don't love you because of what you do, I love you for *you*. You are my peace. You are my home. You are my joy. That's all I ever wanted you to be, and it's what you are. I appreciate all that you've been doing around the ranch to help me, but I'd still love you even if you didn't do any of that. You don't have to do a single thing to *earn* my love. You already have it all. The things you do make me appreciate you more, but nothing could make me love you more. And as long as you never betray my trust, there's nothing you could do to make me love you less. I'm yours— now, tomorrow, the day after, the day after that... forever. Do as much or as little around the ranch as you want. It won't change a thing."

"Thank you for saying that," Laney said softly. "I don't know why I worry so much. I guess I always thought of relationships as the coming together of equals. We're not equals, Alex. Not by a long shot."

"It depends on how you look at it," Alex said. "Yes, we don't bring equal... wealth or stuff into the relationship, and I never expected us to. What we bring is equal respect, equal compassion, equal trust, and an equal desire to please the other. *These* are the things that matter in a relationship, the emotional connections, not the material possessions. Emotionally, we *are* equals, and that's all I ever wanted or expected from a life partner. I've found my life partner, and it's you. All I want is for you to feel the same."

"And I do... I do. In ways I never imagined. When it comes to you, the reality is far better than any fantasy ever could have been. The romance novels have it all wrong. There's no more perfect man alive than you."

"I'm not perfect," Alex said, "but as long as I'm perfect for you, I'm satisfied."

Laney kissed him, and then she put her head on his shoulder. "Do you mind if I ask a personal question?" she asked after several minutes.

"Not at all."

"Did you and my... my *predecessor*... ever have conversations like this?"

Alex burst out laughing. "Penny? No. Penny was too young to understand the deep things in life. She lived in the moment. Being with her was like watching a cat chasing the red dot of a laser pointer. She was all over the place, and every moment was a new experience. It's a good thing that she found life with me too restricting. I think she would have driven me crazy after a while. I crave stability. She never knew the meaning of that word."

"Good. I have to admit... I've wondered how I compare

to her."

"There is *no* comparison," Alex assured her. "You're more emotionally mature, you're more attentive, you're more passionate, you're more trusting, you're more loving, you're not judgmental, you're not self-absorbed, you understand what it means to be a partner, and you make me feel younger than she ever could. You make me a better person, and that, to me, is the true measure of a life partner."

Laney shifted positions so she was on top of Alex, straddling him. "Well, partner, *this* partner needs to feel connected to you again. Feel up to it?"

"You're not too sore?" Alex asked.

"It wouldn't matter. I need to be one with you right now."

Alex smiled. "Then you'd better hold on to something, because it's going to get intense."

"How many towels should I get?" Laney asked.

"All of them."

The week after they returned to the ranch, Alex had his monthly meeting with the partners of his consulting company. The firm was doing quite well, and Alex was impressed with the way the partners had stepped up to run the company the way he wanted it run.

After the meeting, he sat with the Managing Partner, who had been one of the original associates Alex hired when he founded the company.

"I never understood why you had a private jet... until

now," the Managing Partner said. "I now travel almost as much as you did, and dealing with commercial flights or charter planes is such a pain in the ass! The partners discussed purchasing a jet of our own, but it sends the wrong message to our clients, and it's a capital outlay we can't justify while we still have two more buy-out payments for your partner shares."

"They are wonderful to have," Alex noted. Then he thought about what the Managing Partner had said, and something clicked in his mind. "You know, now that I don't travel so much, my jet doesn't get used anywhere near as often as it used to. I have a great crew, but I'm paying them a lot for doing very little. My pilot approached me a while back to see if they could start taking charters as a way to have something to do while keeping the aircraft in top condition. We've been working out the details, but short of actually creating our own airline, it's hard to figure out how to make everything work so I don't absorb liabilities that I don't want."

The Managing Partner remained silent, waiting to see where Alex was going with the conversation.

"I'm just thinking out loud here," Alex continued, "I incorporated the jet under Barclay Aviation, to handle payroll and all the other financial arrangements a private aircraft needs for maintenance, fuel, hangar fees, landing fees, etc. If I were to add a Scheduler, who'd make sure that the jet was available when *I* needed it *and* when the partners needed to use it, AMB Consulting could contract with Barclay Aviation for the use of my jet. You save money by not having to buy a jet, I offset the costs of maintaining the jet and paying the crew by allowing you to charter my plane, and we both win!"

"I'd say that solution has potential," the Managing Partner said cautiously. "We'd need to see a contract that outlines the pricing model, but I'm in favor of exploring this further."

Alex nodded. "I'll get the ball rolling on my end and have a contract outline ready for your review by... say... the end of the month at the latest?"

Alex and the Managing Partner shook hands. They talked for a while longer, and then Alex left the building and returned to the ranch.

On the ride home, he called Henry, his pilot. "Henry, it's Alex. How are you?"

"Doing fine, Mr. Barclay. What can I do for you?"

"Do you remember when we talked about taking charters, since I don't use the jet as much as I used to?"

"Yes, sir."

"And remember how we could never seem to work out the details in a way that made the service attractive to a client without putting me in the airline business?"

"Yes, sir."

"Well, I think I have a solution." Alex outlined what he and the Managing Partner had discussed.

"That sounds perfect, Mr. Barclay," Henry said. "They'd be paying to share your jet with you. I could create a per-flight cost model that would be much easier to manage than a per-charter cost model. I could have it ready for you to review sometime next week, if that's okay."

"That's perfect, Henry, thanks. And I have a new contracts attorney who can take our ideas and formalize them into a document we can present to AMB Consulting."

"Miss Laney?" Henry asked.

Alex laughed. "Right. Give me a call if you need any

242

information or have any questions."

Alex ended the call, happy that the problem of *what to do about the jet* was finally getting solved.

By the end of April, with Laney's help, Alex was able to present a contract to the Managing Partner of his consulting company for use of the Barclay Aviation jet. After walking the partners through the cost model, they agreed to accept the contract, effective at the beginning of July. Alex and Henry immediately began looking for a Scheduler with private aviation experience who could manage Barclay Aviation in a way that balanced the needs of AMB Consulting and Alex, as the owner of the jet.

In late April, Alex received another call from the Director of ICE. "We captured the third aircraft this morning. The TDA members onboard, along with the pilots and the drivers from Dallas, are all on their way to Gitmo right now. Until TDA makes arrangements for new aircrafts, and the Dallas TDA members can acquire new vehicles and drivers, I'd say we've shut down the Alliance pipeline for smuggling these thugs into the country... and past your ranch. We'll keep monitoring the situation, but for now, the main problem may be solved."

"Main problem?" Alex asked.

"You still have the problem of the Dallas TDA

members. They've been recruiting local gangs, and we're hearing chatter that they're planning something major—possibly an act of revenge. Since they shouldn't know about our involvement with the disappearance of their drivers and the members flying into Alliance Airport, they could be talking about you."

"We'll take precautions to prepare for them if they try anything here," Alex stated.

"Good luck with that," the Director of ICE said. "I wish I could have men surrounding your ranch, but we're stretched thin, and without intel specifying when or if they're coming for you, I don't have the resources."

"Director, do you remember what Santa Anna did when his forces approached the Alamo?"

"Didn't he raise a black flag, indicating that there would be no quarter given?"

"Actually, it was a blood red flag, not a black flag," Alex said. "But it meant the same thing. He mounted it on top of the San Fernando Church, and then he proceeded to wipe out the defenders of the Alamo mission. Down here in Texas, the saying "Remember the Alamo," is not just an idol slogan. It's a tradition of fighting against overwhelming odds to defend what's ours. If TDA comes back to my ranch, they'll learn the hard way what it means to face Texans. We won't be flying the black or the red flag, but I can assure you that we'll make them regret they ever tried to step foot on my land. We won't surrender an inch, and we won't let any of the survivors escape. There are signs all over the state that say, 'Don't Mess With Texas.' If TDA comes here to fuck around, they'll find out the hard way what a huge mistake that was."

The Director of ICE chuckled softly. "I pity the fools

who cross you, Mr. Barclay. Good luck, and keep me posted."

"I will, Director. I will."

CHAPTER 19

$\mathcal{A}$lex called a meeting with Chuck Washington, Earl Crawford, the bunkhouse foreman, Art Torino, camera surveillance head, Kate Fleming, drone surveillance head, John Matthews and Eric Fielding, perimeter security heads, and Lewis Todd, rapid response head. The purpose of the meeting was to discuss the potential confrontation with the Dallas TDA members and their new recruits.

"Between the current security staff, and the recently deputized ranch hands, do we have enough people to repel an attack by a gang like this?" Alex asked as he opened the meeting.

"No," Lewis Todd stated firmly.

"Explain," Alex demanded.

"You have forty miles of perimeter fencing surrounding the property," Lewis said. "There are four roads that border the ranch. Since we don't know from what direction they'll come, or what roads they'll use, we'd have to place men all along the perimeter, which would stretch our people too thin to repulse any attack. If they attack in one place, we'd have to move people across the ranch to meet them, and that would expose our flank if they then attacked in multiple places. These guys are thugs, but they're not stupid. They know military tactics. Fifty of them could overwhelm everyone on the ranch, if they hit us in just the right way."

"You mentioned the roads," Chuck noted. "What if we could force them to attack along one road of our choosing? We definitely don't want them anywhere near the road that runs along the west fence, because that runs next to the community and would put too many people at risk. The south road puts them too close to the equestrian center, so we don't want them attacking there, either. That leaves the north road where the main gate is located, and the east road, where the oxy-acetylene incident took place."

"How could we keep them off the south and west roads?" Alex asked. "Those are public roads, so we can't barricade them. Plus TDA could break through any barricades we set up."

No one spoke for a minute.

"We could use spike strips to force them in a direction we choose," Chuck suggested. "We plant the strips at four corners of the property, and we wait for TDA to come. Once the drones see their vehicles approaching, we use the spike strips to keep them away from the west road and the south road. Any vehicle that attempts to turn onto or travel on those roads will be disabled, and the rest of the vehicles should turn off onto another road. If I can get sets of the spike strips that are activated by remote control, we won't have to station men at the four corners, where they'd be exposed and unprotected."

"We could even have the spike strips set up to trap their vehicles right where we want them to attack," John Matthews said. "If we can corral them along the east road, our people could be hidden behind the ridges, which would give us a strong defensive position."

"It would also keep the firefight from happening anywhere near the horses, the facilities, or the residents of the community," Eric Fielding added.

Alex nodded. "Okay. Let's say we're able to use spike strips to force them to a place of our choosing. If they see the spike strips, they'll know we're laying a trap for them, and if they're smart, they'll scatter and try again another time. They'll also be watching the ranch, from the air and using surveillance teams, like they did before. They'll see our preparations and know what we're doing. Then they'll either attack from a different direction or from multiple directions. No, we need to get them to attack in one place that we're ready to defend, without it looking like we're trying to get them to attack there."

John Matthews stood and looked at the estate map on the easel next to the wall. "Where exactly did the oxy-acetylene incident take place?"

Lewis Todd stood and pointed to a spot on the east road. "Right here. Why?"

John bounced his fist against his chin for a moment. "What if the explosion damaged that section of the fence? We'd have to replace it right?"

"Right," Lewis said.

"And anyone watching us would see us examining the fence, then removing the damaged section, and then bringing a replacement section and putting it in place."

"Of course," Lewis said, still not seeing where John was going.

"And if our arc welder was busted, but we didn't know it until *after* the new section was in place, we'd have to use zip ties or some other removable connector to keep that section of fence upright until we could get a working arc welder." John turned around and faced everyone. "And TDA will see that, and they'll know that section of the fence is unsecure. They'll breach the buffer zone at that spot, and our men will be behind the buffer zone's east ridge and the meadow's east ridge, waiting for them."

Alex nodded. "And once they're all inside the fence, we'll trap them, and if they refuse to surrender, then we'll either send them to their maker, or hand them over to ICE in chains."

"Boss?" Lewis asked, sounding surprised.

"As much as I'd like to take the position that no quarter will be given, that's not who we are." Alex said flatly. "If they shoot at us, we shoot back. If any surrender, then ICE can have them. Look, they're coming here to send a message that no one had better mess with them. We're going to send a message right back that no one had better mess with *us*. If we can eliminate TDA's presence in North Texas, no one will ever mess with us again."

"And then we'll be out of a job," Chuck joked.

"Not at all," Alex said as the others laughed. "There are more gangs out there than just TDA, although none as violent and ruthless as TDA is. There will always be threats that will give the security department full employment for the foreseeable future."

Alex looked around the table. "Based on the scenario

that John presented, do we have enough people to protect the ranch and take out whatever TDA sends against us?"

"I still have a couple of concerns," Lewis said. "I like John's plan, and it *should* work, but what if the TDA members from Wichita Falls come down to help Dallas TDA teach us a lesson? That's a lot of armed thugs breaching at one point. Or, what if TDA Wichita Falls comes down, but they attempt to overrun the north gate or somewhere else along the perimeter? We'd have to split our forces, and I'm not sure we can react to two attacks quickly. Santa Anna attacked the Alamo on three sides during the final assault, and it overwhelmed the defenders. If TDA hits us in more than one place, we're in trouble—especially since we won't be able to predict their entry point. And since they could easily blow a hole in the fence with dynamite or C-4, they have forty miles of potential entry points to choose from."

The room fell silent as everyone thought about what Lewis had said.

Finally, Alex spoke. "Okay. We all agree that we can't let TDA anywhere near the west road, right?"

Everyone nodded.

"Then we'll use spike strips to block access to the fences on the west side of the property."

"And if we pop the tires of a neighbor or someone legitimately traveling on that road?" Lewis asked.

"Then I just bought them a new set of tires," Alex answered. "We're only going to block that road once we know TDA is approaching. If we do the same with the south road, then we can limit TDA's options for a breach to the north road and the east road. We have three hundred ranch hands who have been deputized. If we split them along the north perimeter and the east perimeter, and split our security forces along those two perimeters, too, do we have enough people in the right places to defeat TDA once and for all?"

"Potentially," Lewis said. "But I'd be happier if we had more ex-special forces types available when the shooting starts."

"Can we hire more of them?" Chuck asked.

"I wouldn't do that," Lewis said. "We only need them for this one situation. It would be better to contract them from a private security company. That way they come, they help, they leave, and we don't add anyone to the payroll... unless we have to replace someone."

"Do you know of any private security companies with the talent we need that can get people here quickly?" Alex asked.

"I think so," Lewis replied. "I can let you know within twenty-four hours."

Alex looked at Chuck, who nodded.

"All right, Lewis. Do it. And I want you, John, and Earl to work out the details of where and when to deploy our forces. Kate, I need your drones in the air, so we know when TDA puts drone and human surveillance on the property again. Once we know they're watching, we'll let them see us repairing the fence... badly. That should get the ball rolling sooner than later, and it just might keep us in control of the situation."

"Yes, Boss," Kate said.

While Alex was in his meeting, Laney was volunteering with the Special Equestrians program at the equine therapy building. She found it fascinating how the muscles used to stay on a horse helped strengthen the leg muscles in the same way as walking, and the rhythm of movement the horses made actually trained the riders to be able to walk after all other therapy methods had failed.

That day, Laney got to watch a young girl who had never walked without crutches and braces before, take her first steps unassisted, thanks to the Special Equestrians program. Tears ran down Laney's cheeks when she saw the wonder and triumph on the little girl's face. *"This is why I want to volunteer here every day I can,"* Laney thought. *"You don't get to experience things like this in a law office or a courtroom. If the program director and Alex don't mind, this is where I want to spend my days."*

When Laney returned from the equine therapy building a few hours later, she found Alex in the dining room, staring at the maps and aerial photographs of the ranch.

"How did the meeting go?" she asked, sitting across the table from him.

"More questions than answers," Alex replied. "There are forty miles of perimeter fences around the property, which run along four county and state roads. TDA can attempt to breach anywhere, and we have to be able to meet them rapidly. If they breach in multiple places, we have to split our forces and meet them wherever they are."

Alex filled her in on the discussions and the decisions

that were made. Laney began to appreciate the challenge that TDA posed to the ranch.

"Do you feel we'll have enough people to prevent TDA from doing any damage to the ranch?" she asked.

"We have the numbers," Alex replied. "They just need to be in the right place. If we can't match their numbers when they breach, our folks could get overrun, and that would be a disaster."

Alex looked at Laney and asked, "How did your volunteer work go?"

Laney beamed as she told Alex about the little girl she had watched. Then she told him about the decision she had made. "I want to volunteer down there every day that I can, if you're okay with that. The program is so important, and I feel like it can give me a sense of purpose that nothing else can."

"As long as the program director is fine with it, I am too," Alex said, smiling. "The work they do down there is so important, and there's never enough volunteers to help. Maybe you being down there will inspire others to pitch in, so we can help even more people like the girl you watched today. I just wish I had the time to volunteer, too, but hopefully, when I'm fully retired, I can join you down there."

For the rest of April and into early May, the weather turned rainy and cool. Drones couldn't fly because of the lightning and the winds, but the fixed cameras around the property were able to monitor all traffic along the four perimeter roads.

No TDA surveillance teams were spotted.

Lewis was able to locate a private security company that could send a team to the ranch immediately. Forty former soldiers arrived and were assigned housing in the community apartment building. Their team leaders worked with Lewis, John, and Earl to formulate detailed plans for rapid deployment in the event of one or multiple TDA breaches, and they also provided suggestions for luring TDA to specific breaching points where the defenders would be waiting. These suggestions were incorporated into the plans.

"The private security guys are an interesting bunch," Lewis said to Alex one afternoon the week before Mother's Day. "They're looking forward to fighting TDA. They all volunteered for this assignment."

"At least they're motivated," Alex said after he approved the plans for defending the ranch. "We need that right now."

Over the next several days, the weather improved considerably. The days were sunny and warm, and the winds were light. Kate was able to send up her drones, and on the second day of aerial patrols, she spotted people watching the ranch.

Art's ground cameras also spotted the watchers, and the images not only proved that all of the watchers were Hispanic, but they also verified that one of the watchers had participated in the first car chase when Laney brought the rest of her clothes to the ranch from her townhouse.

Chuck called a meeting between Alex, Art, Kate, Lewis, John, and Eric. The team leaders from the private security group were there, too. At that meeting, Art and Kate confirmed that the ranch was under surveillance, and that TDA was involved.

Alex leaned back and scratched the back of his head. Then he breathed in deeply and let it out slowly. "Okay. We've been planning for this, and now it's happening. I'll notify ICE and the State Police, but I doubt they'll be able to send anyone to help. Notify your people to be prepared, and try not to frighten our patients, clients, and the training teams. For them, it's business as usual. For the rest of us... well, you all know what to do."

"Yes, Boss," Chuck said.

"May I make a suggestion?" one of the private security team leaders asked.

"Of course," Alex replied.

"Since you're expecting a firefight, you should have medics to treat your wounded until you can get them to the hospital. There's an outfit outside of Houston that provides support to military units in hot zones, when their own medics can't be deployed fast enough. I can contact them for you. You'll need them."

"I wish I had thought of that," Alex said. "Yes, please contact them and have them deploy here as soon as possible. Tell them to keep it low key. I don't want anyone seeing us bringing in medical staff—especially our TDA watchers."

"Yes, sir."

Alex called the Commander of the State Police and the Director of ICE to let them know about the current plans for dealing with a TDA incursion.

"You think you can entice them to breach your property at locations of your own choosing?" the Director asked.

"It's worth a try," Alex replied. "Otherwise we have to patrol forty miles of fences, find the breach points, and then intercept TDA by moving our people from all over the ranch. There's too much risk with that."

"I agree," the Commander said. "If you can give them a reason to breach where you're waiting, they'll be easier to intercept and contain."

"That's our thinking," Alex confirmed. "But I'm worried about the TDA members in Lawton and Wichita Falls. If they join in, and breach from the opposite direction, the ranch will be overrun, and we'll be lucky to live through it."

The Director of ICE said, "I'm still not sure about your plans for the Dallas TDA members, but there's probably something we can do about the Wichita Falls and Lawton members, if they choose to help breach your ranch."

The Director outlined his idea, and both the Commander and Alex agreed that it should work. The three agreed to talk daily and keep in touch until TDA made their move.

Two days later, members of John Matthews' and Eric Fielding's perimeter security teams were dispatched to two places along the north and east roads. One spot was where the oxy-acetylene incident took place, and one was near the northeast corner of the property, where it looked like part of the fencing had suffered storm damage.

The teams made a great show of examining the damaged fencing and determining that they both needed to be replaced. The watchers saw everything.

The next day, the teams returned to the "damaged" segments of fencing with replacement segments from storage. They removed the damaged fence segments, unloaded the new segments, put them in place, and then couldn't get the arc welder to work.

The teams made an even greater show of calling a local welding company for help, and then yelling at them for not being able to come out for another two days. The teams then secured the new fence segments with removable straps, loaded the damaged segments into their vehicles, and headed back to the ranch.

The TDA watchers notified the Dallas TDA members immediately.

Alex notified the Director of ICE and the Commander of the State Police to let them know that things had been set in motion.

The traps had been set.

When Laney returned from volunteering at the equine therapy building later that afternoon, Alex told her that the attack would probably come in the next two days. The weather was perfect, and if the TDA watchers heard that the repairs to the fence would be finished in two days, they might move quickly to take advantage of the fence being unsecure. Not having to blow the fence would allow TDA to breach the property without alerting anyone.

Laney let the news sink in for a minute. Then she asked, "Are you going to be out there for the next two nights?"

Alex nodded. "I have to be. I can't ask my people to risk their lives if I'm not willing to do the same for them."

"How does Mike feel about that?"

"He's beside himself," Alex answered, amused. "He has been trying to talk me out of it ever since I told him my decision."

"Then I imagine he'll react the same to me being out there with you," Laney commented.

"What?"

"I'm going to be out there with you, Alex. Shoulder to shoulder? Back to back? Those weren't just words. I meant what I said. It's you and me together, or there is no you and me."

"You're not a soldier," Alex protested.

"Neither are you. Look, if we're going to build a future together, then the people here need to see me the same way they see you. We're partners, so we're in this together."

"If you're doing this just to keep up appearances—"

"You know me better than that," Laney snapped. "I have your back, and you have my back. I can't sit in this house all alone waiting to find out what's going on, just like you couldn't sit here either. I'm going to be with you wherever you are. We'll have each other's backs, just like Mike's team will also have yours, and Ken's team will also have mine. We'll be the safest two people out there, but we'll still be there with *our* people, defending *our* ranch from these monsters."

Alex smiled. "You really do think of this place as ours and not just mine, don't you?"

Laney nodded. "You bet I do. My mind is made up about us. I hope yours is, too."

"It is," Alex confirmed.

"Good." Laney smiled and kissed him. "How long before we have to be at our posts?"

"Not until nightfall," Alex replied.

Laney looked at her watch. Then she stood and held out her hand. "That gives us plenty of time."

Alex took her hand and stood. "Just what do you have in mind?"

"Something to remember me by."

"Don't joke about that," Alex said sharply.

Laney stopped and put her arms around him. "I wasn't trying to be morbid. I was just thinking about how, in ancient times, the men were sent off to battle by their wives after great sex. Since we're both going off to battle, I thought we could send each other off with great sex."

"Then why didn't you just say that?" Alex asked, leading her up the stairs two at a time.

There were no sightings of TDA on the first night, nor were any of the watchers visible on the second day.

On the second night, the ranch hands, security, and the private security contractors, were in position by 11:30 PM. Fifty ranch hands were guarding the horse stables and the equestrian center buildings. Thirty ranch hands were protecting the trucks that had brought the defenders from the ranch to the buffer zone, where they were now deployed. The trucks were parked on the road that ran between the meadow and the buffer zone.

The defenders on the north end of the buffer zone, under the direction of Chuck Washington, all wore red jackets with the ranch logo on them, so the defenders could identify friend from foe. There were twenty of the contract security personnel, twenty-five ranch security personnel, and just over a hundred ranch hands hiding on top of and behind the hills and ridges close to the unattached fence segment along the north road. Half of the contract medics were deployed with the ranch hands.

The defenders on the east side of the buffer zone, under the direction of Lewis Todd, wore the same red jackets and had the same numbers of ranch hands, ranch security, contract security personnel, and contract medics as the defenders to the north. Alex, Laney, and their individual security details were also with the defenders on the east side of the buffer zone.

It was chilly that night, as it had been the night before, and Alex hoped that the ranch's preparations wouldn't be wasted for a second night. The defenders were cold and tired, and everyone was anxious to end the TDA threat to the ranch.

However, just after midnight on the second day, Kate alerted all of the defenders that her drones had spotted vehicles approaching the ranch.

"There's a long column of vehicles approaching the ranch from the east along the north perimeter road. Repeat, there's a long column of vehicles approaching the ranch from the east along the north perimeter road."

CHAPTER 20

lex heard Chuck Washington ask over his communication earpiece, "What types of vehicles and how many?"

"Most appear to be pickup trucks with close to a dozen men riding in the backs," he heard Kate reply. "I estimate twenty-five to twenty-six vehicles altogether."

"Can you tell where they're heading?" Chuck asked.

"Stand by," Kate said.

The defenders waited to hear Kate confirm which sections of the fence were being targeted.

Finally, Alex heard Kate say, "They're splitting into two groups. One is heading south on the east perimeter road, and the other is continuing west along the north perimeter road."

"If they don't stop where expected, alert us where they're heading so we can redeploy," Chuck said.

"Rodger that," Kate confirmed. "The spike strips have

been deployed on the west and south perimeter roads, and the gates have been locked down."

A few minutes later, Alex saw the line of vehicles heading in their direction. They came to a stop near the section of fence that had been left disconnected. TDA had taken the bait.

Kate confirmed that both groups of TDA members had stopped exactly where Alex and the defenders had hoped they would.

Alex smiled. The defenders were evenly matched with the TDA thugs getting ready to breach the buffer zone, but Alex's people had several advantages. First, they knew the land quite well. Two, the Dallas TDA members didn't know that Alex's people were waiting for them. And three, if the Dallas TDA members were expecting reinforcements from Wichita Falls or Lawton, they were in for a major disappointment.

Two hours earlier, Alex received a call from the Director of ICE. Thanks to aerial surveillance by the State Police, a column of vehicles was spotted crossing into Texas from Lawton, Oklahoma. It joined up with another column of vehicles just outside Wichita Falls, and both groups headed southeast toward Alex's ranch.

The aerial surveillance confirmed that the vehicles were mostly pickup trucks, with as many as a dozen Hispanic males sitting in the back. Weapons were visible from the helicopters.

ICE and the State Police intercepted the vehicles. Several TDA members were killed while resisting arrest, but the survivors were arrested and would be transported to Gitmo in the morning to be with their compadres already being detained there.

ICE and the State Police were less than an hour from the ranch, waiting for word from Alex to move in and arrest the Dallas TDA members breaching the buffer zone.

Alex watched the TDA members cut the straps holding the fence segment in place, and then move the segment aside so the trucks could enter the property.

The contract security personnel had automatic weapons, firing a combination of armor-piercing rounds and tracer rounds. They were going to aim for the gas tanks of each vehicle.

Half of the ranch hands were firing 30-30 rounds, and their job was to shoot at the vehicle engines and try to disable them. The other half of the ranch hands were firing .45 Long Colts, and their job was to shoot into the cabs of the vehicles, taking out the drivers and any passengers.

The ranch security personnel had pump-action shotguns, but rather than shooting regular shot, the shells were filled with darts, called flechettes, that were designed to be anti-personnel shot. These would be fired into the beds of the trucks.

"East defenders, wait until all of the trucks are in the buffer zone and I give the order before firing," Lewis Todd said over the communication earpieces. Chuck Washington gave the same instructions to the north defenders.

Alex looked over at Laney. In the moonlight, he saw the grim determination on her face. He reached out and rubber the center of her back. She smiled, but she kept her eyes on the TDA trucks, which had started entering the buffer zone through the open fence.

Alex heard the familiar sound of lever action rifles chambering the first round. The ranch hands were getting ready to open fire. Rifles raised and aimed at the TDA vehicles.

Apart from the trucks and a light breeze blowing through the tree leaves, there was no sound, and there was no indication that the TDA members had seen the defenders.

As the TDA trucks moved around the ridge between the fence and far side of the buffer zone, the order to open fire was given.

The roar of the rifles was deafening as they began firing at the engines and cabs of the trucks. The lead trucks stopped dead from the 30-30 rounds that pierced and disabled the engines.

Automatic gunfire sounded, and Alex saw the tracer rounds aimed underneath the truck, trying to hit the gas tanks. Two tanks exploded as the tracers ignited the fuel.

TDA members leaped out of the back of the trucks and began returning fire, aiming at the muzzle flashes since they couldn't see the shooters clearly.

Security opened fire with their shotguns, and the darts dropped several of the TDA members rapidly.

Alex saw someone escape from the cab of the lead truck and pull out a weapon that looked like a grenade launcher. He aimed his lever action, using 30-30 rounds, at the grenade the TDA member was trying to attach to the launcher. Alex fired, and a second later, the grenade dropped from the TDA member's hand as Alex's bullet hit it dead center. Alex chambered a second round and fired at the TDA member, who was still holding the launcher. He fell backwards and didn't move.

"Good shot," Laney said.

"Thanks."

Alex heard someone call for a medic, but it didn't look like any other defenders had been injured. Rifles, shotguns, and automatic weapons continued firing at the TDA members. Fewer and fewer TDA members were returning fire, though.

Some of the TDA members started running back toward the open fence, but ranch security personnel intercepted them and prevented their escape. They were quickly disarmed and forced to lay down on the ground.

A few raised their hands as a sign of surrender, and ranch security took them into custody with those who tried to escape. As for the rest of the TDA members, the defenders continued firing until no TDA members were returning fire.

Several of the pickup trucks were on fire, and the rest were no longer running or able to run.

The contract security personnel began searching the wreckage for survivors. The occasional gunshot was heard, but not many.

After thirty minutes, the head of the contract security personnel reported that there were no survivors. Ranch security reported that there were 25 captured TDA members who had been disarmed and handcuffed. The east defenders had taken on almost 170 TDA members, the most dangerous gang of criminals in the western hemisphere, who had driven right into a trap from which there was no escape.

Alex and Laney hugged each other. Then they checked to make sure that their security details were okay.

"We're okay, Boss," Mike confirmed.

"So are we, Miss Laney," Ken stated.

Alex and Laney began checking on the ranch hands while the contract security and the ranch security personnel disarmed and collected all of the weapons from the dead TDA members, and then they dragged the TDA bodies away from the trucks. Four ranch hands had been injured, but none of the injuries were serious.

Alex spoke to Lewis Todd over his communications device. "Lewis, this Alex. How are your people, and how are the contract personnel? Any injuries?"

"No, Boss, no injuries," Lewis replied. "A couple of the guys were hit, but their vests protected them. They'll have some bruising, but nothing else. The contractors are all okay. I doubt the TDA weapons would have pierced their body armor."

"Good. I shot what looked like a RPG round that someone from the front truck was trying to load. Someone might want to secure that and see if there are more grenades in any of the trucks."

"Will do, Boss. Thanks for the heads up."

"What happened up north?" Laney asked.

"That's a good question," Alex said. "I'll find out."

"Chuck, it's Alex," Alex said into his communications device. "Can you give me an update on what's happening up there?"

"Sorry about that, Boss," Chuck responded. "The worst is over. We're just mopping up now. Eleven ranch hands were injured, one seriously. No deaths. Two security team members injured, none seriously. One contract security team member killed, none injured. The injured ranch hand has been treated by the medics and is already on his way to the hospital. The rest of the injured are still being treated by the medics. That was a good idea, having them on hand. We took thirty prisoners altogether. The contract security team members are looking for survivors. We don't expect that they'll find any."

"Understood. Thanks, Chuck."

Laney looked at Alex. "Sounds like they had a rougher time than we did."

"They didn't have the terrain that we did," Alex said. "This was the perfect spot for an ambush. We just had to find the best available spot up there."

Alex spoke into his communications device again. "Kate, this is Alex."

"Yes, Boss," Kate responded.

"Notify ICE and the State Police that they can move in to collect the prisoners, bodies, weapons, and wrecks of the Dallas TDA members."

"Rodger that, Boss."

Chuck's voice came over the communications earpieces. "All ranch hands are dismissed. Return to the bunkhouses and clean your weapons, if they were fired. Shuttle busses to the community will be running for the next several hours. Security details, escort your protectees back to the residence. Medics and contract security personnel, you're dismissed as soon as you complete your current tasks. Ranch security team members will remain on the scene to secure the prisoners and coordinate with ICE and the State Police when they arrive to clean up. Horse stable security patrols are to return to their normal posts."

Alex looked at Laney. "I want to take another look around here, and then I want to look at what happened up north before I go back to the residence."

"I'm coming with you," Laney said.

Alex looked at Mike and Ken. "Sorry fellas. Looks like you'll have to stay awake a little longer."

It took all night and well into the morning for ICE and the State Police to remove the prisoners and the bodies of the dead TDA members, collect all of the firearms and other weapons, and start hauling off the wrecked vehicles.

Once the last of the vehicles had been removed, the perimeter security teams moved in to repair the fences, ensuring the integrity of the ranch's perimeter.

At 11:00 AM, Alex and Laney met with the senior ICE officer, the senior State Police officer, Chuck, Lewis, and Earl Crawford. The contract security personnel and medics had left during the night, taking their gear and their dead operative with them.

Alex, Chuck, and Lewis answered all of ICE's and the State Police's questions about the operation and the results.

"Why didn't you contact us sooner?" the senior State Police officer asked.

"There was no time," Alex replied. "The Dallas TDA members arrived, breached the fence, and then the firefight started. I had security contact you as soon as the TDA members stopped shooting at us."

"And there were only 55 survivors?" the senior ICE officer asked. "Against almost three-hundred-and-fifty TDA members on a revenge mission? I find that a little hard to believe."

"It's not like we got out unscathed," Alex countered. "One of my men is in the hospital, several were injured, and one of the contract guys was killed."

"But the rest of your people are all okay," the State Police officer pointed out.

"Because we were ready for them," Alex said. "We knew the terrain, we had a plan, and they walked right into the trap we set for them. And thanks to *your* efforts to prevent their reinforcements coming from Wichita Falls and Lawton, they were foolishly optimistic about their chances. If they weren't expecting reinforcements, I doubt they would have been so easy to defeat."

"You were lucky," the ICE officer said.

"I'm okay with that," Alex said. "I'd rather be lucky and alive, than something else and dead."

After the ICE and State Police had left, Alex turned to Chuck, Lewis, and Earl. "Everyone did a great job, and I thank you. There will be bonuses paid to everyone who participated last night, and if anyone needs any counseling related to what we went through, let me know, and I'll make that available to whoever needs it for as long as they need it. I also want to make certain that all weapons have been put away clean and have been secured back into their cases, and I want an inventory of all ammunition used so I can have it replaced."

"Will do, Boss," they responded.

Once that meeting was over, Alex and Laney met with Nathan Diaz, who was responsible for the grounds in the meadow and the buffer zone.

"I don't know if it's possible, but I'd like as much of the used ammunition from last night to be picked up. I don't want any of it winding up in the hay bales, and I don't want any of it damaging any of the equipment. Much of the ammunition was jacketed, but there was a lot of unjacketed lead flying around, not to mention those flechette darts. There's no telling how wide an area is now contaminated with bullets and shell casings, wadding, and other ammunition."

Nathan nodded. "I've seen attachments that can hook to the rear of a tractor that can recover ammo, as long as it hasn't been pushed into the ground. Outdoor shooting ranges use them. If I can acquire one or two of those, I should be able to clean up the area nicely. Then a bit of reseeding, and in a month or two, you won't know anything ever happened."

Alex nodded. "Perfect. If you can't borrow or rent those attachments, then go ahead and purchase two of them. Hopefully they'll never be needed again, but it might be a good idea to have them, just in case."

"I'm on it, Boss!"

"Thanks, Nathan."

After lunch, Alex and Laney walked toward Alex's office.

"I want to go swimming and get some sun this afternoon," Laney said as they passed the pool. "I need to relax, and I need to be warm after last night."

"Sounds like a good idea," Alex said. "I'll join you."

When they reached his office, Alex dialed a number and put it on speaker so Laney could hear.

"Office of the Vice President of the United States," a voice answered. "How may I direct your call?"

"The Vice President, please. Alexander Barclay calling."

"One moment, Mr. Barclay."

Several minutes later, Vice President Glass came on the line. "Hello, Alex. To what do I owe the pleasure?"

"I wanted to tell you that the Great Barclay Ranch Range War is officially over."

"Outstanding!" the Vice President exclaimed. "Who won?"

"We did."

The Vice President laughed. "ICE has been keeping me informed. I saw the press release they're putting out today about the three aircraft they intercepted, the incoming TDA members they captured, and the capture of the TDA members from Lawton, Oklahoma and Wichita Falls, Texas. They mentioned that several of those TDA members were killed while resisting arrest. They also mention that most of the Dallas TDA members were killed resisting arrest, but they don't mention anything about your involvement."

"I hope not," Alex said. "That was one of the stipulations, that we could never be named as having been involved. I don't need any more TDA thugs coming here for revenge or to send a message that they're untouchable."

"How many raided your ranch?" the Vice President asked.

"I think the final tally was three-hundred-and-forty-three."

"And how many were killed resisting arrest?

"Two-hundred-and-eighty-eight. Fifty-Five were taken prisoner."

There was a pause on the line. "That many resisted arrest?"

"That's what I told ICE and the State Police," Alex

replied blandly.

"Jesus, Alex! Are there any TDA members left in Texas?"

"Just around Houston, and ICE and the State Police have redeployed down there until any more show up here. Alliance Airport is still being watched, but no new planeloads of TDA members have been seen since the last plane was intercepted."

"So it really is over?" the Vice President asked.

"It seems so. I hope so, anyway."

"What does Laney think?"

"That it'll be good for things to get back to normal," Laney answered.

"I agree," Alex said.

"Well, congratulations, you two. I hope you get the peace you're looking for."

After the Vice President ended the call, Laney looked at Alex. "The Great Barclay Ranch Range War?"

"We have to call it something. It's as good a name as any, don't you think?"

Laney giggled. "I like it. Barclay's Brigade and the Great Barclay Ranch Range War. That would make a great title for this chapter in the history of the ranch."

Alex laughed. "I guess I'll have to write it all down at some point. We did accomplish quite a bit, and even though the good people of North Texas will never know we were involved, they're all better off now that TDA is gone."

"And we can all get back to normal," Laney added.

"Yes." Alex pressed a button on his desk, and the blinds all closed, the lights turned off, and the fireplace lit up. "Speaking of normal, what did the victorious soldiers get upon their return home?"

"In Rome, they had orgies. In other nations, they were welcomed home into the arms of adoring women."

"And since we're both victorious soldiers returning from our range war, shouldn't we welcome each other home into our loving arms... and other things?"

Laney stood and moved to one of the couches by the fireplace. "I thought you'd never ask."

Alex joined her on the couch, and soon they were undressed, letting their tongues please each other. Then Laney, who was on top, spun around and guided Alex inside of her. Her first orgasm was almost immediate.

Alex shifted positions so he was sitting up on the couch, with Laney on top and facing him. He kissed her as she moved up and down, and when she leaned back, he held onto her and nuzzled her breasts.

He felt his first climax building, and she squealed with delight when she felt it shooting deep inside of her.

They continued making love for another thirty minutes, enjoying giving pleasure to each other. Once they were finished, they walked back to the house, changed into their swimwear, and went swimming.

Alex floated underneath one of the waterfalls at the far end of the pool from the house, letting the water fall on his chest. Laney swam laps, and then she joined him underneath the waterfall.

"I never asked you how you felt after last night," she said. "I'm sorry about that. You were so concerned about how I was feeling that I never checked on you."

"You never did give me an answer," Alex noted.

"I know. I needed time to process, and I still don't understand why I feel the way I feel."

"I don't understand."

"I'm not upset," Laney said. "I killed people last night, and it doesn't bother me. I know I was defending myself, and you, and the ranch, but shouldn't I feel... something? But I don't. I'm not upset, I'm not sad about killing someone trying to kill me. It's like... it was a perfectly normal, natural thing to do, and I'd do it again in the same circumstance. Isn't that strange?"

"Only you can answer that," Alex said. "And to answer your question, I feel the same way you do. I defended the ranch, I defended you, and I defended the people who live here on the ranch. It's what had to be done, so I did it. I didn't think about it, other than to figure out how to do it. I wanted TDA destroyed for the sake of all of us, and now it's destroyed here in North Texas. That's how I feel."

"But don't you think that's strange?"

Alex shook his head. "I don't think you can define normal or strange in the situation we just faced. I think you can only decide one thing: Can I live with what I had to do? For me, the answer is yes. You'll have to decide what your answer is."

"For me it's yes, too," Laney stated. "I just feel like I should feel something for those men we killed."

"I do feel something," Alex said. "I feel victorious."

Laney shook her head. "I'm being serious."

"So am I. They came here to pillage, steal, destroy, rape, murder... and we stopped them. We saved the ranch, we saved the families living in the community, we saved the trainees living in the community, we protected our facilities, and we saved each other. How could I feel anything other than victorious unless part of me thought they should get away with what they were attempting."

Laney thought about this as she let the water from the

waterfall pour all over her head. Then she said, "I never thought about it that way, but you're right. There's no part of me that thinks they should have gotten away with doing what they came here to do. They fucked around, and they found out. They got exactly what they deserved."

"Exactly."

Are You Sure About This?

CHAPTER 21

The rest of May was certainly calmer than the three months preceding it. Alex and Laney were able to settle into a routine that they both enjoyed. There were no more signs of TDA in North Texas, and no one appeared to be watching the ranch.

On Memorial Day Weekend, like every year, the junior rodeo teams and individuals training at the ranch put on an exhibition for their families and the people living on the ranch. Bo and his team had the pits and smokers running all weekend, making great barbeque for the guests and the staff.

Laney loved watching the various age categories compete and demonstrate what they had been learning from Sam Stewart and his rodeo trainers.

But more than that, she loved being on the ranch, and being part of its family. She loved riding with Alex every day, she loved volunteering with the equine therapy practice, and she loved using her talents as an attorney to help Alex and the ranch, rather than helping the clients of Dwight's law firm.

She dreaded the idea of going back there, and she dreaded the thought of possibly having to leave the ranch behind.

But the first Saturday of June was only twelve days away, and that was the day of the last checkpoint with Alex. That was the day they'd decide officially if the relationship was going to continue or end. That was the day she'd know whether her career was with Alex and the ranch or with Dwight and the law firm.

Dwight had already given her partnership to one of the other associates, leaving her feeling uncomfortable with the idea of returning to the law office. She was certain that it would be better for her to go into private practice, but she wasn't excited about having to find her own clients or handle her own billing—all the things that Dwight had people to handle.

For the next week-and-a-half, Laney felt anxious. She knew what she wanted, and she was sure that Alex wanted the same thing, but until they both sat down and said the words, there was uncertainty.

She and Alex made love several times in the days leading up to the checkpoint, and each time was better than the previous time. This helped her feel more confident, but she was still anxious.

When the first Saturday finally arrived, Laney maintained the appearance of being calm, but inside she was a wreck.

She and Alex sat at the conference table in his office. He had a stack of papers, a couple of notebooks, and a closed box with him that was large enough to hold a number of file folders.

Alex slid one of the notebooks over to Laney and handed her a pen. "This is in case you want to take notes for later."

Laney was confused by this, but she accepted the pen and put it down on the notebook.

Alex cleared his throat. "Okay. Today is the final checkpoint. I don't know about you, but I've been a bit nervous about today. The last time I made it to the final checkpoint, things didn't end well for me. Two failures in a row is not something I want to deal with, as you can imagine."

Laney nodded.

"Would you like to go first?"

"I went first last time," Laney said. "Why don't you go first this time?"

"Are you sure?"

"Yes."

"Okay..." Alex shifted in his seat. "You know that I love you, right?"

She nodded.

"Do you know that I also want to marry you?"

Laney's jaw dropped for a minute, and then her face lit up. "You do?"

Alex nodded. "I decided this a while back, but since we're following the process, I couldn't say anything until today. I want to marry you, Delaney Connor, and I hope you still love me and want to marry me, too."

"Of course I still love you and want to marry you!"

Alex looked relieved. "Thank God. So you do want to continue the relationship, living with me here at the ranch?"

"Absolutely yes," Laney confirmed.

Alex was grinning ear to ear as he picked up his pen and started writing a list of things that needed to happen quickly. "Okay, you need to tell Dwight you're not coming back. We need to select the décor for your office." He tapped the box next to him. "This has all the samples the decorator sent over. We need to get everything ordered that you want. We need to move the rest of your stuff out of your home and put the townhouse on the market, and we need to pick out the ring. I wanted to buy you one and give it to you today, but after what happened last time with your predecessor, I decided against that. We also need to discuss prenups. But before we do all of that, we need to discuss finances."

Alex slid a folder over to Laney. "This is all the information regarding my net worth. I have no debt, so this is all assets, investments, companies, and cash.

Laney read through the information. Alex's companies, which included AMB Consulting, Barclay Aerospace, and Barclay Aviation, were worth a total of $12.6 Billion. His real estate holdings, including the ranch, were worth $2.3 Billion. His cash and investments, including the ranch operations trust that Laney had helped set up two years prior, totaled $27 Billion. Alex's total net worth was $41.9 Billion.

"I had no idea," she said softly as she closed the folder and slid it back across the table. She looked Alex in the eye. "I would have believed this back in DC at the ball. I would have believed this if I had only seen the residence and not the rest of what you do here. But seeing you in this environment, being a rancher, it just doesn't seem possible.

You're so down-to-earth. You're so... normal."

"Thank you," Alex said. "I try."

Laney explained her net worth, which was the cash in her bank accounts, her 401(k), and the equity in her townhouse.

Once the financial conversation was concluded, Alex stood. "Come with me," he said.

Laney gestured to the papers and the box of samples. "But—"

"We're coming back, but there's something I need to show you. It's related to what we've been talking about."

Curious, Laney stood and followed Alex back to the house. They took the stairs to the basement, and then Alex led her through the doors leading to the storage area, where the holiday decorations, tables and chairs for parties and events, and spare pieces of furniture were kept. Alex turned on the lights as he entered.

Just to the left of the door was an enclosure that Laney thought was part of the elevator, since the elevator was right next to it. Alex approached the enclosure and opened its door. Inside was a large vault. Alex entered the combination and opened the vault door. The vault lights came on automatically. Alex stepped back so Laney could see inside.

When she saw the contents of the vault, her jaw dropped. On the lowest level were gold bricks. Above that were gold bars in various sizes. Above that were gold coins. Above that were papers that looked like stock certificates and bonds. In the top compartment were bundles of cash.

Laney looked at Alex. "How much...?"

"Enough to run the ranch for almost a year," Alex replied. "With money left over for other emergencies. I trust my banks, but I also believe in being prepared."

Alex gestured for Laney to touch it. She picked up one of the bricks and then put it back down quickly. "How much does this weigh?"

"The largest bricks are 400 Troy ounces, or about twenty-seven pounds. The medium size bars are one kilogram each, or about 2.2 pounds. The smaller bars are ten ounces each. The bars in the plastic cases are one ounce each. All of the cash is in one-hundred dollar bills."

Laney picked up some of the smaller gold bars, and then she ran her hand over the stacks of cash. "No wonder you keep the vault down here where no one can see it."

"Like everything else on the ranch, I try to keep it safe," he said, closing the vault and then the enclosure door.

They walked back to the office and sat down at the conference table. Laney was still speechless from what she had just seen. Alex pulled out all of the samples from the decorator, along with all the specifications for what was in his office—as if the trip to the vault had never happened.

"Shall we talk about your office?" he asked.

Laney nodded, but it took her a minute to reorganize her thoughts. "I want the same layout and types of furniture, and I want it all in the same place as in here, but I think I want different colors. I definitely want your desk furniture, but I want a different desk chair and a more oval conference table. Same conference table chairs, though. And I like the two couches in front of the fireplace, but maybe a lighter color—British tan would look nice. I want the desk chair to match—the same leather."

She looked through the books and picked out the desk chair she wanted. Then she selected the curtains and the rug. They were similar to Alex's, but lighter and more... happy, as Laney put it.

Alex wrote down everything she said and promised to get the decorator working on acquiring the pieces immediately.

They spent about thirty minutes going over prenup items that Alex's other attorneys were insisting on. Laney found the terms and conditions reasonable. "I understand all of these and I don't object to any of it. Have them draw up the papers."

Alex wrote that down, and then he asked, "What kind of wedding do you want, and when do you want it?"

Laney had no family, her friends were work friends or people she knew through the Party. Everyone else was on the ranch. "Do we need a large affair?" she asked.

"We can have whatever you want."

Laney reached for Alex's hand. "I want to be married to you. I don't need an elaborate wedding to do that. I've never understood wasting so much time and money on huge weddings just to impress people who won't be impressed. I don't care what people think, and we *clearly* don't need any gifts, so let's just get married and be done with it. Keep it small, keep it simple."

"If that's what you truly want, I'll make it happen."

"That's what I truly want. You're what I want, not a bunch of pomp and ceremony."

"I have a friend who's a minister down in Austin," Alex said. "I'll bet I can get him to marry us, either here or down there. Then we can have a nice honeymoon somewhere, and then get down to living the rest of our lives together."

"Sounds perfect," Laney said. "How about the Florida Keys for a honeymoon? I'd like to stay in America for some reason."

"Let's see what's available, and then we can set the date for the wedding based on that." Alex grabbed his tablet off the desk and started looking at resorts in The Keys. Laney leaned over so she could see what he was seeing.

"We know next weekend is out," she reminded Alex. "That's the fundraiser for the Equine Therapy charity."

Alex nodded. "The top donors will be spending the night in the guest wing, including the Governor. I've made arrangements for everyone else to stay in hotels in North Tarrant County, and we'll have a shuttle service running between here and there so no one will have to drive all the way out here."

"Good thinking," Laney said. "It's an auction, isn't it?"

Alex nodded.

"What's being auctioned?"

"Remember that day we went to Mount Vernon, and we stopped in those little galleries in Alexandria?"

Laney nodded.

"I made arrangements to purchase several original painting and furniture pieces. Those are being auctioned, along with a couple of cruises. I'm also auctioning off a couple of historical weapons from the wild west."

Laney laughed. "Ones from your collection?"

"Sort of. They're part of my overflow collection— valuable to own, but not enough room to display. I always auction off a few of them each year."

"How many guns are in your overflow collection?"

Alex thought about it for a moment. "About thirty. Ten pistols and twenty lever action rifles. They're stored in special cases near the vault. That's where the paintings and furniture are being stored, too."

"They're here already?"

"Oh, yes. I made sure they were here a month before the auction. That way I had time to replace anything that was damaged."

Alex pointed at the tablet. "Well, since we know next weekend is booked, let's see what's available in the Keys for later this month." Laney agreed, and Alex entered the search parameters into the travel site he used. After a moment, the site returned several pages of results, and they started scrolling through the listings of available resorts.

"Look at that," she said, pointing at a resort on Key Largo. "I've heard of that place."

Alex checked availability, and the last week in June was available—a private bungalow for Laney and Alex, and another bungalow next door for the Security Detail. Alex booked it, and then he called his minister friend. After confirming that his friend could marry them in Austin the morning they could check in at the resort, Laney agreed with the plans and the date of their wedding. Then Alex called Henry to make certain that the jet and crew were available.

"It's all set," Alex said when he ended the call. "We just need to go to the courthouse and get a marriage license. We can worry about name changes after we get back."

Laney leaned back and shook her head. "That was fast!"

"We still need to get the rings," Alex said. "Any plans for this afternoon?"

"Are you serious?"

Alex nodded. "There's a jeweler in downtown Fort

Worth. I should be able to get an appointment today. If you want, I can send a team to your apartment to pack everything and move it up here, if you'd like."

"There's really not much that's moving," Laney said. "I don't need any of the furniture or anything in the kitchen, so I can sell the townhouse as furnished. I just need the rest of my clothes and everything on my shelves, in my drawers... Tell you what. Let's go look at rings, and then go by my office and pack up my things from there today. We can deal with the townhouse tomorrow. I'd like to be there for that."

Alex nodded and called the jeweler. He agreed to meet with Alex and Laney at one o'clock that afternoon.

The visit to the jeweler's store was an interesting experience for Laney. The older gentleman specialized in custom work, and Laney was fascinated by the process.

Mike and Ken entered the jeweler's store with Alex and Laney. The rest of the security detail remained outside, either standing outside the door, or inside the three vehicles in the motorcade.

"Are you two looking for matching rings?" the jeweler asked Alex and Laney once they were seated at the counter.

Alex looked at Laney, who nodded. "Yes, we'd like matching rings."

"And will there be a separate engagement ring and wedding band, a single wedding ring, or an engagement ring with a ring guard?" the gentleman asked, showing Laney examples of each.

Laney looked at Alex. "If I'm going to be riding horses every day, and working with the Equine Therapy practice, a big diamond engagement ring would be a bother and could get damaged easily. I think a band with maybe a couple of smaller stones might work better."

"Are you sure?" Alex asked. "You can have whatever you want."

Laney smiled. "I don't need anything fancy or glitzy if I'm going to be a rancher for the rest of my life. Just something to show that I'm yours is all I want or need."

Alex shrugged and looked at the jeweler. "Whatever she wants."

The jeweler flipped through a small sketchbook until he found what he was looking for. He turned the book around so Alex and Laney could see. On the page was the sketch of two bands. One was wide—smooth on the outer part, and textured on the inner part. The other was more narrow, but also smooth on the outer part and textured on the inner part. The smaller band also had three stones: one emerald and two diamonds.

The jeweler explained the design. "We can use any stones on the lady's band—diamonds, sapphires, emeralds, your birthstones... anything you like."

"I love the design," Laney said.

"So do I," Alex echoed.

"And I love the emeralds, since my family's from Ireland," Laney added. "Would it look better with three emeralds, or two emeralds and a diamond in the center?"

"It's entirely up to you," the jeweler said. "I can do it either way. Three emeralds might look better, but either way it will be stunning."

Laney looked at Alex. "What do you think. And don't

say I can have whatever I want. I need your honest opinion."

Alex grinned. "Well, if you insist, I prefer three emeralds."

Laney looked at the jeweler. "Three emeralds it is."

"Beautiful choice. I have everything I need here in the shop. I can have the rings cast and the stones set by... a week from Tuesday. Does that work for you?"

Alex and Laney both nodded. The jeweler took measurements of Alex and Laney's ring fingers, and then he wrote up the sale. When he was finished, he showed Alex the price.

"Done," Alex said.

The jeweler nodded. "Payment is due when you approve the rings and pick them up next Tuesday."

Alex shook the jeweler's hand, and then Alex, Laney, Mike, and Ken left the store.

CHAPTER 22

Packing Laney's office only took an hour, but as they were leaving, Dwight arrived to pick up some papers that he had left the night before. Seeing Laney and Alex carrying boxes, he immediately knew that she was quitting.

Laney handed Dwight an envelope that she had planned to leave on his desk. "My resignation, Dwight. Effective immediately. I want you to know that I truly enjoyed working here, and I appreciate all that you taught me, but..." she looked at Alex, "I received a better offer."

"You've stolen my best attorney, Mr. Barclay," Dwight accused.

"Not sorry, Dwight," Alex responded. "She has a better future waiting for her with me at the ranch."

Dwight looked at Laney. "You're sure about this?"

She nodded. "And it's all thanks to you."

"What do you mean?" he demanded.

"You're the one who gave me the invitation to a ball. That's where we met. That's where this all began. So... thank you, and goodbye."

Laney and Alex left the law office with Dwight still wrestling with the fact that he had set everything in motion by giving Laney his inauguration tickets.

"It's interesting, isn't it?" Alex asked as they loaded Laney's boxes into the back of the SUVs.

"What is?" Laney asked.

"I broke up with your predecessor, and my cousin's children got sick, forcing me to attend the inauguration solo. Dwight's wife broke her leg, causing him to give you his tickets, and then your boyfriend broke up with you, forcing you to attend the inauguration solo. And then we both sat next to each other at the ball, danced all night, and then a winter storm kept us in DC long enough to really get to know each other and want to test out entering into a relationship. And now... we're getting married! That's a lot of things that had to happen in a very short period of time to bring the two of us together and set us on the path that brought us to today. If that's not fate, or a higher power at work, then I don't know what is."

"So you're saying that we were destined to be together?" Laney asked.

"It certainly feels that way," Alex replied. "I don't believe in random chance—not where two souls are involved. Think about it. We both knew each other already, we were both half-way across the country at the same time and in the same place, we were both alone, and we were both willing to take a chance with each other. Things like this don't just happen. There were too many pieces that had to line up *just* right. I don't think it was a coincidence.

Do you?"

Laney shook her head slowly. "I see what you mean." She put her arms around his neck. "We *were* destined to be together, weren't we?"

"Yes we were, and if a budding relationship can survive what we went through over the past four months, there's no question in my mind that we're destined to stay together."

Laney gave Alex a kiss.

When Mike cleared his throat, Alex realized that they were still standing in the law office parking lot. "Sorry about that, Mike," Alex said. Then he turned to Laney. "Let's head back to the ranch."

Laney got into the middle SUV, followed by Alex. Soon, the motorcade was heading north away from Fort Worth.

The next three weeks were a whirlwind of activity.

The weekend after selecting the rings, and moving Laney's things from her office and townhouse to the ranch, was the annual fundraiser for the Equine Therapy charity. The VIPs staying at the residence started to arrive in the early afternoon. Shuttle buses from the hotels began bringing the rest of the guests to the ranch later that afternoon.

Alex and Laney greeted each guest as they arrived. Fran and her team were busy preparing hors d'oeuvres for the cocktail hour, a full multi-course dinner, and a variety of desserts. An army of servers had been hired for the evening to help serve the food and remove the dishes, and a bar team had been brought in to pour, serve, and refill drinks until the auction was over.

Extra tables had been set up in every available space on the first floor, including the library, where the couches and sitting areas had been removed to make room.

During the cocktail hour before supper, the lead trainers and therapists from the Equine Therapy practice spoke about the successes they'd had over the previous year, and the plans they had for the future. Alex also spoke about his commitment for the practice to continue being state-of-the-art and the finest practice of its kind anywhere in the United States.

Once dinner was ready, the guests found their seats, and the servers began bringing out trays of food for each table. Fran and her team had outdone themselves on the meal, and the guests all raved about the food.

After dinner, the tables in the library were removed, and extra chairs were brought in for the auction. Ranch hands helped bring up the auction items from downstairs and place them in the library in front of the main fireplace.

Alex served as the auctioneer, and the ranch hands helped move the items forward before Alex opened the floor for bidding. Each item sold for well over twice what Alex paid for them, but it was the western firearms that sold for the highest prices.

Even after the auction items had been sold, the guests continued making pledges to fund the Equine Therapy operations for the coming year. Between the auction sales and the pledges, the Equine Therapy practice more than exceeded its goals for the evening, ensuring full funding for another year with money left over for additional equipment, staff, and services.

As the shuttle buses began taking the guests back to their hotels, and the top donors had retired to their suites in the guest wing, Alex and Laney sat in the lounge with the governor and his wife.

"Another successful evening?" the governor asked.

Alex nodded. "We exceeded all of our goals, Governor. Our Equine Therapy practice will be able to help even more people than planned over the next year."

Alex gestured toward Laney. "And with people, like my fiancé here, becoming volunteers with our Special Equestrians program, we're able to provide more hands-on assistance to those who need it."

"Fiancé?" the governor asked.

Alex nodded and took Laney by the hand. "We're getting married on the twenty-first."

The governor and his wife smiled. "Texas' most eligible bachelor is finally off the market," she said. "The Lone Star State's finest socialites will be terribly upset when they hear the news."

Alex and Laney laughed. "They'll just have to go back to chasing oil barons," Alex said. "I'm looking forward to settling down as a rancher full-time. Hardly the life for one of those highbrows."

The next morning, Alex and Laney had breakfast with the top donors. Once they had all left the residence, heading back to their homes, Kelly Fernandez's housekeeping team, along with several ranch hands, descended on the residence, cleaned the guest rooms and dining areas, and took the extra tables and chairs to their storage racks in the basement. Lastly, the furniture that had been removed was returned to its proper place.

Alex and Laney went riding as soon as the last guest had left, and when they returned to the residence hours later, they went upstairs to stay out of everyone's way.

They made love in the shower, enjoying the sensation of being one while the water sprayed all over them. Then they spent the rest of the day curled up next to each other on the couch in the den, watching movies and enjoying just being together.

On Tuesday, they drove back to the jeweler's store to see the rings. The older gentleman had done an incredible job with both rings, and when Alex and Laney tried them on, they both fit perfectly.

"Do I have to take it off?" Laney asked as Alex placed his ring back in its box.

"I'm afraid so," Alex said. "You need something for our wedding day. If you wear the ring now, what will you have?"

"You." Laney looked at the ring one more time, and then reluctantly took it off and put it in its box. "You're right."

Alex paid for the rings, thanked the jeweler, and they headed back for the ranch.

Laney, Alex, Ken, Mike, Gordon, Travis, and Hans flew to Austin in Alex's jet early in the morning of June 21st. They drove to the home of Alex's friend, who performed the wedding ceremony in his living room.

Alex handed his friend the wedding license, and he promised to complete the information and file it with the state.

They then returned to the airport, boarded the jet, and flew to Key West, which was the closest airport to the resort on Key Largo. Jenny served champagne and wedding cake on the flight to celebrate the marriage.

That night, as the newlyweds relaxed in bed from a marathon of lovemaking, Alex drained the last of the champagne bottle into Laney's glass. "How are you feeling, Mrs. Barclay?" he asked, nuzzling her neck behind the ear.

"Wonderful, Mr. Barclay," she purred. She drained her glass. Then she put the glass down and moved on top of him. Looking him in the eyes, she said, "You know, I just realized something."

"What's that?"

Laney had a wicked look in her eyes. "You never *actually* asked me to marry you. Did you know that?"

Alex stared at her, replaying the final checkpoint in his mind, and realized that she was correct. "Well, we should do something about that. We want this marriage to be *official*, don't we? Mrs. Delaney Erica Connor Barclay, will you marry me and do me the honor of being my wife and my life partner in all things?"

Laney smiled, but said nothing, pretending she was thinking about it. Then she giggled. "Yes, a thousand... a million times yes! I will marry you and be your wife and life partner in all things, Mr. Alexander McIntyre Barclay."

She felt something move between her legs. "Seriously? You're not tired after all we've done already?"

"Our marriage needs to be official, now that we're finally and formally engaged," Alex said.

Laney laughed. Then she wrapped her arms around him and kissed him as she felt him slip inside of her.

"You'd better hold on to something," he whispered, "because it's going to get intense."

The End

ABOUT THE AUTHOR

W. B. Speir is an Award-winning author. Born in Alabama, W. B. has lived in Michigan, Connecticut, Florida, and now resides in Texas. W. B. has 26 published novels, six of which are Royal Palm Literary Award Gold and Silver winners. W. B.'s novels span the Romance, Romantasy, Fantasy, Historical Fiction, Science Fiction, Espionage, Suspense, and Action-Adventure genres. *Invitation to a Ball* is W. B.'s fourth Romance novel.

For more information about W. B., please visit the publisher's website at progressiverisingphoenix.com.